COCO'S GAMBIT

A Novel

Peter T. Treadway

Copyright © 2021 Treadway Publishing

All rights reserved. No part of this publication may be reproduced, distributed, or transmitted in any form or by any means, including photocopying, recording, or other electronic or mechanical methods, without the prior written permission of the publisher, except in the case of brief quotations embodied in critical reviews and certain other noncommercial uses permitted by copyright law. For permission requests, write to the publisher, addressed "Attention: Book Rights and Permission," at the address below.

Published in the United States of America

ISBN 978-1-953904-50-8 (SC)

Treadway Publishing
550 Okeechobee Blvd,
PHL 17 West Palm Beach, Florida 33401
www.stellarliterary.com

Ordering Information and Rights Permission:
Quantity sales. Special discounts might be available on quantity purchases by corporations, associations, and others. For details, contact the publisher at the address above.

For Book Rights Adaptation and other Rights Permission. Call us at toll-free 1-888-945-8513 or send us an email at admin@stellarliterary.com.

Contents

Chapter One 5

Chapter Two 18

Chapter Three 24

Chapter Four 39

Chapter Five 45

Chapter Six 63

Chapter Seven 76

Chapter Eight 80

Chapter Nine 83

Chapter Ten 89

Chapter Eleven 92

Chapter Twelve 109

Chapter Thirteen 118

Chapter Fourteen 124

Chapter Fifteen 131

Chapter Sixteen 139

Chapter Seventeen 151

Chapter Eighteen 160

Chapter Nineteen 170

Chapter Twenty 184

Chapter Twenty-One 197

Chapter Twenty-Two 206

Chapter Twenty-Three 219

Chapter Twenty-Four 230

Chapter Twenty-Five 236

Chapter Twenty-Six 249

Chapter Twenty-Seven 256

Chapter Twenty-Eight 262

Chapter Twenty-Nine 266

Chapter Thirty 270

Chapter Thirty-One 274

Chapter Thirty-Two 278

Author's Bio 280

Chapter One

If I were permitted to choose amidst the jumble of books that will be published a hundred years after my death, do you know which one I would pick?... I would simply pick, my friend, a fashion magazine in order to see how women will dress a century after my passing. And these rags will tell me more about humanity's future than philosophers, novelists, preachers or scholars.

— Anatole France

"Shit," Ian Blakely said aloud, "where's the damn helicopter?" Ian was lost. He was wandering around the Shun Tak building looking for the heliport. He had been the keynote luncheon speaker at an investment conference in Hong Kong. Now he was rushing over to Macau to buy a painting. He had to be back in Singapore that evening for a dinner. The ferries and the helicopters to Macau leave from the Shun Tak Building and Ian had gotten off the elevator on the wrong floor.

He approached a young Chinese man wearing a uniform. The man looked official. "Which way is the elevator for the helicopter to Macau?"

The man stared at Ian, his blank eyes exuding incomprehension. "Boat," he replied, pointing to several ferries berthed outside the window.

"No, the lift to the helicopter." Ian switched to the British 'lift' on the absurd chance the young man was confused by his American usage. Ian pointed up. Helicopters usually take off from the roof.

"Boat," the young man said again, still pointing at ferries berthed outside and doing a good imitation of a malfunctioning robot.

Ian realized the problem. He wasn't in Singapore where everybody spoke English. The young man in the uniform wasn't a malfunctioning robot. He just didn't understand. A hundred and fifty years as a British Royal Crown Colony had come and gone. Ian had seven minutes. He hurried back to the elevator where he finally saw a big sign in English for the heliport. It was staring him in the face. He cursed. His firm managed over $9 billion dollars, he was the keynote speaker at a very high level investment conference, and he couldn't read a simple goddamn sign.

Two minutes later he was in the heliport waiting lounge. Finally. His kind of place. Pretty Chinese attendants who spoke English, sandwiches that served as the lunch he had missed while he was speaking at the conference, an assortment of travel magazines with pictures of spas and resorts for rich people who could speak English.

Five minutes later he was on board. One of the pretty lounge attendants help strap him in. The AgustaWestland AW 139 s, used on the Hong Kong Macau route, seats twelve and has three rows, four seats across. The first two rows face one another. Ian had a window seat, on the left side, second row. Directly in front of him with her knees about a half inch from his was a drop dead gorgeous young woman. Next to her was seated an older man, probably her husband. He was dressed elegantly, with a shirt Ian recognized as Brioni. The man and the woman seemed engrossed in their iPhones, oblivious to requests that could barely be heard over the speaker system requesting that electronic devices be turned off. Ian assumed they were Mainland Chinese or *Comrades*, as his Singaporean Chinese assistant derisively called all Mainlanders. Ian could not help noticing the pave diamond Piaget watch that the woman wore prominently on her wrist. Or the smart skin tight jeans and stylish ultra-high heels. Maybe Louboutins? Then he spied her bag. Hermes. Was it a Birkin? Like the one Lady Gaga supposedly paid US $100,000 for?

Ian wasn't sure. But he wasn't ignorant in these matters. His Blakely Funds had done well investing in the stocks of the global luxury brands that had become de rigueur for Asia's multitudes of newly rich. He had gotten to know these firms' products and some of their designers and executives. The Piaget made him especially happy as the Blakely Funds had done particularly well in the stock of the parent company. Of course the Blakely Funds had done well owning Apple as well. The Pope had visited Korea and told his audiences not to be so materialistic. What planet was he on?

And besides, being a rich bachelor in Asia required some knowledge of these products. Gifts were always appreciated. The gifts had to be real, not fakes like the ones the Philippine helpers bought in Shenzhen.

Unfortunately this woman in front of him was going to pose a problem. Ian couldn't help staring at her. She was stunning with big gorgeous brown eyes. Ian couldn't control his own eyes which automatically locked on to hers. What could he do for the next fifteen minutes that the flight would take? The AW139 dipped its nose as it lifted off and then headed out over Victoria Harbour. Ian finally forced his head to turn. He looked out the window to his left at the ho-hum buildings in Kennedy Town. An endless sea of boring apartment buildings. Then he forced his head to make a one hundred eighty degree turn to his right. Sitting there next to him was a middle aged woman who had a giant Chanel shopping bag on her lap that presumably was filled with Chanel goodies. She had to be a *Comrade*. She had a north China peasant look— ex-peasant would be a more accurate description—with a round plain face, terrible teeth and very little make-up. She clutched the shopping bag like a hungry eagle with a tasty rabbit in its talons. Ian wouldn't be staring at her for fifteen minutes.

All of this was what Ian had wished for. He had relocated to Asia from the US. He had come to Asia to be in the epicenter of where the new global wealth was cooking. In mid-life he had heard the call, "Go East young man," and followed it. And – although he would never admit it --maybe he had found it a way to start a new life after his beautiful blond English model wife had left him for another woman. He missed their infant daughter of course. But Asia had its own overwhelming appeal. Ian was obsessed with Asia's immensity and vitality. Unlike the Holy Father, he was fascinated with its unbridled materialism. Temples, monks, spiritual gurus and the like— they were all bullshit as far as he was concerned. He was far more interested in what was *new* in Asia – the new over-the-top outré gargantuan buildings that the Western intelligentsia so detested, the wonderful tasteless displays of wealth, the airports as big as cities, the lust for global brands like Piaget, Gucci and Apple. Ian was definitely impressed by the man with the beautiful woman in front of him, whoever he was. However crass, sexist or whatever, a man knows he has made it in life when the woman who holds his dick is a young knockout wearing a Piaget.

Before he was a successful global hedge fund manager, Ian had been a professor of financial history at the Harvard Business School. Business school professors often serve as advisors to the captains of industry. Unlike the leftish English and sociology professors, they are pro-business to the core. Business professors are considered the philistines of the academic world by their jealous liberal arts colleagues. The liberal arts crowd have no choice but to revel in their penury and hate the rich. Ian was partial to philistines.

It was a nice day. The trip to Macau was going to be a smooth one. Ian closed his eyes. If he continued to stare at the woman, the man next to her might take serious umbrage. His eyes closed, he tried a meditation technique he learned in the States from some CDs he had picked up one time in an airport bookstore in San Francisco. He invited the future price of gold to float into his mind. His meditation instructor on the CDs had suggested letting the idea of world peace float in. But there was no rule you *had* to meditate for world peace. The technique failed him. The vision of the beautiful woman in front of him kept floating into his mind instead of the future price of gold. Luckily the whine of the engines helped put him into a quick catnap. He woke up when he felt the helicopter bank left. He opened his eyes. The beautiful lady with the Piaget was still right in front of him, still engrossed in her iPhone. She looked up with her beautiful eyes and met Ian's gaze for a split second. Then Ian looked out the window. They had just passed directly over the runway for the Macau Airport. Then the big sign for the downtown Sands casino came up.

Then some kind of statue out in the water. Ian thought it might be a statue of the Blessed Virgin that the Portuguese had left. But later he found out it was the statue of a Chinese goddess. He would reflect that sooner or later some Harvard Divinity School graduate female student, desperate for a "new" dissertation theme, would write a dissertation saying that this Chinese goddess and the Blessed Virgin really *were* the same person. And ready to kick ass.

Thirty seconds later they were down. As he got up, he heard the beautiful lady and her companion speak. He couldn't understand but he knew that were speaking Korean, not Chinese. He laughed to himself. He could hear his Singaporean Chinese assistant commenting, "Of course they're not *Comrades*. They're much too elegant."

Going through Macau Customs seemed to take forever even though the helicopter passengers got special treatment. Ian was behind schedule. His dinner later that night in Singapore was with an important client. But it was a short ride from the Macau Marine Terminal to the Galeria Wang Qiang, located on a little side street near the St. Paul ruin. Ian got in a quick glance of the new Macau from his limo although even with the tinted window he had to squint because of the strong sun. So many new hotels and casinos. The boxy Sands, the multicolored MGM, the Wynn towers, the lotus shaped New Lisboa, all shining in the sun. A new "terracotta" army representing the new Asia. Ian smiled. His mind added one small footnote. In 1999 Macau supposedly was given back to China by the Portuguese who had run the place since 1557. Ian had concluded Macau's new rulers weren't really Chinese. Instead they were two Jews from Las Vegas and a Eurasian (and his many wives and children). They were the ones that built the new terracotta army of casinos and hotels. The Blakely Funds had done well trading their stocks.

One nice thing about Macau. Most stores have Portuguese and Chinese names. This is a charming colonial holdover. No doubt it's good for tourism although it serves no other purpose. Ian was reasonably competent in Spanish. He therefore could figure out the Portuguese signs on the stores along the way.

That put him into a select group in Macau. Most of its Chinese residents could not read or speak Portuguese. Nor did they give a shit about the matter.

Ian arrived at the Galeria. He hopped out of his limo and walked in. He could smell the paint. The gallery featured paintings by the artist himself, Wang Qiang. It was a working gallery. Wang's paintings were on exhibition in the front while he painted in the back in a large studio. Wang Qiang painted China's new nihilistic materialism and its obsession with wealth and global brands. And its flagrant but silent sexual revolution, which the grey Mandarins in Beijing either were unaware of or, if rumors were correct, were secret but enthusiastic participants.

Wang had developed a style which he called "*Luxury Realism.*" Once upon a time in the Mao era China had a slogan "*Xue Xi Lei Feng*" or *Learn from Lei Feng*. Lei Feng was some kind of revolutionary model citizen who regrettably died from being run over by a truck. Wang's gallery had a big sign over its front door that said *Learn from Coco Chanel*. Not that Wang was partial to one brand. In the back of the gallery was another sign. *Learn from Louis Vuitton*.

Ian regarded Wang as a prophet of the new order. Wang put on canvas what Ian was seeing with his own eyes. No peasants, no dour Cultural Revolution scenes, no brand X international abstractions. Rather a celebration of the new Chinese bourgeoisie and its lust for the latest global brands. And its lust for lust itself. Wang had been quoted in the media as saying that China had had three major religions in the last two thousand years. First Buddhism, then Communism and now Louisvuittonism.

Most Chinese artists have studios in Beijing or Shanghai. But somehow Wang belonged in the louche atmosphere of Macau. Ian had read a review of Wang in a Hong Kong underground art magazine. "Fuck politics, long live sex, money and luxury brands, that's Wang." the reviewer summarized. Ian shared some of the same sentiments himself.

Wang was expecting Ian. He greeted him with a big smile. The two men shook hands. Ian at six foot three towered over the diminutive Wang. Ian was wearing a dark blue light sports jacket with no tie and had a slightly disheveled absent-minded professor look which he consciously maintained despite having long since given up being a professor. Wang, on the other hand, was short and stocky, had a round middle aged face and wore a green surgical gown that was covered with paint. He stunk of paint and cigarettes. His smile revealed yellow nicotine stained misshapen teeth long overdue for a serious surgical upgrade.

"I'm sorry I'm late but my Hong Kong conference ran late," Ian said. It ran late because several investors wanted to talk to him personally about investing money with him. "I was lucky to get a helicopter flight. And now unfortunately I'm in a bit of a hurry. I've got a dinner later tonight in Singapore."

Wang just smiled. Without saying a word, Wang simply motioned to Ian to look around. An assistant came up to Ian and gave him a cup of green tea. Ian assumed Wang's English was poor. He reminded himself that in Asia that he should *never* judge someone by their English. Some of the smartest Chinese businessmen that he had met spoke lousy English. Perhaps that was on purpose.

Ian immediately saw something that interested him. It was the type of painting he had come for. It was a large 36" by 72" painting of a beautiful young Chinese woman getting into a black Mercedes. She had on a leather miniskirt and a Chanel bag slung over her right shoulder. Her bare left leg was in full view as she slid sideways into the car. And she was obviously tall. Ian felt like her eyes were focused directly on him and that they said "come fuck me." *Come fuck me-- if you can afford me,* that is. The painting was entitled *Woman in Mercedes.*

He pointed to the painting. "How much is this listed for?"

Wang's assistant, a young man who had been quiet up to this point, interjected. "Mr. Wang sell painting two hour ago."

Ian was disappointed. "How much did it go for?"

The young man first spoke with Wang in Mandarin. "Two hundred thousand dollar."

"I thought it might have gone for more," Ian said. Sales of Wang's paintings in international markets had gone for more. Ian had done some checking on Wang. Wang was a naturalized American citizen who it seemed had some public problems with the IRS. Also it had become known in art circles that Wang had lost a great deal of money gambling in Macau. Maybe he would be flexible.

Ian began to walk around the gallery. He saw a number of paintings he liked but nothing he wanted to spend two hundred thousand dollars on. He momentarily was interested in a painting of a miniature Caucasian girl in a bikini sitting in a giant open Gucci bag. That painting was ungraciously titled *Buy Bag, Get Girl Free*. But the girl looked a little like his ex-wife. No, he didn't want that one. His eyes then fell on a large painting that depicted a large ring on some woman's finger. Written in cursive English on the bottom of the painting was a quote from Andy Warhol. "It would be very glamorous to be reincarnated as a great big ring on Liz Taylor's finger." A little too cute for Ian. Another painting that caught his eye showed an attractive Chinese couple sitting and taking high tea. The woman was trying to choose among stacked trays of assorted nibbles as her companion approvingly gazed at her. Except the nibbles in the trays weren't cucumber sandwiches or little sweets. Rather they were diamonds and various precious stones. That painting was entitled appropriately enough *High Tea*. Ian lingered for a few moments but that wasn't quite what he wanted either.

Ian couldn't get the *Woman in Mercedes* out of his head. Nothing else was going to do. He was disappointed. He had researched Wang and had made a special trip to his gallery. He had come determined to buy something but it was starting to look like that wasn't going to happen. A long climb for a short slide, as his father used to say.

Ian turned to Wang. "I'm sorry. I don't see anything I'm ready to buy right now. But thanks for your time."

Wang said something in Mandarin to his assistant. The assistant then said in English, "One minute."

Wang headed for his studio in the back room. A few minutes later he came out. He was carrying another 36" by 72" painting. This one was a frontal nude. Or almost nude. Another gorgeous young Chinese woman. Actually she looked a little dark to be pure Chinese. And her eyes though beautiful were somehow just a bit rounder. The woman, probably no more than twenty, had a gold chain with a diamond pendant hanging down between smallish breasts. Slung over her left shoulder was a Chanel bag. She was standing in high cage heels that went almost all the way up her calf. Ian's eyes darted between the diamond and two large deep-pink nipples. She wore a tiny pair of shorts that were partly opened in the front just enough to reveal a glimpse of her pubic hair. Incongruously, in her left hand she held a lit small cigarillo. She had a slight smile on her lower lip. Her hair had a disheveled look, but it stopped at her shoulders. Not the Suzie Wong hair down to her waist look. Unlike the Mercedes woman who seemed to be inviting a sexual adventure, this woman seemed to be taunting her onlookers. *I'm a slut, I like it, deal with it.*

Ian had to have this painting. It was way over the top and he had no idea where he would hang it, but this was the artistic fulfillment of a hedgie's wettest dream. He checked his iPhone. He only had a few minutes or he would miss the return helicopter and be late for his dinner in Singapore.

"Cartier," Wang said pointing at the pendant on the woman's necklace. "I borrow it."

"What's the English name for this painting?"

"*Bad Girl,*" replied the assistant. "Only English name. No Chinese."

"So what price would you put on it?" Ian asked.

Wang answered. "Three hundred."

"Three hundred thousand dollar," the assistant immediately corrected.

Ian laughed. "That's too much. The other one is the same size and that went for two hundred thousand dollars."

Wang and the assistant looked at one another. "Mr. Wang's price are final," the assistant said.

Ian replied. "I will offer two hundred thousand. My final and only offer. I shouldn't pay more than the other buyer. Even though I think he got a bargain. The paintings are the same artist, same theme, same size."

Wang and the assistant spoke to one another again in Mandarin. "You respected financial man and have high art taste. Mr. Wang want you for client for future. Two hundred fifty thousand dollar. Nude worth more."

Ian looked at the now stone faced Wang. "Two hundred thousand. I'm not paying more than the other guy."

Wang said nothing for about ten seconds. Then he shook his head, "Okay." Wang might not be Shakespeare but it seemed he could get by in English.

Ian and Wang shook hands. Ian realized he was purchasing an expensive painting at the same light speed he bought stocks. He never did this with paintings. He was not a visual person. He could remember dates and prices of stocks, but not faces. Every painting he had bought he had looked at least twice. But this time he had no time, no choice. "The painting will need to be shipped," Ian said. "I presume you will want a letter of credit, against the receipt of a bill of lading."

Wang shook his head no. "I know who you are. Famous financial man. We ship painting. Just wire money after painting arrive. We have our own shipper. Very reliable. Fully insured. Next time you come back, you buy more."

Ian was surprised by the answer but of course he didn't argue. "I can assure you payment will be forthcoming as soon as the painting is received in good condition. Send the painting to this address." He handed Wang a card. "It's a frame shop I've used in Singapore. That's where I live. I want to put my own frame on it."

The assistant then pulled out a sheet with wiring instructions. Wang's account was in the Banco Soares in Macau.

"No problem with Atherton's?" Ian asked as he looked over the wiring instructions. Atherton Global was Wang's agent and handled the sales of Wang's paintings internationally.

"No problem," Wang himself replied. "Part of agreement. What I sell here my business."

Ian figured Atherton's would list *Bad Girl* for at least three hundred fifty thousand dollars. If Wang sold it through Atherton's, Wang would have to report the sale as income to the American government. And pay Atherton maybe a fifty percent commission. *Not Ian's problem.*

"Can you tell me who bought the other painting?" Ian asked.

"We cannot," the assistant said. "Buyer want privacy."

Ian shrugged. "Okay".

"Painting ship Art Services International," the assistant said.

"They're the best," Ian said.

The assistant then carried both paintings, one in each hand, into the studio in the back. As the assistant did this, Ian noticed a sticker on the back of the Mercedes painting. It read "Henry Ashton." So much for privacy. Ian knew Henry Ashton. Ashton was the Vice Chairman of Standard Commerce Bank, Singapore. Scion of a Sephardic Jewish family originally from Syria that had Anglicized its name and prospered first in British and then independent Singapore, Ashton was a well-known collector of art. Ian was happy. He was in good company.

"You American, right?" said Wang.

"No, Mr. Wang. Nowadays, I'm a Singaporean."

Wang sighed and pointed to himself. "American. Not good for taxes."

"Not good," Ian said.

"IRS worse than Chinese Communist Party. And you can't give up American citizen. I make big mistake."

Ian nodded agreement. "The US is 'do as we say, not as we do on this.' In 1974 Congress passed something called the Jackson Vanik Amendment which punished the Soviet Union for imposing an exit tax on departing Soviet Jews. Apparently Americans are not accorded the same rights as Soviet Jews. The exit tax for Americans is quite high. I can personally attest to that. The so-called Heroes Earnings Assistance and Relief Act, passed in 2008 and signed by Republican President Bush and sponsored by the noted crook Representative Charles Rangel, imposes what can be considered an exit tax."

Wang stared at Ian. Ian's professorial lecture might have been a little too much for Wang's English. But then Wang may not have cared. He was a man who had just made $200,000 tax free dollars. Actually with Henry Ashton's contribution he would be making $400,000 tax free dollars. Americans have to pay US taxes on income earned outside the United States even when the taxpayer resides abroad. No other country imposes this. Ian guessed that, contrary to US law, Wang might not be reporting these transactions. Ian laughed. He was familiar with Wang's bank. Its original Portuguese owners – the Soares family – had sold out and departed for Portugal just before Macau's handover back to China in 1999. Nobody today in that bank from the CEO on down could string a full English sentence together. Its information systems were not exactly state of the art. And its CEO, a Eugene Cheung, was a wily old fox. The IRS would have to work to get its money on this. But Wang was taking a chance if he did not report this transaction. The IRS was leaving no stone unturned nowadays. The bank under new laws was supposed to report large account transactions to the American authorities. *Not Ian's problem.*

"You are teaching in the US now?" Ian asked. Before he became famous Wang had spent time in the States teaching art.

"No," Wang said. "I teach at Rhode Island School of Design. Next to Brown, famous Ivy university."

"Yes I know. I'm an ex college professor myself. When did you do my painting?" Ian asked.

"Ten year ago. In US."

"Who's the girl?"

"Just model. Not important."

"I guess in your business you see lots of naked girls."

Wang grinned. "Like doctor. But more fun." Wang's jagged tooth grin bespoke lechery not art.

"So you kept it all this time?" Ian said. He found himself suddenly jealous. This woman in the painting now belonged to him.

"Yes," Wang laughed. "I don't know why."

"It's not important," Ian said.

It would be.

Chapter Two

All portraiture is intimate. It involves careful examination of the faces, bodies, and clothes of figures that can neither leave nor turn away. Likewise, to paint a portrait requires intimacy.

— *Justine De Young*

Her land line phone was ringing. *Caller Unknown.* "It fucking better not be that asshole," she said aloud to herself in English.

"Coco, how are you," the caller said in Mandarin.

It *was* that asshole. "I told you not to call me." She looked around nervously. "I have enemies. This phone could be tapped. People in the house can hear us talking." She looked around. Actually she wasn't too worried about the servants although you never knew. Or the people who worked for her in her business. She had made sure they were all ethnic Chinese like her. They were loyal. They were *her* spies. She looked out the window. Some military guys in a jeep outside. Nothing unusual. But who knew what toys they had? Maybe they could listen. Su Myat was capable of so many tricks. The woman was insane. She could hear the workman on the roof of the house. They were all dumbass Burmese, all shirtless with their dirty longyis. She didn't have to worry about them.

She moved to a corner of the room and put her hand over her other ear. She looked out the window. The soldiers with their truck. Were they listening? Was her phone somehow tapped? "What do you want?" she said, finally.

"I thought you should know," Wang Qiang said. "I sold the painting. Wang Qiang paintings get a great price."

"You bastard." She bit her tongue. *The scumbag had just identified himself.* She had told him never to do that.

"Do you want me to repeat it?"

"Fuck your mother," she yelled in English.

Wang laughed. "I got two hundred thousand US dollars. That's big money for your little tits. No taxes, no fifty percent to Atherton Gallery, no need for handouts from you."

"You blackmailing bastard. Now my life is in danger. Why did you do this?"

"I owe some debts. They wanted the money now. Right now. I didn't have time for all your bullshit. Dealing with you always a negotiation."

"Fuck you" she shouted again in English. She looked around.

Wang laughed again and continued in Mandarin. "Now you don't have to send me money anymore. Think of what you are saving. I'm doing you a favor."

"You are really stupid. If they are listening on this call, they will come after you."

"I'm not afraid of some deranged woman from some southeast Asian shithole," Wang replied. "She's your problem, not mine. You should be proud. The buyer's name is Ian Blakely. The Blakely Funds. Big financial name. You'll be famous. And he's a good looking guy. He can fuck you and look up at the painting. Just like I did."

"Go to hell." She hung up. That was enough. If Su Myat was listening, everything would be ruined. If Su Myat got a hold of this stupid painting, her husband would be humiliated. And she would be dead. Or as good as dead. This was so unfair. Her whole marriage was something out of the Dark Ages. She could have said no. She saw opportunity, but she hadn't bargained on all the Burmese intrigue with Su Myat, her husband's daughter by his first marriage. Now this.

Coco called Major Nyan Myint. The Major had been seconded to her husband and was his personal assistant. She didn't trust the Major but who else was she going to call? "What are those military guys doing on our grounds," she asked speaking in Burmese.

"It's basically just routine, Madame," the Major responded, "You had complained your Bloomberg service wasn't working right. They are just doing some tests."

That wasn't what she wanted to hear. It was true she had a satellite dish on the roof to get the Bloomberg financial news service. It seemed to be suffering from some kind of interference. But these military guys were electronic guys. They could do electronic evesdropping. Maybe they weren't listening. But she couldn't take the chance. She couldn't trust the Major. His loyalties were to her husband, not to her.

She would have to move fast. She had to get the painting. But she couldn't just call up Ian Blakely out of the blue and offer to buy it. This financial guy. She knew very well who he was. He was on the list of possible investors that Devan had sent her for Project Zafar. What a twist of fate! To think that Ian Blakely had now bought the painting.

Her husband had allowed her to do as she pleased about business. Although born in Myanmar, or Burma as it was called then, Coco was Chinese enough. Her husband conveniently thought all Chinese were business geniuses. A prejudice of which Coco did not wish to disabuse him. He took care of the politics. He was former head of the army, now retired, but still active. There was one good thing about Myanmar. Women were a lot freer than places like India. And her husband was eighty five. She had saved his life. It was the divine wish that he marry her. That's what the monks said. And the stars were all properly lined up. That's what the astrologers said. And that's what her father said. She should have told them all to fuck off. She should have gone back to New York and worked for that goddamn bank and put up with their mind numbing politically correct bullshit. But here she was: Chinese, smarter than her husband's evil daughter, Su Myat. She had been Phi Beta Kappa at Brown.

She had an idea.

It was a long shot, but maybe she could kill two birds with one stone. Their Project Zafar had a loose end. What was going to happen to all the money that the government would receive? Ian Blakely was perfect. Why hadn't she thought of this before? Why not create a sovereign wealth fund? Blakely could invest the money abroad from the Project Zafar until the government needed it. Like they do in Norway and Singapore and lots of other places. Blakely would be the manager and train the Burmese. He was not only a world famous money manager but perfect for the job. He was a former professor. The government would like him. It would answer the Opposition's objections that the money from Project Zafar would just be wasted.

Ian Blakely was a Westerner, an American who had become a citizen of Singapore. He had been on her short list of investors for their project. They needed one more investor. Apparently Blakely's family was British on his father's side. Her husband would like him. He would think he was a Brit. Her husband had gone to Sandhurst. The fucking Brits had brainwashed him. General Maung Myo loved the Brits even though he would go on and on about the evils of British colonial imperialism. So Blakely would be perfect for Myanmar. Singaporean citizen, world famous fund manager, British ancestors, former professor—perfect.

Blakely had the painting. If she could just bring him in as investor and dangle this idea of running a sovereign wealth fund before him, he'd be on her side.

But what if he recognized her from the painting? Coco went to the mirror. The *Bad Girl* painting was done ten years ago. She was just a skinny kid then. She may have been Phi Beta Kappa, but she had been stupid enough to fall in love with a horny middle aged artist. She knew even at the time that she shouldn't have posed for that painting. But she was stoned on weed. The painting was bad luck. It was on July 4 that she posed. The fourth is a big deal for Americans. But the number four is bad luck for Chinese.

The mirror was giving her bad news. It said she didn't look that different from when she was twenty. That normally would have been good news. She looked pretty damn good when she was twenty. But that wasn't good news this time. When she was twenty she was five foot seven with a slender model-like figure. Now she was a thirty years old with the same five foot seven slender model-like figure. No change in weight. To the nearest pound. And she had the same taut darkish skin. Well, maybe when she was twenty her skin was slightly more taut. But really she was the only one that would notice that. She always wanted a boob job but she had never got around to it. Too late now. Same small tits. Yes she had replaced her third world teeth with a full set of shiny white crowns. But her teeth weren't a big deal in the painting. And what man ever remembered teeth anyway? Except for that one time when she got a little carried away with a blow job. She couldn't change her big eyes. She was always so proud of the fact that they were so entrancing, so unforgettable. That's what Western men said. Especially the older ones that she was attracted to. She used to like to hear it. Western men went crazy over her eyes. Chinese men didn't give a shit. Or at least they didn't say so. Or maybe they even looked down on her because she wasn't one hundred percent Han Chinese, the dominant ethnic group in China. Her mother was from a minority group that looked more like Thais and lived in Northern Myanmar and neighboring Yunnan province in China. A Chinese man could see it in her eyes. And her slightly darkish skin. She had never dated a Burmese man.

But sunglasses would take care of her big eyes. She had a huge really old dark pair of Guccis. She would wear her hair put up to look different from the disheveled look in the painting. She would add a few additional Burmese touches like a heavy dose of thanaka . She often wore thanaka anyway. It really did protect you from the sun and keep your face white. Of course she would look demure and traditional in a colorful longyi, the sarong-like garment that was standard dress for both men and women in Myanmar. And sandals of course. No Jimmy Choo high cage heels. She was really into them in college, unlike the American kids who all wore sneakers and dressed like homeless people. And, God forbid, no cigarillo.

Coco had to get Blakely on her side. Once his money was in the deal and he agreed to manage the sovereign wealth fund, she could manage him. She could get the painting back. He would be an ally. There was no choice. He might be in danger too. But that was his reward for being a horny *gweilo*. *These white guys come to Asia and think they can fuck every woman they see. He was probably holding his dick when he bought the painting. His dick, his problem.*

She had to call Devan now and set things in motion. She was sure he would cooperate. Devan had the Indians. Su Myat had the Chinese. The Indians were the only alternative. The whole project was going to cost a billion US dollars. At least Devan didn't smell like the Indians she knew in Yangon. And he had gone to Harvard Business School. And Devan was close to Ian Blakely. He was Ian Blakely's student. He had told her that. Of course he was a Chetty. Not the best pedigree for Myanmar. And he even had a crush on her. She was sure of that. But now he was getting married. Thank God.

She had to move fast. Before Su Myat figured out who Wang Qiang was.

Chapter Three

I didn't go to business school.

—Sheldon Adelson
Billionaire CEO of Las Vegas Sands

It was eleven a.m. Saturday morning in Singapore. Ian had got ahead of the day's heat and taken his morning swim. He was about to embark on his high speed Saturday morning walk. Ian took exercise seriously and regarded it as a necessary maintenance program to keep his fifty nine year old body in twenty five year old condition. Singapore is right on the equator and at sea level. For some people it is too hot and sticky. Not for Ian. He had dry skin. After four days on an airplane and in the ultra-dry Persian Gulf, sticky was just what he needed. On this walk, as he always did, he luxuriated in the riot of tropical flowers that surrounded his and most of the other apartment buildings in his neighborhood. Birds of paradise, bromeliads, chalice vines, canna lilies—his neighborhood was a botanical garden. And it wasn't that far from the world famous Singapore Botanic Garden. So many flowers, so much color, so many beautiful green leaves. The occasional lizard that scurried out of his way added to the tropical touch. The snakes and the rats – Ian had never actually seen either one – tended to mind their own business. The monkeys and tigers, alas, hadn't been seen recently.

Singapore was Ian's adopted home. It seemed like the perfect place for him. A place where he could meet by chance his fellow one percenters. A place where there were millionaires on every corner. A place where the government didn't demonize rich people. A multiracial meritocracy. An Asian Switzerland—efficient, English speaking and beautiful, although unlike Switzerland they didn't make cheese in Singapore . A place whose motto could be *Give me your talented, your rich, your huddled achievers yearning to be free of confiscation.* A place where one could comfortably be, like Ian, free, white, rich and fifty nine. Not the Holy Father's or Obama's kind of place.

As was his wont on his walk he detoured over a block to Orchard Road to pick up a vegetarian falafalel from one of the street vendors. And to ogle all the hot young girls. Nothing like a tropical climate with its minimal need for clothing. *A dirty old man needs his eye candy.* He passed by two particularly good looking Chinese girls. About twenty, they were speaking the local version of English which took a little listening to for a foreigner. They didn't have umbrellas like the Mainland girls who were never without them rain or shine. The girls were attired in tee shirts, the shortest of shorts and what Ian perceived to be the latest trend in high heeled sneakers. Definitely locals. He was much too old for them, he had to admit. But they were not too young for him.

Ian had spent the week mostly in the Persian Gulf, chasing potential clients, not girls. Friday's seven hour flight from Dubai had actually been quite pleasant overall. Ian had been to Hong Kong, Singapore, Macau, Dubai, Doha, Abu Dhabi, and then back to Singapore in four days. He had slept in his plane three of the four nights he was traveling. The one night he didn't stay in the plane he stayed in the apartment he owned in Dubai. Ian's Dubai apartment was in the Burj Khalifa, at one time the world's tallest building and an icon for the entire city. Like the plane, Ian had gotten the apartment at a knockdown price, again courtesy of the 2008 crisis. Ian's apartment was almost two thirds the way up. Not the top but higher than the Empire State Building. He had a panoramic view of the Persian Gulf and the city and was happily insulated from the city's death inducing dry July heat.

Girl watching in Singapore was definitely different from the Persian Gulf. There, the local women tended to dress head to toe in black abayas and burqas. All you could see were eyes and sometimes even the eyes were covered. And even with all that camouflage a curious foreigner could still get killed for staring too much. Burqa Babes were definitely off limits. Ian had had a recent taxi ride in Singapore where the driver told him Middle Eastern passengers drove him crazy. Why? Because more than one client from the Middle East had told him to cover up his rear view mirror so that the taxi driver couldn't stare at the client's all black covered wife. This taxi driver, a somewhat loquacious Sikh, told Ian, "Everyone has wife. Why do I want to stare at theirs?" Good point. Although at the moment Ian didn't have a wife.

Dubai and the other nouveau riche Gulf states were definitely places to stare at the incredible new buildings, not the local girls. Singapore, which also had its share of incredible new buildings, was a more relaxed and sluttier place. As luck would have it this morning he ran into the good looking Filipina who was the live-in helper for his downstairs British banker neighbor and his wife and child. A brown woman with a flirtatious manner, she often took their five year old and their dog out walking. This morning she was attired in the tiniest of shorts and a really tight green tank top. "You look more yummy every time I see you," Ian said, while offering silent thanks for stores like Guess and H&M. Cheap and sexy. The helper and the five year old both gave him a big smile. "Say good morning to Uncle," the helper said to her young charge, which he did. The dog licked Ian's hand, which he hated but tolerated. What men will do to indulge their lust! Amazing that the neighbor's wife – a rather unattractive and frumpy British woman – would let such a gorgeous creature be around her husband on a daily basis. Just to be on the safe side and knowing his own weaknesses, Ian had deliberately selected a rather plain but efficient middle aged Philippine woman to be his own helper. She actually had a college degree from someplace in the Philippines. The last thing he needed in his new homeland was a headline saying "MAID SUES RICH WESTERN HEDGE FUND MANAGER FOR SEXUAL HARRASSMENT." It had happened to a friend of his. *Never fuck the help.*

Despite all of his travels and the morning's exercise, Ian was brimming with energy. Of course, he had a little help. Nothing like flying at Mach .8 in the comfort of your own twin engine Gulfstream G450 at turbulence-free cruising altitude of 45,000 feet, at least a mile above the *hoi polloi* in commercial airliners bouncing below. Especially, when like Ian, you are six foot three and prone to back problems from sitting in cramped commercial seats on so many long distance plane flights. Ian had picked up the plane on the cheap. Its prior owner was a major global bank that fire-saled it in a downsizing exercise forced on them after 2008. Although it really was bigger than he needed, the G450 had the range Ian wanted as it could easily make it nonstop from Singapore to the Persian Gulf or to just about anywhere in Asia. He had had the cabin configured to his needs with an on-board Bloomberg screen, WiFi and a high speed internet connection. And of course a large reclining bed that could be pulled down when needed. Ian since his divorce had discovered that female guests on a man's private plane were always in the mood to show their appreciation.

When he wasn't on the phone, Ian had spent the time on the plane reading Constantino Bresciani-Turroni's *The Economics of Inflation—A Study of Currency Depreciation in Post War Germany*. In those bygone days the dollar was as good as gold. As a former financial historian, Ian was fascinated with the book. But he also was taken with the author's name. He decided if he ever got a dog he would name him Constantino. And have his neighbors' Filipina come walk Constantino.

His walk finished, Ian was at his desk replying to emails and nibbling on his falafel. In recent years Middle Eastern guys had suddenly made their appearance on the sidewalks of global cities selling falafel. Only a month ago on a trip to New York he had managed to buy a falafel while rushing between meetings. He wondered if the guys selling him falafel in Singapore were brothers of the falafel guys in New York.

Ian had given his helper a week off to go home to the Philippines so he was by himself. A stack of research reports awaited his perusal. As he looked out his window, he could just see the top of the massive hotel towers of the Sands complex down on Marina Bay. Some artsy fartsy architectural critics pretended to hate the Sands complex, perhaps because it is dedicated to a low life pursuit like gambling, or perhaps because the company's CEO was thought to be a crass right wing Jew. Some critics claimed this man had help ruin Macau and now it was Singapore's turn. Ian however loved the Sands complex. And he liked crass right wing Jews. Actually, he liked right wing people of any sort. He looked away from the Sands. The strong tropical sun was hurting his eyes. Lying on his desk was an old copy of Nicholas Taleb's *The Black Swan*. Another one of his favorites. Black swans in Taleb's book were giant unexpected economic events that turned the investment world upside down. The 2008 financial crisis was such an event. Ian had seen the world in a similar fashion as Taleb and had read the book several times. The only problem was that recently, while eating breakfast at a hotel in Colombo, Sri Lanka, he thought he had seen not only *one* but *two* black swans swimming in the pond outside the hotel's restaurant. That was a lot of black swans for one day. Taleb had portrayed them as being extremely rare. Maybe Ian was mistaken. He wasn't a biologist; perhaps the birds he saw were ducks. On the other hand, perhaps Taleb should travel more.

Ian's iPhone beeped and interrupted his reverie. It was Devangar Saravanan.

"Devan, how are you?"

"Great. I'm sorry to be bothering you on a Saturday…" Devan, reflecting his years in the US, spoke with the lightest of Singaporean -Indian accents.

Ian interrupted him. "For me Saturday's no different from any other day. No bother." That was true. Ian didn't play golf and he didn't care about professional sports. His work was his hobby. And despite occasionally being photographed in the company of one beautiful woman or another, in the last year he had been relatively quiet on the social front. His wife of two years had taken their child and left him just before he moved to Asia. His final divorce had only come through six months ago. Lucky for him she was independently wealthy from her own career. So he didn't get hosed by his ex-wife on the property front. The IRS was enough. But he wasn't ready for another relationship.

Devan continued. "Remember that offshore liquid natural gas investment in Myanmar that I told you about for your new Asian energy fund?"

"You mean Project Zafar?" With the recent decline in energy prices energy producing assets globally had become cheaper. Ian had concluded that picking up energy assets on the cheap might be a good strategy for the Blakely Funds. So, just like he had bought his Dubai condo and Gulfstream in the depths of the 2008 crisis, he had launched a new energy fund.

"Yes," Devan replied. "They are very interested in having you on board as an investor. You are apparently a legend in Myanmar."

"How did that happen?"

"I don't know. But your fame is spreading wider and wider."

"You know my great grandfather served for a brief time in Burma. He was a lieutenant colonel in the colonial Indian army. Actually a 'leftenant' in British lexicon."

"Commanding his sepoys no doubt," Devan added.

"Sepoys? Now there's a word you don't hear anymore. One of your ancestors by chance?"

"No, remember I'm Chettiar. My ancestors were all bankers and moneylenders. We didn't enter the army. We left shooting people to the Sikhs, the Gurkhas and the Moslems. And the British."

"So separating innocents from their money is in your DNA," Ian said. "Now, how much do you want out of me?"

"It's up to you but at least fifty million. US. This project all in will require close to a billion dollars. You will make at least a twenty percent annual rate of return on your investment over ten years. And that's assuming no increase in LNG prices. But you only have to put in ten million dollars initially."

"LNG. That's liquid natural gas," Ian said.

"Yes."

"How can you offer a return like that? The price of energy has declined so much lately."

The enthusiasm in Devan's voice was palpable. "Technology and technology and technology. Calcutta Global Oil, which I'm sure you know, will be the heavyweight investor in and operator of Project Zafar. They have made some amazing breakthroughs in FLNG technology. That's the trade acronym --Floating Liquid Natural Gas. The big oil companies – Exxon, Chevron and the like – all want to license Calcutta Global's technology. We Indians are really good at technology, even if we can't build toilets. Do you want me to go on?"

"Of course, Devan. Go on. I'm well aware of the sophistication of Indian technology. And Indian shortcomings in the toilet space."

"The Calcutta Global Oil Company will actually run the project. The Indian government wants it to happen and the Indian National Development Bank will be financing the bulk of the capital investment on very favorable terms. We've got the Indians. We are now awaiting the approval of the government of Myanmar."

"The new Indian government is definitely on board for this?"

"Yes, absolutely."

"I've actually read something about Calcutta Global's new technology. But the prices of oil and gas have dropped so much."

"That's what's so amazing about the new Calcutta Global technology! We still make a killing even at the lower prices. Do you want to hear more?"

"Yes, Devan, go on."

"We Indians can be quite creative when our government isn't standing in our way. Anyway, our group purchased options from the government of Myanmar on two contiguous offshore blocks. A 'block' covers a specific territory in offshore Myanmar waters. Everybody thought these particular blocks were worthless. But we know now they are in fact worth a great deal."

Ian's Blakely Funds had now had nine billion dollars under management, not counting the billion that he had just gathered from rich oil sheiks on his visit to the Persian Gulf. His problem was where to invest it all. Devan had approached Ian once before on Zafar. But Ian hadn't had time to deal with it.

"This project will be really a big deal in Myanmar," Devan added. "And it will be a big deal in India too. Our firm is going to put in a significant amount of our own money. But that's only the half of it."

"How so?"

"Ian, Myanmar is overflowing with oil and gas. The Chinese have some huge projects. The Myanmar government is going to be overflowing with money. At least in the short term. They really don't have the personnel to handle all this money right now."

"So."

"We are selling this to the government that the money they earned from Zafar will be put in a special fund perhaps for a rainy day. The money will be invested abroad."

"Sounds like a sovereign wealth fund or SWF as they are called," Ian said.

"Exactly. Ian, we want you to manage the money from this project. You are going to set up Myanmar's SWF. We are talking about over half a billion within five years. Minimum. You of course will get a separate fee for managing this fund."

"Come off it, Devan. There must be somebody in all of Myanmar who can do this. Why do they need me?"

"Take my word for it. There's nobody in all of Myanmar who can do this. Training your eventual successor will be part of your job. Can we get together and talk about this?"

"Sure, Devan. How about dinner tonight?"

"Great idea."

"It's Saturday night. I see neither one of us has a social life."

"My fiancée is visiting her parents in Calcutta. What's your excuse?"

"Can't meet the right girl."

"Ian, that's not believable in your case." Devan continued. "Shall we meet at the Tanglin Club? It's right down the road from you."

"How about something a little more adventurous? You know how the Brits are. They don't like you to talk business at" -- Ian hesitated for emphasis—'The Club.'"

"Okay. How about a nice south Indian fish head curry on banana leaves at my favorite hole-in-the-ground in Little India? I know a little place where we can get a side booth and have privacy."

"Will the smell kill me?"

"It will make you stronger. I'll drop by at eight and pick you up. I'll drive."

"Is this real time or Indian time? I mean are you really coming by at ten?"

Devan laughed. "I'll be there exactly at eight. If not sooner. Meanwhile, I'll email you the business plan and the summary of a report that concludes area of Myanmar we are talking about is loaded with natural gas. And maybe oil."

Ian leaned back in his chair. His energy fund was his new pet project and he was very enthused about it. The Blakely Funds had made over a billion dollars in 2008 shorting subprime mortgages and financial companies like Citibank and Fannie Mae. When the world tanked of course he went short. He would do it again. But deep down he was an idealist. He liked investing in areas that could improve the world. The Blakely Group had added funds investing in telecommunications, software, social media and education. Energy was the latest. Ian was also thinking of starting a biotech fund if he could find the right person to run it. Globalization and technology were a religion for Ian, the next phase of human evolution. He wanted to finance evolution and perhaps have a little fun along the way. Ian detested the do-gooders, Luddites and anti-technology environmentalists, who he felt did enormous harm and were on the wrong side of evolution. If his Funds continued to do well, he would set up a trust in a few years that would further in biotech research. No charity handouts. As far as Myanmar went, the idea of investing in a backward country that had just decided to rejoin the modern world excited him. And he was to run a SWF. That had a certain cachet in the investment world.

The phone rang again. There were only a limited number of people who had his private number. This call was from Mr. Lee from the frame shop. Ian had almost forgotten about *Bad Girl*.

"Mr. Lee. How are you? Has the painting arrived?"

"Yes/no."

The Chinese are known for their binary approach to information. Concepts like "if" or "perhaps" are not favored. The answer is either "yes" or "no". *Yao bu yao*, "like/not like?" But Lee's answer was a little over the top even by Chinese standards. "What do you mean?"

"You told me that painting was nude. This painting is Chinese lady getting into Mercedes. Not nude."

"Oh shit." Wang had mixed up the paintings. Ian had gotten Henry Ashton's. Hopefully Ashton had his.

"Okay, just hold on to it. I think I know where mine is. I'll get back to you."

"Okay-lah."

Ian called Ashton immediately on his private number. He got a recording with a woman with a very British accent who said "Mr. Ashton is otherwise engaged at the moment." Mr. Ashton was probably at one of his snooty clubs where they had a heart attack if you spoke on a cell phone. Maybe he was in the middle of a golf round. He left a message that he had Ashton's painting and wondered if Ashton had his. He had a feeling Ashton would be calling him back quickly.

It took five minutes. "I have to speak softly," Ashton said. "I'm in the men's locker room at my club. They don't approve of cell phones."

Ian could hear the flushing of a toilet in the background. What would the Club say if they knew one of their most prominent members was furtively huddled in a toilet stall and flagrantly violating one of their most sacred rules?

"Ian, is your painting one of an almost nude Chinese girl with a cigarillo?"

"That's the one. It looks like Wang Qiang got things mixed up. I've got your *Woman in Mercedes*."

"Indeed. I must say yours is pretty racy compared to mine."

"I'm a hedgie. You're a banker. Different rules." Another toilet flush in the background. Ian wanted to ask what they were serving for lunch at the Club that was causing this run on the men's toilets. "I'll bring your painting over next Tuesday myself and we'll make the switch. How about four o'clock."

"As you wish." Ashton clicked off.

Ian sat back and laughed. The rich, F Scott is supposed to have said to Ernest, are different from you and me. Turns out the rich don't have a choice. They have to huddle in the men's rooms of their snooty private clubs to discuss their latest art purchase. Poor people don't have to do that. And in Ian's case the rich actually have to change countries. The avalanche of money he was making had changed his life. For starters when he lived in Miami he was named in an article in *Rolling Stone* as one of the ten most evil persons in America. He had had the audacity to defend his shorting mortgage related securities in an op-ed Wall Street piece. He had had to hire a bodyguard. In 2009 he moved to Singapore, and became a Permanent Resident. Then at great cost he gave up his American citizenship and became a Singaporean citizen. He had tried to get a British passport since his father was British but that proved too complicated. But he wanted to be in Asia which in his opinion would be the center of economic growth in the twenty first century. And now even the Republicans were calling for increases in taxes. As if Obama needed egging on.

Led by Warren Buffet, the Democrats were asking the "rich" in the name of patriotism to contribute ten percent of their wealth. *Fuck that.*

Ian wasn't that patriotic. He figured his investments did far more for humanity than what he viewed as wasteful spending by the US government. Ironically, some people in Singapore felt sorry for him. In Singapore he was a refugee of sorts. A rich refugee, but a refugee nevertheless. Things hadn't been so bad for the white man's image since the British surrender of the city to the Japanese in 1942. But Singapore was Asia's new Switzerland. Aspiring Switzerlands don't fuck with rich people.

Ian called Mr. Lee back and told him he would pick up the painting on Tuesday afternoon. Wang could wait for his money. Then he went back to his research reports. He enjoyed the solitude. He enjoyed the phone not ringing.

Except the phone did ring again. It was someone called Adrian Cairncross. "It's awfully good of you to take my call, Mr. Blakely."

"How did you get my number?"

"Wang Qiang gave it to me. He's one of our artists. I'm with Atherton's."

"I see."

"I won't take much of your time. I understand you have purchased a painting by Wang called *Bad Girl*."

"That's right."

"I'm so sorry. Mr. Wang is a bit disorganized. It seems that painting was already purchased by someone else."

"Mr. Wang didn't mention that." Ian was starting to get unhappy.

Cairncross continued. "Well, he gets a little distracted sometimes, like all artists. I reminded him again today and he's very embarrassed. You've paid already?"

"Yes," Ian lied. "I own the painting."

"Ah, perhaps we could talk about this. Our buyer is very upset. He believes he owns the painting. In our minds there is no question. He purchased it first. Our client really wants this painting. He is a gentleman. He could go to court but I'm sure he'd rather not. He's a reasonable man and very, very rich. No doubt he would be willing to make it worthwhile to let him take it off your hands. It is our understanding you got a good price. You will make a nice profit. Our client understands Mr. Wang is, shall we say, a little eccentric."

"I'm very rich myself. Your client must really want this painting. Who is he? Where is he from?"

"I'm afraid I can't tell you that. My client requires absolute secrecy. You are in Singapore?"

"Yes. And where are you?"

"I'm in London. But as it turns out I have business in Singapore. I'm leaving tomorrow."

Ian thought the call was a little fuzzy for a London connection. Nowadays, unless your party is in some ass-backward fourth world country, everybody you talk to sounds crystal clear like they were next door.

"Could I stop by your office Monday afternoon? May I repeat. You will find our client to be a very determined but a very reasonable man. I'm sure we can straighten this out."

Ian hesitated for a moment. "Do you know where my office is?"

"Yes, you are in our computer."

"Great."

"It's our business." Cairncross said. "We have already identified you as an up and coming heavyweight in the collecting world."

"That makes my day."

"Indeed. See you Monday in Singapore. You are very kind." Cairncross clicked off.

Ian was very disappointed. He wanted the painting but of course if someone else had bought it first then he would have to relinquish it. But there was something about Cairncross he didn't like. Too much bullshit. He spoke with an upper class English accent. But underneath there was another accent, something vaguely un- English.

Ian called Wang Qiang. No answer. Not even a recording.

Ian called his assistant, Anita Ng. Other than the fact he could never pronounce her last name correctly and her political views were to the left of his, Anita was perfect for him. Anita was Singaporean Chinese but had spent half her life in the US. She was twenty seven, had an MA in art history from Columbia, an MBA from Pace University and spoke reasonably good Mandarin and passable Cantonese. She was married to a professor of genetics at Nanyang Technological University and was about five months pregnant. Anita had returned to Asia after finally finishing her studies, and, with her language background and high level of efficiency, was very useful to Ian who spoke no Chinese languages. She spoke to Ian as if they were equals which he liked. Some of the Chinese in his office treated him with the reverential respect due a Confucian father. A great trait for running a harmonious society. A real drawback for a hedge fund when twenty- four hours a day you had to think outside the box.

Anita served also as Ian's unofficial art advisor. It was she who had brought Wang to Ian's attention. But he hadn't told her about the purchase. Ian wanted to save that for when he actually showed Anita the painting. An almost nude Chinese girl. Ian couldn't wait to hear her insult him for having been overwhelmed by his pathetic case of yellow fever.

Ian began. "I'm calling about an Adrian Cairncross. He works at Atherton's. I want to know about him ASAP."

"Spell the name," Anita said. She was used to Ian's seven day a week work schedule.

Ian spelled the name.

"Why do you want to know about him?"

Ian told Anita how he had bought a painting and now there was some mixup both as to ownership.

"What's the painting like?"

"It's a frontal nude of a young Chinese girl. Well almost nude."

"Oh shit," Anita said. "You're hopeless. What's wrong with a nice nude white girl?"

Ian could see Anita rolling her eyes. This he was enjoying. "Been there. Done that."

Anita continued. "Why am I not surprised. Well, you're in luck. My best friend in the States works for Atherton. She's number two in their New York office."

"I don't know what this guy's game really is."

"We'll find out," Anita said.

"We have two mixups for this painting. First the delivery switch and then a new buyer. I'll get back to you as soon as I know something. This is very odd."

"What do you mean delivery switch?" Anita asked.

Ian explained to Anita how his painting had gotten mixed up with Henry Ashton's.

"Very odd indeed," Anita said. "I'll be back to you as soon as I learn something."

Ian called Wang Qiang again. No answer. No recording.

Chapter Four

"Husband," Coco said, "I want you to trust me on this." They were speaking in English. The General liked to practice his English. She always called him Husband although she really wanted to say Grandpa. But it was her deal. She had to put up with the downside. And there were major advantages. She had made her choice. She just had to play the cards the way they were dealt. She lit up a cigarillo. Her husband had a certain basic animal cunning. And shrewdness and wisdom that came from experience. She admired these qualities. And she had to make sure he was okay with what she was doing.

"Coco, you know I trust you. You have proved your loyalty to me as no one else has." General Maung Myo – or U Maung Myo, using the honorary title often attached to his name --was eighty five but still mentally sharp. He could only walk with a cane thanks to a small stroke he'd had six months ago. He was about the same height as Coco -- five foot seven-- which forced her to give up wearing her beloved 160 millimeter heels. She had to wear traditional Burmese sandals or Adidas running sneakers, at least when she was around him. A woman in Asia cannot tower over her husband. There were some advantages to the sandals and sneakers, she had to admit. At least she could walk.

The General spoke, projecting the authority of a man used to being obeyed. "Su Myat opposes everything I do. I am so disappointed in my daughter." The General shook his head. "The monks said you were sent by the Buddha himself. The astrologer said the stars were on your side. She has no right to doubt them."

Coco sighed. *Always the monks and astrologer.* Luckily the monks and the astrologer hadn't figured out that she was planning to destroy Su Myat. "Husband, we have another potential investor here. He's an American who operates a major set of hedge funds out of Singapore. He would partner with the Saravanan Group and the Calcutta Global Oil Company."

The General's mouth twisted. "The Saravanans are Chettys. That still bothers me."

Coco's large brown eyes studied him. "You've known the Saravanan family for at least fifty years. They've always been honest with you. They've helped you. You've met Devan Saravanan twice. You were impressed with him. He has put this whole thing together. He's a Harvard MBA. Times have changed. This is a new country. The Chettys haven't been a big deal here since the 1930s. Remember, we need the Indians. Su Myat has her Chinese group. The Indian National Development Bank will make a huge loan on this project. Calcutta Global is number one in FLNG technology. We've discussed this so many times."

"Su Myat will use this against us. And now the opposition is saying we don't need another oil and gas project. Myanmar has more money than we know what to do with. Leave the gas in the ground for now."

"I have an answer for that. We will propose a Sovereign Wealth Fund, or SWF as they are called, be created. This new investor is a world famous investor. He will manage the Sovereign Wealth Fund until it can be turned over to the Myanmar people. I've just written a memo outlining how this would work. There's a lot of natural gas in the world with all the new technologies. The people here have to understand that leaving the gas in the ground may not be the best strategy." She handed her husband the memo. "This is a form of diversification. There's so much oil and gas in Myanmar earning nothing in the ground. But nobody can be sure how much it will be worth in ten years. The price could just as easily go down further as well as up. The Americans with their fracking and horizontal drilling and the new technology in liquid natural gas shipping are driving down the global price of natural gas. And -- our Indian partners have some spectacular new technology of their own. We still make money even at current lower prices for energy. So, with our project some gas gets taken out of the ground and monetized right now for Myanmar. And the waters in our two blocks are so shallow. This is a very simple project. We will have a long term contract with an inflation adjusted price from the Indians. The Sovereign Wealth Fund will be a piggy bank for Myanmar to be used in the future."

Coco wondered if he understood all this. Sometimes it seemed what she said to him on financial matters was of no interest or went straight over his aged head. Other times, he seemed to understand perfectly.

For a few moments the General said nothing while fiddling with the memo Coco had just handed him. Then the old spark filled his eyes. "I think this Sovereign Wealth Fund is a brilliant idea. The Singaporeans have two of them, right?"

"So you knew that. Great. And so do the Kuwaitis, the Saudis and the Abu Dhabians have SWFs. There are lots more."

The General watched her. "You are a financial wizard, Coco. Like all Chinese. It amazes me how someone so young and so pretty can know about these things."

Coco put her hand over her face. "Make believe I'm ugly."

"I cannot," the General said solemnly. "But I wonder about my daughter. I think she is another Supayalat."

Coco immediately liked the Supayalat reference. Anybody from Myanmar would understand it. Queen Supayalat was the last Queen of Burma and is revered by many in Myanmar today. But she did have one "minor" negative in her history. She reportedly had 80 to 100 of her husband's relatives-- and therefore potential rivals of her husband -- murdered in order to avoid succession problems. After the third Anglo Burmese War, the British abolished the monarchy, deposed King Thibaw and Supayalat and banished them to exile in India. That was another way to avoid succession problems. In Su Myat's case, several years ago her younger brother had disappeared under mysterious circumstances. Several years prior to that, her younger sister had been killed in London by a hit and run driver. That eliminated Su Myat's siblings as heirs to the General. Until Coco showed up.

The General continued. "I don't know why my daughter is doing this. This project was your idea, not hers."

Coco tried to pull him back tactfully to the subject at hand. "This new investor is a white guy. He is very rich. He was an American but now he's a Singaporean."

The General interrupted. "He's an ASEAN citizen. That's good." Myanmar was a member ASEAN, or the Association of Southeast Asian Nations, and took its membership very seriously.

"I believe his family's British on his father's side," Coco said. "Used to be a Harvard professor. He manages a lot of money. Devan says at least nine billion US."

"What's his name?"

"Ian Blakely."

The General pointed to the cigarillo in his wife's hand. "That will kill you."

"I'm going to give it up." She had been saying this for the last ten years. "Right after Chinese New Year."

"This Ian Blakely. His name sounds British. That's good. I like British people. Even though they invaded our country."

The General could go on and on about the evils of British colonialism. But he had been trained at Sandhurst. He did love British people and was almost deferential around them. After listening to her husband and other Asians of his generation, Coco had concluded that before the British had left Asia, they had inserted a secret gene in the natives' DNA which made the natives look up to them nostalgically and kiss their ass.

The General continued. "You know him?"

"I have not met him yet."

The General seemed relieved. "Okay. I want to meet Blakely. By himself, man to man. Not with the Chetty."

Mission accomplished. Coco heaved a sigh of relief. "I'm sure he will want to come here and meet with you." The General would approve of Ian Blakely. And he was right about Devan. Chettiars still were hated in some quarters in Myanmar. And for some people in Myanmar, all Indians were Chettys. But in Coco's opinion these people were stupid. Myanmar needed the Indians to offset the Chinese. And there could be no deal without Devan. His firm was an investor and he had done an incredible job putting everything together. He was the glue. *Fuck Burmese prejudices.*

The General wasn't finished. "You must not give Su Myat anything to use against you. She will be watching. You must be beyond reproach."

"I know." The General was right. And of course she knew full well that, like any old man with a young good looking wife, the General was paranoid about his young good looking wife going off to fuck some good looking young man. Especially when sex with this old man was like playing pool with a limp hose, even after a bottle of Viagra. And that was before his stroke. She had fucked her brains out in college. It never occurred to her that at age thirty she would be married and celibate. She knew her husband was happy she had never met Blakely.

The General was telling her something else. The General was finally acknowledging that his daughter was a threat to him. Coco had been waiting to hear these words. "Should we use our information and move on her husband?" she asked.

"Not yet."

So the General still wasn't ready to get really nasty. But the time would come. She had the dirt on Su Myat's husband. She was ready. She was putting together a special video. Chinese history was filled with scheming concubines and eunuchs. Court treachery was a Chinese tradition. Her father, a one-time though now reformed drug warlord, had taught her a few things in the treachery department. And she was an apt pupil. She would get her painting back and then she would finish off Su Myat. Everything in due time. With Su Myat it was either kill or be killed.

Chapter Five

Tersely and pointedly speaking, Chettiar banks are fiery dragons that parch every land that has the misfortune of coming under their wicked creeping.

They are a hard-hearted lot that will ring out every drop of blood from the victims without compunction for the sake of their own interest...[T]he swindling, cheating, deception and oppression of the Chettiars in the country, particularly among the ignorant folks, are well known and these are, to a large extent, responsible for the present impoverishment in the land.

—***Testimony of a Karen witness to the Burma Provincial Banking Enquiry, 1929.***

Devangar Saravanan had managed to find a small room off to the side of the restaurant where they had some privacy. The strong smell of curry permeated the only partly air conditioned air. If you don't like the smell of curry, don't go to Little India in Singapore. On the way to be seated Ian noticed a Chinese family seated right next to the room where he and Devan were to eat. They had a little boy who kept yelling *"Bu yao, bu yao"* --I don't like, I don't like".

You can't please everyone. Probably, in parts of China, serving Indian food to Chinese children would qualify as child abuse. But in multicultural Singapore, it is no doubt a civic duty.

At any rate Ian wasn't yelling *bu yao*. He liked Indian food.

A painting of what perhaps was some maharaja's wife hung on the wall. She was a buxom woman, fully clothed in a colorful though sensuous native dress. The painting was probably a cheap reproduction that you could pick up in any shop in Little India. But Ian couldn't help mentally comparing this well-endowed but decorously attired Indian lady with the indecorously nude but less endowed Chinese lady in his *Bad Girl* painting.

"The Indian girls always have such big boobs in these traditional paintings and look so sexy," Ian remarked to Devan, pointing at the painting. "The Chinese girls in traditional scroll paintings always look so scrawny. At least that's the way they look in the Chinese and Indian galleries at the Metropolitan in New York." Of course *Bad Girl* was not exactly a traditional oeuvre.

"That's about the only thing India beats China in," Devan replied grinning. "Anyway, we Indian men like a little more 'meat on the bone', so to speak."

"More to love."

"Yes," Devan replied. He looked away as if he was a little embarrassed by conversation.

Two smiling male waiters, both with dark South Indian faces, entered with the food. The fish head came in a big dish swimming in a soup of curry flavored okra, tomatoes, and eggplant. The fish's open mouth revealed a row of pointy teeth. Ian and Devan scooped out portions of the fish and the curry and placed it on the banana leaves in front of them, which served as their plates. Ian dipped his naan bread into the curry.

"If I eat the head, will I get smarter?" Ian asked.

"Hasn't worked for me," Devan replied. "Not too spicy?"

"No problem. I'm an *hombre del mundo*," Ian replied taking a sip of his Kingfisher beer.

"The last time I was in Los Angeles," Devan said, poking at his banana leaf, "people spoke to me in Spanish. I'm dark and short. They thought I was Latino."

"I'm sure all the Latinas thought you were short, dark and handsome."

"Maybe. I guess from living in Miami with all the Cubans you acquired a taste for spicy food."

Ian said nothing. Cuban food in Miami isn't spicy. It isn't overwhelmed with hot peppers like Mexican food. But Ian hadn't come to have a long discussion about the pros and cons of hot peppers. Eating the fish head curry was enough. "I think this place is far better than some snooty ex-British club," Ian said. "In colonial times of course the Brits – my ancestors – would sit around and drink gin and talk about how the natives could never run the country. Didn't matter what country they were in. The conversation was the same."

Devan nodded. "My fiancée has relatives who belong to one of those snooty clubs in Kolkata, as it's called today. The club's survived, but now it is filled with Indians. They drink plenty of gin."

"What do they talk about?" Ian asked.

"They talk about how the natives cannot run the country. But now they have sixty years of proof."

"Devan," Ian said solemnly. "Maybe you shouldn't run for office in India."

"Let me begin by telling you about my family. I belong to a South Indian group called the *Chettiars*. We're from Tamil Nadu in south India. We have been in the money lending business for centuries. Actually, I am part of the *Nattukkotai Chettiars* who are the moneylenders. It's a little complicated."

"What isn't complicated in India? The Chettiars are all Brahmins, I presume?"

"Actually not. We are considered a Vaishya or mercantile clan. I can explain all this in greater detail if you like."

Ian smiled. "Perhaps some other time."

"Anyway, under the British the Chettiars prospered, especially in places like Burma and Ceylon. In Burma we set up banks that dealt with the native

Burmese. The big British exchange banks, as they were called, would not deal with the locals. My grandfather started a bank. The Nattukottai Chettiars financed the expansion of agriculture along the Irrawaddy delta in Burma."

"I've heard a little about the Chettiars. You're sort of like the Jews."

"We're in the money business and everybody hates us. And we are spread out all over formerly British southeast Asia. In colonial days there were Chettiars even in Vietnam. There are two Nattukottai Chettiar temples in Singapore. Maybe you've been to one?"

Ian shook his head. "I'll put it on my to-do list. Actually, all Hindu temples look pretty much alike to me. A lot of colors."

"I'll take you sometime," Devan said.

"Nowadays everybody hates money men. Especially hedge fund guys like me. You don't have to be Jewish to be hated anymore. Or Chettiar."

Devan nodded. "When the Depression came in the 1930s the prices of rice and other commodities collapsed. The Irrawaddy Delta farmers defaulted. The Irrawaddy Delta is just north of Rangoon or Yangon as its now called. I guess you know that."

"I do," Ian said.

"The Chettiars always took land as collateral from the farmers. Chettiars always lent on collateral. In the twenties agricultural activity expanded in the Delta. But in the Thirties during the Depression there were a lot of foreclosures. The Chettiars wound up owning a substantial part of the land in the Delta. Our people never wanted this to happen. We aren't farmers. We didn't want to own farmland. But the world collapsed on us."

"I can guess what happened next," Ian said.

"Everybody turned on us." Devan said, going at the okra, tomatoes and eggplant. "The Burmese and the British colonial officials all made us into bad guys. There were riots. Then the Japanese invaded in 1942 and after that came independence in 1948. The Chettiars lost almost everything, including in many cases their lives."

"But now you are telling me to invest in Myanmar." As he said this Ian helped himself to another portion of fish head. He was trying to eat moderately. People in America joke that with Chinese food you are hungry a half hour after eating. Nobody ever said that about Indian food. Indian food is seductive. You wind up eating too much. You wind up gorging yourself on a riot of curries, spices and breads. A half hour later you can hardly walk.

"We Chettiars don't give up easily. Yes, I'm telling you to invest in Myanmar. Despite all the setbacks and local prejudices, my family has retained a presence there. I grew up in Singapore but I was actually born in Rangoon. My family has been helpful to General Maung Myo over the years."

"That's why you got this deal."

"Off the record, yes. But it was his new wife who pushed on this. She saw the potential. I'm the glue with the Indians. I'm always in the background. The General never lets me forget I'm Chetty. But enough of this ethnic stuff. Look at the map." Devan pulled out a preliminary prospectus from his briefcase. He had already emailed Ian a copy. He opened it to the first page, right alongside his banana leaves. "Myanmar is situated in southeast Asian right between China and India. 'Strategic' understates Myanmar's geopolitical importance. And, although more exploratory work needs to be done, it's almost certain that Myanmar is replete with oil and gas as well as all kinds of minerals. On shore and offshore. It is of course famous for jade. And there are beaches waiting to be discovered."

"So how did it get to be so backward?"

"Well, of course the Japanese invasion in 1942 was very destructive. Then after World War II came independence, then a civil war among conflicting ethnic groups and then, in 1962, the military coup. The country went into a long dark hibernation. But now it is opening up. That's why Obama came here."

"And made me ill."

"It was the smart thing. You have to give the guy credit."

"Okay, I'll give him credit. One credit. Wasn't Burma part of British India at one time?"

"Yes, until 1937 Burma was part of the British Raj and ruled from India. But in 1937 the British split it off and it became a separate Royal Crown Colony. The local people did not want to be part of India. In the Twenties, Rangoon was more than 50% Indian. Mandalay was heavily Chinese. But with the Japanese invasion, independence, and then the military coup in 1962, the majority of Indians and Chinese had to leave."

"A sad story."

"Ask any Indian or Chinese in Southeast Asia. It was a sad day when the British left."

Ian smiled. He hadn't heard a pro-colonial speech like that before. "But now the Chinese have come back."

Devan leaned forward from his open briefcase and prospectus. "That's exactly the opportunity. Myanmar doesn't want the Chinese to take over. The American boycott has been an invitation to let the Chinese do just that. That's why they are opening up and why they let Aung San Suu Kyi out. Burma like Vietnam has spent a lot of time in the past fighting the Chinese. In the eighteenth century the Chinese actually invaded Burma."

"But they got their butts kicked," Ian interrupted.

"So you know the history." Devan lowered his voice as if there was a Chinese spy listening. "The Chinese don't know how to spell 'soft power.' It's too subtle for them. And the Indian government has finally awakened to the Chinese threat. Under a new leadership. Indian needs oil and gas." The briefcase snapped closed. "India needs to keep Myanmar out of Chinese hands."

"And the British aren't coming back to help them."

"That's why the Indian government is giving us such a good deal on this. They desperately want this deal to happen. Look," Devan pointed to the map in the prospectus. "The Chinese are building twin oil and gas pipelines running from Kyaukphyu Sittwe adjoining the Bay of Bengal to Kunming in Yunnan province of China. This is up in north Myanmar." Devan lifted his arm and pointed north, forgetting he was in Singapore. "Our project is further south in offshore waters in the Andaman Sea. It's well within Myanmar's Exclusive Economic Zone, or EEZ as it's called. The gas will come up from the offshore wells. The waters are no more than one thousand feet in some places in our blocks. The gas is compressed by 60,000% and liquefied. That's why it's called liquefied natural gas or LNG. It is loaded onto special refrigerated tankers. The gas is cooled down to -260 degrees Fahrenheit. Each tanker can carry at least 4 billion cubic feet of LNG. All of this concentrated energy can then be shipped thousands of miles to the highest bidder. In this case it will only have to be shipped over the Bay of Bengal to floating terminals our Indian partners are building near Kolkata."

Ian interrupted. "And if Myanmar needs the gas?"

Devan shrugged. "If Myanmar needs the gas we can ship it the other way inland, although Myanmar right now does not have the infrastructure to handle it. Myanmar of course gets first priority but they won't need our gas for years. Maybe decades."

"Can't you just pipe the gas into a land based facility in Myanmar?"

"Too expensive. Not practical."

"You're making Myanmar sound like a real bonanza."

"Ian, we think the place is overflowing with gas. And possibly oil. We think Myanmar will be like the Persian Gulf. With the new state of the art floating liquefied natural gas technology, or FLNG. With FLNG natural gas is condensed and stored in floating terminals. It's price competitive with on-shore pipelines. You read the report done by Burton and Company. They are the world's leading LNG consultants. They did a geological survey. We paid for that. Your ten million goes towards that. Except you are getting in after the positive results have come back. You are getting a great deal. The gas is there. We are sure of that. It's no more than a thousand feet down in some places. Piece of cake with today's technology."

"What about all the new natural gas technologies like fracking and horizontal drilling? Natural gas prices have collapsed in the US. Won't the long term price of natural gas come down?'

Devan shrugged. "It could go down and it could go up. That's an unknown although with the growth of Asian economies long run it is more likely to go up. Natural gas is environmentally cleaner than coal and safer than nuclear. We are getting a ten year contract from India set at a very profitable price that adjusts for inflation but has a floor which will protect us. Natural gas isn't like wheat which basically has the same price all over the world. India will be paying a much higher price for some time. Because of transportation and liquefaction costs, the law of one price is not operative globally in the case of natural gas. Myanmar should pocket some profits now rather than leave the gas in the ground for a later day."

"No argument here. You're preaching to the choir on this."

With his right hand Devan tapped the prospectus on the table. "Prices could continue to come down in real inflation adjusted terms in the long run even in India. The sovereign wealth fund converts the gas under the sea at today's prices into productive non-energy global investments. It's a way for Myanmar to diversify its assets."

"But what about all the people that are forecasting the world will run out of energy? These people are all bullshit but they never go away. Have they had any impact in Myanmar?"

"We've tried to take a low key approach with the Myanmar government. I think we have convinced the Myanmar government of this. They are aware that the gloom and doomers, who said the world would run out of energy, have been whining for the last decades and have been wrong. The famous 'peak oil' forecast has turned out to be completely wrong."

"And the greens? What about them?"

"Solar and wind in Myanmar can't compete with natural gas on price or total energy supplied."

"So the alternative energy zealots are not a problem?"

"They do their own thing. But Myanmar can't rely solely on alternative energy and it can't afford to let substantial oil and gas resources just sit in the ground. As you know, natural gas is far less dirty than coal and less risky than nuclear."

At that point the two waiters returned, this time to clear the table and to bring a special south Indian desert that Devan had ordered. The deserts came in two glass dishes which the waiters placed before Ian and Devan.

"This is a south Indian dish called Chakra Pongol," Devan said. "It's made with rice, cashew nuts, some clarified butter called ghee and…" Devan laughed. "I don't know, a lot more stuff. I'm not a chef. But it's really delicious."

Ian took a deep breath. He hadn't planned on desert. He was stuffed. *But the Chakra whatever looked so good.* He dug in. "It's definitely good. A perfect accompaniment to a discussion of liquefied natural gas."

"That's why I chose it," Devan deadpanned. "Now back to our discussion."

"What about the proposal to run additional pipelines north through Bangladesh and into India?" Ian asked.

"It will never happen. The Chinese are opposed since they think they own all the oil and gas in northwest Myanmar. And Bangladesh will always find a reason to screw what they think of as Hindu India."

"And one more thing," Ian asked. "Why does this gas project have a name like Project Zafar?"

"Bahador Shah Zafar was the last Mughal Emperor in India. He was deposed by the British in 1857 after India's First War of Independence was put down. The British exiled him to Rangoon. His burial place in Rangoon has become a shrine. He was a poet. Zafar means victory. You should visit his shrine if you go to Myanmar. He's an anti-colonial connection between Burma and India."

"Wasn't he a Moslem?"

"He had Hindu wives. And he was considered a Sufi saint. He was not a jihadist."

"You'll have to explain to me sometime what a Sufi saint is."

Devan smiled. "When I take you to the Chettiar temples."

"And this First War of Independence. Wasn't that the Sepoy Rebellion?" Now Ian was smiling.

"Sepoy of course. Only proper talk for *pukka sahib* gentleman."

"*Pukka?*... I've never been called that before. So what comes next?"

"Well, Ian, our group has negotiated a Production Sharing Contract, or PSC, with the Myanmar government. It's awaiting the President's final signature. The General assures us the President will sign."

"You've talked to the President yourself?"

"Are you kidding? I'm Chetty. Ian, I have to hide when I go to Myanmar."

"And what happens to my $10 million if he doesn't sign?"

"Then you lose the $10 million. You will put in the other $40 million once the President signs and the PSC is formalized. Look, Ian, I've got all my firm's and my family's money in this. This has a risk but it's a great investment. We got the first option on these blocks from the government. We paid for these options."

"Are you sure there's natural gas down there?"

"In this business you are never sure," Devan said. "But Burton and Company is super confident on our blocks. There may be oil as well."

"I see."

"Well maybe you don't see everything." Devan tapped on the prospectus. "You really are getting a great deal on this. Our group. Project Zafar paid to explore these blocks. We didn't know what was down there. Now we have a pretty good idea. We are letting you buy in for the same price but after the positive preliminary exploration results are in."

"And why are you giving me this deal?" Ian's smile killed the sting to his words. "I feel like there is something you are not telling me."

"Ian, stop being so suspicious. We want your financial respectability. We want to show the government we will invest the money wisely for it with the Sovereign Wealth Fund. The General's wife is insistent that you join this project."

"Really. I don't know who in hell she is."

"Your fame has travelled wide," Devan said.

"I can see where this would really make your firm if it goes through. Didn't anyone else see the value in these blocks?"

Devan shook his head. "Believe it or not, they didn't. Now word has gotten out and another group would like in. But they are too late."

"I can't believe there won't be some last minute dirty tricks. After all, this is Myanmar," Ian said.

"I cannot guarantee there will not be. But we are on solid legal grounds and we've got the General."

"Who's this other group?"

"It's led by the General's daughter by his first marriage. His first wife passed away several years ago, by the way. The daughter's name's Su Myat," Devan said.

"Family feud? I need to know more about this before I put in a nickel."

"I think you should talk directly to the General and his wife about it."

"Devan," Ian said slowly. "what's your opinion?"

"Our group is highly confident this other group can't win. They are backed by the Chinese. The Myanmar government wants to balance the Chinese and the Indians. There's too much Chinese investment in Myanmar now. And we paid for the options. Even in Myanmar they can't take this away from us."

"I definitely want to meet the General and this new wife."

"And they want to meet you." Devan leaned forward. "Ian, if you decide to get into the deal and you hit it off with General and his wife, I will need a ten million dollar check from you immediately. Call it an option on the right to make a twenty percent annual rate of return. When the government gives the final approval and the PSC is signed, you will put in an additional forty million dollars. That will give you a ten percent ownership in Project Zafar LLC. General Maung Myo and his wife will own fifteen percent, my company will own ten percent, and Calcutta Global Oil will own sixty five percent. The Indian Development Bank has extended a five hundred million dollar credit to the Calcutta Global Oil Company to buy tankers and equipment. The Myanmar government gets a huge cut in tax royalties. Myanmar makes out like a bandit on this."

"And if the Myanmar government doesn't approve?"

"If the government doesn't approve, then you've lost ten million. But legally they have to approve if we come with the right financing and technology. The Zafar Group—that's us-- already has a preliminary permit and options that we bid for in the auction."

"How many others bid in that auction?"

Devan smiled. "Nobody else was interested."

"You mean they didn't want to go up against General Maung Myo. But his daughter has no inhibitions."

Devan shrugged. "Look, everything was done legally. The bidding process was announced in the newspapers. Of course it helps to have General Maung Myo on our side. The daughter only became interested when she found out the results of our preliminary study."

"How did she find out?"

"That's a mystery, but the study is now public information as part of the PSC application."

"So the daughter has her spies."

Devan shrugged. "You will need to go to Yangon as soon as possible to meet with General Maung Myo and his wife. The old man wants to meet you."

"And I want to meet him. But I'm not committing to anything right now."

"Understood."

"Isn't the new capital in Nap..." Ian stuttered. "Whatever it is."

"Naypyidaw," Devan said, completing the sentence. "The General is officially retired. He and his new wife like Yangon. They didn't want to move."

"So I go to Yangon."

"Assuming you and he and his wife get along and you want in, you write the ten million check. All the investors will meet in Singapore the week after next in the offices of Calcutta Global. You should be at this meeting if you are in the deal."

Ian sat and thought for a moment. Then he spoke. "Look, this is Asia. All this intrigue is a bit complicated for an innocent white guy like me."

"Innocence is not a quality that I associate with you." Devan was smiling.

"I've read your documents. They are impressive. But my gut tells me this family stuff is a bit too much for me. And Myanmar isn't exactly the pinnacle of good governance."

"Ian, go up to Myanmar. Talk to the General and his wife. Then decide. Let them explain the family stuff."

"And the Chinese government?"

"Officially neutral but of course they are not."

"And the daughter and the General's wife?"

"You ask the right questions. Su Myat hates her father's new wife. She is a great deal younger than her husband."

"How much younger?"

"I think she's thirty. He's eighty five."

"Wow! A man after my own heart. So she's a thirty year old promoting a liquid natural gas project? This doesn't sound believable."

"How old is Mark Zuckerberg?" Devan asked. "You say this because she's a woman?"

"Touche."

"Reserve judgement until you meet her," Devan replied. "Look this is Myanmar. Tricks can be played. The daughter Su Myat hates the new wife and thinks she has deprived her of her inheritance. The daughter's husband is number three in the army. General Maung Myo got him the job but that's apparently history. No gratitude there. Her husband can be dangerous although he's quite stupid. But legally the daughter doesn't have a leg to stand on."

"Devan." Ian smiled." The Myanmar legal structure is a joke and you know it."

"That's changing. Really, the country is changing. And General Maung Myo was in the Cabinet for many years and was head of the army at one time. He's still a big deal. As long as he supports this project, it goes through. Once the government gives final approval on the PSC, there's no turning back. So all you will have at risk until then is the ten million. Surely, for this kind of return that's peanuts."

"There are no peanuts in this business," Ian said. "Only blood, sweat and tears."

"The General's daughter has lined up a Chinese group of investors. The Chinese want to ship the gas north up to their pipeline. Their plan is total bullshit."

"What does the government think about that?"

"They don't say officially, but off the record they hate it." Devan said. "As one minister put it to me so elegantly, 'the Chinks want to take over our whole fucking country.'"

"Tell me more about this younger wife. Some bimbo the General picked up in a bar in Phuket?"

Devan laughed. "You are in for a surprise. She is really good looking. She's of Chinese descent. She went to Brown, Phi Beta Kappa. She's one of the smartest people I have ever met. She likes to surprise people. Throw them off balance. She's got a mind for business."

"So how did she surprise you?"

"Well, she has a very frank way of speaking. And she doesn't care whose listening."

"What's her background besides Brown?"

"Her father was a young soldier who fled with his unit into North Burma in 1949 when the Communists took over and then for a while ran a drug trade. With CIA support. He is out of that now."

"You're sure? That's all I need. To be mixed up with a Burmese drug lord."

"Completely sure. The father is a born again Christian. He goes around Taiwan giving speeches against drugs. I checked him out with the American embassy people here in Singapore. He's a born again good guy."

"And Madame is a born again Christian too?"

Devan laughed. "God no. You'll understand what I mean when you meet her."

"But she's Chinese. Wouldn't she favor the Chinese?"

"I'm pretty sure she was born in Myanmar. Besides, she only thinks money. Chinese, Indians, it's all the same to her. Oh and by the way, she likes to be called Coco, not Madame Maung Myo."

"Coco?"

"You know how some Chinese are, especially those that live outside China in places like Southeast Asia. They like to have a Western name that they choose. This name fits her."

"Why?"

Devan thought about it. "She's a bit of a fashionista. She chose the name as an undergraduate."

"Fashionista?"

"As in Coco Chanel."

"She named herself after Coco Chanel?"

"You got it."

"And she understands natural gas liquification?"

"Ian, she's not an engineer. That's the job of our Indian partners. But she's a finance whiz. She's good with numbers. She worked on Wall Street for a few years where she did discounted cash flow modeling. She's done all the financial modeling for Zafar. She's going to fool you. Looks can deceive."

Ian smiled. "Now you're telling me only stupid women can be beautiful?"

Devan threw up his hands. "Your turn. Political correctness from the most unlikely of people."

"So how does a good looking, brilliant thirty year old Brown Phi Beta Kappa become the wife of an eighty five year old presumably decrepit Burmese retired general?"

"The rumor is she somehow saved the General's life."

"How did she do that? And what difference should that make?"

"I don't know. Ask her."

"I will."

"Just be careful with her. She likes to throw people off balance."

"Devan, did you know the original Coco Chanel had some Nazi sympathies? Or so it is alleged."

"Really? Nobody out here in Asia knows or gives a damn about that. I didn't know that. Most of us weren't history professors like you."

"A financial history professor, as you know. You're right. All the *Comrades* lined up to get into the Chanel stores in Hong Kong and Singapore don't know or give a damn about such matters."

Devan laughed. "Our Coco may be many things but I can assure you she's neither a born again Christian nor a Nazi."

"'Our Coco?' Devan, I think you've got the hots for her."

"I'm going to be a married man before too long. Look, you need to meet Coco and the General. You'll need the General's blessing on this. But don't worry. You come off as a Brit. I don't know why but he loves Brits. And Coco has been pushing for you to join this project."

"Why? I don't know her."

Devan just shrugged. "Ian, if this goes well there will be more opportunities. Myanmar is booming. Go up there. Take a look. You won't regret it. It's a quick trip. You have your own plane."

"You'll set up the trip?"

"No problem. Next weekend okay?"

"Sounds good."

"By the way Devan, is your future wife Chettiar?"

"No. Actually, she's Bengali. I met her in Boston in the US. She was in medical school at the time."

"Not an arranged marriage?"

"No way. Modern Indians aren't doing that."

"Is she Brahmin?"

Devan seemed a little annoyed by the question. "Caste is of no consequence for modern Indians. Why do you ask?"

"India's so complicated. I'm just trying to learn the basics."

"Myanmar is simpler than India."

"I hope so."

Chapter Six

We shall sing the love of danger, of habitual energy and daring...

—*From Founding Manifesto of Futurism,*
F. T. Marinetti, 1909

Ian was back in his apartment. It was ten Sunday night. He was talking by phone with his assistant, Anita.

"Nobody at Athertons knows anything about an Adrian Cairncross. Nothing." Anita said. "Remember I told you my girlfriend is number two in their office in New York? I woke her up by the way. She would know. She double checked on their computer system."

"Did you look on the usual places on the Internet?" Ian asked.

"Nothing. Nada."

"Then who the hell is he?"

"Beats me."

"Anita, what does he want with this painting?"

"I don't know. Something isn't right."

"He's coming to our office on Monday. He said he was flying in from London."

"Ian, are you sure you want to do this meeting? He's some kind of fraud."

"Of course," Ian replied. "I have to find out what he really wants. This guy has an intimidating way on the phone. There's something I don't like about him. Why don't you sit in on the meeting?"

"Maybe we need some protection."

"What am I? A hundred fifty pound weakling?"

"I still haven't seen that painting. Does it have some hidden meaning? I mean there must be more to it than just some Chinese boobs."

"If it has a hidden meaning, I missed it."

It was exactly four p.m. Monday afternoon, Singapore time. Several calls to Wang Qiang once again had gone unanswered. But it had been a good day for Ian's public funds in the Asian markets. The markets had gone down. Ian's flagship hedge fund was net short. Now London was trading down. There was every indication that when they opened the markets in New York would build on the downward global momentum.

Time for Ian to get up and stretch his fifty nine year old body. He had been sitting at his desk hiding behind computer screens and on the phone just about all day. He even ate his lunch at his desk. Today lunch consisted of some take out samosas from a local restaurant. After stretching he got down on the floor and did his twenty pushups. Then he stood up and picked up his Leica Ultravid HD binoculars. The binoculars were a gift. Almost ritualistically he took them out every day after the Asian markets closed. From his office in Singapore's new office district off Marina Bay, he could just see the domes from Gardens by the Bay and make out some of the faces and cameras of all the tourists in the famous infinity pool on top of Marina Bay Sands. And spot an occasional gorgeous bikini clad young lady. Nice after staring at numbers on a screen all day.

But no bikinis today. No matter. Ian felt the view alone was reason enough to move to Singapore.

He turned to admire the Boccioni painting that he had acquired about a month before he bought *Bad Girl*. The painting was entitled *Dynamism of a Soccer Player II*. He had acquired it at a private estate sale of a deceased Swiss banker. Nobody had known this painting existed, but with Anita's help he had verified its provenance. Umberto Boccioni was an Italian futurist who painted just before World War I. Italian futurism stood for an unqualified enthusiasm for technology, an enthusiasm which Ian shared. The painting itself was an abstract riot of reds, blues and yellows and burst with energy. The new technologies in the days of the Italian futurists were things like autos and airplanes. The fact that Ian was unable to locate the soccer player in his painting bothered him not in the least.

Refreshed, Ian went back to his desk. Then Anita knocked on his door and entered his office. Anita was about five four and wore glasses. She was one of those women who wasn't really beautiful but who could be considered attractive when she was properly made up and dressed for the office. Her pregnancy was just starting to show.

"Adrian Cairncross is here now," Anita said.

"Send him in."

Anita signaled Cairncross to enter. Ian motioned for him to sit down. Neither man offered to shake hands.

Ian remained at his desk, fiddling with his binoculars while saying nothing.

"Nice binoculars," Cairncross finally said. "I have a pair like that myself." Ian reflexively put the binoculars down.

Anita handed both men small cups of espresso. As planned, Anita joined the meeting. She sat down on the couch away from Cairncross.

"It's a bit sweet," Cairncross said, almost choking on his coffee. In Miami Ian had acquired a taste for Cuban espresso which is served laced with sugar. He usually asked his guests if they wanted the sugar. But he omitted this courtesy with Cairncross.

"I'm addicted to Cuban coffee," Ian said. "It's always sweet."

Anita sat smiling sipping her coffee. She was enjoying Cairncross' discomfort.

Without asking anybody's permission or for any ashtray, Cairncross lit up a cigarette. Both Ian and Anita were non-smokers. Anita belatedly provided the ashtray.

Ian was already pissed off.

"It's very kind of you to make this time available to me," Cairncross began.

Ian studied Cairncross. He was a stocky man of medium height. Perhaps forty years of age. He had a muscular appearance. His head was completely shaved. He could have been a Buddhist monk or maybe an extreme fighter. From looking at his face, Ian judged him to be Eurasian. Cairncross didn't smile as he spoke and his words had a threatening tone built into them. Like his voice, his dark almost black eyes had an intimidating quality. Ian could just smell he was trouble.

"I'll get right to the point," Ian said. "I lived in Miami for a while. Besides Cuban coffee I acquired a nose for bullshitters. They have lots of them there. And you sir have nothing to do with Atherton's. We checked. Tell me who you are and why this painting is so goddamn important. And skip the bullshit."

Cairncross managed a grudging smile. "I like people who do their homework. Very well, You're right. I have nothing to do with Atherton's. But I do represent an extremely wealthy client who likes paintings of naked Chinese girls. He has a collection. I can't tell you who he is but I can tell you he always gets what he wants."

Ian was puzzled by Cairncross' accent. Just like on the phone, he was hearing Brit plus someplace in Asia. "So why doesn't he just have Wang find another naked Chinese girl and paint her? Wang would be very enthused about a commission like that."

"He wants this one."

"Why?"

"That's not your business. Now come on, Mr. Blakely. I'm prepared to offer you three hundred thousand dollars. A refund of $200,000 plus another $100,000. We'll work this out with Wang Qiang."

"Three hundred thousand dollars?" Ian asked.

"That's probably the market price. You got a bargain."

"And if I say no?"

Cairncross flicked ashes onto the floor. "Then we will procure the painting by some other means. My client has access to other means. He will use them." Cairncross's eyes were cold. "You should think about the welfare of your firm's employees." He momentarily glared sideways at Anita. "And your own welfare."

"Wow. You get right to the point, don't you. You're threatening me, Mr. Cairncross. All for a painting of some naked girl?"

"You told me to skip the bullshit." Cairncross put out his lit cigarette in his mostly unfinished espresso. He turned to Anita. "Lovely earrings you have on. My client has a painting of a Chinese girl with earrings just like that. That's all she's wearing. He likes naked Chinese girls. He's especially fascinated with pregnant ones. He's a little perverted." He turned back to Ian. "Please don't tell me you are going to be stupid?"

Ian looked over at Anita. The color had left her face. "Mr. Cairncross," he said, holding his binoculars by the strap "I will not sell you the painting. Our meeting is over. You may get the fuck out of here."

Cairncross stood up. He walked over to Anita who was still sitting. He reached down and fondled the earring hanging from her left ear. "Lovely," he said. He turned and dropped his card on Ian's desk. The card contained only a name and phone number with a country code that Ian didn't recognize. Then he pulled out a piece of paper which he laid on Ian's desk. "Bill of sale. My client purchased the painting two days before you."

Ian looked down at the paper. It was a photocopy of a bill of sale for *Bad Girl* with Wang's signature. But the buyer's name had been blacked out.

Cairncross said. "Think about it. You may want to reconsider your decision. Call me. But do it quickly." He turned to Anita and smiled again. "I'll find my way out. Perhaps I will see you again." But before leaving, Cairncross turned to look at the Boccioni painting. "This is a real piece of shit," he said. "Don't worry. My client will not want this."

"Fuck you and your client," Ian said.

Cairncross smiled and walked out the door.

Ian looked at Anita. "That son of a bitch. I will never sell him *Bad Girl*. Who the hell does he think he is."

"He could be dangerous," Anita said.

Ian wasn't listening. "I don't care. This bill of sale is a copy. I think it's fake."

"He threatened me," Anita said, eyes wet behind her glasses. "Why don't you just sell him the painting? You make $100,000 and get rid of trouble. Three hundred thousand is a good price. This guy might represent the Japanese Yakuza or the Italian Mafia or someone like that."

"Why would the Yakuza or the Mafia need this painting so badly?" Ian asked.

"Look, sell the painting and you make $100,000 and you get rid of trouble."

"Anita, you're right of course. But I don't take shit from anybody. And I've been trading for too long. My nose tells me nobody goes crazy like this for a painting of a naked girl. I know all Chinese women are beautiful. But not this beautiful. I'm not letting go. I just don't like some asshole coming in here and threatening me and my staff. And dumping his cigarettes into my Alessi espresso cups. I made a special trip to Bal Harbor in Miami to get those."

He picked up his phone and got Mr. Lee from the frame shop on line. "I'll be over in ten minutes. I'm going to pick up the painting." He then called Henry Ashton, telling him he was delivering his painting.

"Anita, see if you can find out more on our Mr. Cairncross. He's got that strange accent underneath that British veneer. Where's it from?"

"Just guessing, but I would say Thailand."

"Go fishing on him. You noticed he had an Oxford University ring on?"

"I didn't know they had Oxford rings," Anita said.

"Probably fake. Like everything else about this guy."

"I'll see what I can find."

Ian dropped by Mr. Lee's shop and picked up Henry Ashton's painting with the woman getting into the Mercedes. He told Mr. Lee nothing about the switch or where the painting was going. He figured the less Lee knew about the paintings, the better. For Lee. He then proceeded to Ashton's office.

Henry Ashton stood up to meet Ian. Ashton was a short, square man with a vaguely Middle Eastern look reflecting his Sephardic roots. He looked every bit the banker in his dark blue pinstriped suit, light blue shirt, Hermes tie and matching pocket handkerchief. The fact that Singapore was practically on the equator and might get a little hot did not seem to bother him in the least. His attire contrasted with Ian's who, as he frequently did, came attired in a sport coat and jeans. Or maybe no sports coat at all. The American hedge fund look. Not that Ashton cared. Ian could have come dressed in a Speedo swimsuit and Ashton would have been happy. Ian had an account at Standard Commerce but the Blakely Funds did not use Standard as its prime broker. Prime brokers are the main bank for hedge funds. That would be a great business for Ashton's bank. Ashton would welcome any opportunity to ingratiate himself with Ian and the Blakely Funds. He didn't know it but events were about to soon present him with such an opportunity.

Ian thought when he entered Ashton's office that he had walked into a museum. Ashton's office itself was quite spacious but had a view that was blocked by a newer, taller adjacent building. No matter. The office walls were covered with a variety of fine art paintings, ranging from Western traditional and contemporary to traditional and contemporary Chinese. It was easy to see that art for Henry Ashton was more than decoration. Directly behind Ashton's desk was a large dark painting of a stern looking bearded man, which Ian knew was that of the bank's Scottish founder. Directly adjacent to that painting was a faded photograph of a boxer. The young Henry Ashton had a brief career as a professional boxer.

"Awfully glad to see you," Ashton said with his cultured Oxbridge accent which somehow came off even stuffier than normal, thanks to the broken nose Ashton had sustained long ago in the ring. "Wish I could offer you a better view." Ashton gestured towards the window. "We were here first. But the new business district has stolen our view. Progress I guess. The Lion City has to grow."

"Your artwork even beats a view of Marina Bay," Ian replied. "Well Henry, here's your painting and your sexy lady getting into the Mercedes. Shall we take the wrapping off and admire it? You know I wanted to buy it myself but you must have gotten to Wang's gallery just before me. Wang has such a delicate touch with his brush. And he really relates to women."

"Leave it wrapped. It's a little too much for me to hang here. You know. Older white man with Asian trophy woman. Some of my older Chinese clients get a bit upset by such things. I'm going to put it in my gallery at home. My little Jewish wife allows me freedom in the art area."

"As you wish."

"Ian, I think Wang is emerging as one of China's greatest painters. Of course he's a bloody degenerate. You know, I can't get a hold of him. I haven't paid him yet. I guess you've told him about the mix-up?"

"Actually, I haven't been able to get hold of him either. And I haven't paid him."

"How odd," Ashton said, rubbing the side of his once broken nose.

"To say the least."

"Well, anyway, here's your nude." Ashton pointed to the rolled up painting behind his desk. He smiled. "I don't get to deal with nudes too often in my daily business."

"I'm glad I could brighten up your day," Ian replied, also smiling.

"I had it rewrapped. Wang has such an incredible touch. The perfect painting for a dirty old man who loves art. What made him show it to you, if I may ask?"

"I think he just needed the money. He'd been holding that painting back for some reason. He'd already sold yours."

"Do you want me to unwrap it for your inspection?"

"No. Henry, I wonder if you can do me a favor?"

"Certainly."

"There's been some kind of screw-up on my painting. A gentleman turned up in my office and claimed his client had bought the painting first. I may have to relinquish it but he's going to have to provide some proof. He wasn't polite, to put it mildly. And he didn't provide much in the way of documentation or proof. I need to speak to Wang."

"I see."

"I wonder if I might leave the painting here with your bank? I presume you have a vault."

"Of course, I'd be delighted to offer our facility. Just let me give you a receipt for your painting. That's our usual procedure."

Ashton took out some stationery with the Bank's name on it, and in his own hand wrote out the receipt which he handed to Ian.

"Ian, your painting is perfectly safe with us. Leave it with us as long as you like. I should tell you our vault is brand new, quite large and climate controlled. Perfect for your painting."

"Thank you. Oh, and Henry? If anyone comes around asking, no information is to be given out on my painting. No one is to know it's here."

"Understood," Ashton said. "And as far as our bank. We've been in business since 1830, shortly after Sir Stamford Raffles founded Singapore. Unlike some of the bigger global banks, we still rely first and foremost on a sense of trust and discretion between ourselves and our clients. And don't worry. People don't push us around." He made a fist with his right hand. "The old right still works."

"Thank you, Henry." Henry was so nineteenth century. Just what Ian needed. "I guess you could say a Singaporean's word is his bond," Ian added.

Henry laughed. "Indeed. You could say that. You're a naturalized Singaporean, am I correct?"

"Yes."

"Well, no zeal like that of a convert."

Later that evening Ian received a phone call. It was Mr. Lee. He sounded agitated and very upset.

"Two men come in my shop. Just as I close. They want know about nude painting. I tell them I don't have it. That there was no nude painting. They ask about you. I tell them you took another painting. But I don't know where. They put gun at my head! They spend hour searching my shop. Make big mess."

Mr. Lee was becoming hysterical. He kept mumbling things in what Ian guessed was his native Fukienese dialect.

"They left?"

"Finally. Big man slap me in face. Slap me! Say I know where you take painting. Finally they give up. They say they kill me if I call police." The more upset Lee got, the worse his English became.

"Do you need to see a doctor?"

"No. Why do this? Why you not tell me?"

"I'm sorry Mr. Lee. I didn't know something like this would happen. For now, it's better you don't know anything. I'll explain when I know more and it's safe."

"I very scare."

"What did these men look like?"

"One man very well dressed. Very gentleman. But smoke cigarette. The other man dressed like worker. The other man Asian but not Chinese. I sure of that. All bald. Like monk. The gentleman I don't know. Eurasian, I think."

"Look, Mr. Lee. You have relatives in China. Why don't you and Mrs. Lee just get on a plane and spend two or three weeks there? I'll pay your expenses and replace any income you may have lost. I really don't think these men will bother you again. But just to be safe."

"They hurt me if I call police."

"Then it's better you don't. These men want the painting. They know you don't have it. They will leave you alone as long as you aren't a threat to them."

"I have other clients waiting for frame," Mr. Lee said finally. "I cannot spend two weeks away. But I go for week. Thank you."

Mr. Lee clicked off. Ian was deeply troubled. How did Adrian Cairncross know about Lee's shop? Why would he threaten Lee with a gun? Had Cairncross had gotten the information from Wang Qiang? Would Cairncross figure out the paintings had been switched? Was Henry Ashton their next stop?

What kind of shit had he stepped into when he bought this painting?

Ian called Wang. The response this time was by a telephone company operator in Cantonese, then Portuguese, then English. "This is no longer a working number."

He called Henry Ashton and explained what had happened. From beginning to end. "I don't know whether they will connect this to you, Henry. They may figure out there was a switch. If you want me to take the painting back, I will."

"Too late, old boy," Henry replied. "If they find out the painting is here, they will pay me a visit anyway. The hell with them, I say. What are they going to do? Rob the vault? But what is it about this painting, if I may ask?"

"I really don't know."

"You really don't?" The disbelief in Henry Ashton's voice was tangible.

Ian found himself yelling. "I really don't know, Henry!"

"It's clear that this painting has a great deal of meaning to somebody. I'll give you a guess."

"What's that?" Ian said.

"Someone wants to embarrass this lady. This is about money and power, not about tits, if you will pardon my crudeness."

"Wang said she was just a model," Ian said. "You think Wang was lying?"

"Yes, I do. This painting was done some time ago. Perhaps the lady has become more respectable. Perhaps the lady is now in a position of power. Or money."

"Or her husband is," Ian said. "Do you think the husband is some high ranking guy?"

"I'd bet on it. Probably in the PRC. These Chinese boys play rough sometimes. The lady – girl – is probably Chinese."

"So what we may have, Henry," Ian mused," is another Bo Xilai in the making? That PRC big shot whose wife murdered her lover."

"Anything's possible."

"So why did Wang sell me the painting now?"

"Ian, Wang was broke with gambling debts. That is well known. And he apparently owed your IRS some money."

"Henry, please. Not my IRS anymore. So the lady didn't pay up. An old story."

"Wang is a brilliant artist. But, shall we say, he's not the most honorable of men."

"Now Wang's phone is disconnected. Maybe somebody shot him."

Ashton laughed. "If they did, the prices on his paintings will go up."

"Well there's something to look forward to."

Ashton exaggerated his British accent. "At any rate, your painting is safe with us. Laying down our lives for a lady's honor is just one of the services our bank provides."

"I hope it doesn't come to that but I'll send flowers if it does."

"That's very reassuring." Ashton laughed.

Ian thanked Ashton again. It was clear Standard Commercial would be getting more business from the Blakely Funds. That is if Ian didn't have to lay down his own life.

Chapter Seven

"Coco, would you like your soup put on your desk?" Khin Chit asked in Chinese, but in English, Chinese or Burmese "Coco" was the name Coco preferred. That was what her staff called her. Khit Chin was a middle aged woman about forty five. Her mother was from China, her father from Myanmar. In that way, Coco and Khin Chit had similar backgrounds. She had only worked for Coco for two years but Coco's father had recommended her and Coco trusted her.

Coco always had the same thing for lunch. A light soup and that was it. Today it was a shrimp soup, flavored Vietnamese style with lemon grass. Coco sat, cigarillo in one hand, with her little short haired Abyssinian cat Samantha sitting on her lap. On her computer screen were projections of the profits she expected from Project Zafar. She was tweaking the numbers and adjusting the assumptions on the ten year discounted cash flow model that she had developed. She had done so many of these models as a slave on Wall Street. This time it was for her. She liked what she saw.

"Coco is going to win big on Zafar, Sam. The return is fantastic", she said in English. "Even with the big royalty payment to the government." She always spoke to Sam in English and she never used the cat's full name 'Samantha'." And the cat like everyone else only knew her as Coco and presumably was only fluent in English. Coco and Sam had their own private girl talk. "That cunt Su Myat is going to fucking regret she ever laid eyes on me. Sam, you are going to be one sexy rich little cat. Only the best fish for you. We'll import fish for you from Bulgari. The best." She laughed at her own joke. Bulgari, at least up to now, is known for jewelry, not cat food.

Khin Chit started to set the tray on the desk. Coco didn't notice that Khin Chit's hands were shaking. Suddenly, Khin Chit let go of the tray and it dropped with a thud on the desk. The soup bowl slid off and fell to the floor. It broke in half and spilled its contents over the big Persian rug that covered half the room. In an instant Sam bolted down and began lapping up the soup. Coco looked down angrily. The rug was priceless. She had found it in an upstairs attic when she and General Maung Myo had bought the house. The British officer who originally owned the house so many years ago had left it. Coco guessed he had picked it up in a campaign in Rajasthan or Sind or someplace like that.

Coco screamed at Khin Chit. "Shit! What has gotten into you? Now the rug will have to be cleaned."

"I'm sorry," Khin Chit said. "I didn't want to do it. Forgive me." She was shaking uncontrollably and had started to cry.

Coco looked down at the cat. "Sam, you're not supposed to eat human food. You are only a cat. We have our rules. We've talked about this. You and I agreed."

Except Sam wasn't listening. She was wretching onto the rug. And Khin Chit's longyi was becoming wet in the front as she urinated uncontrollably.

Coco looked at the cat in horror. The cat suddenly rolled over onto its back, paws up. She was either dead or doing a good imitation. Coco stared at Sam and then looked up at the shaking Khin Chit, with her soiled longyi. Khin Chit was a heavy set woman, and by appearance more of a physical threat the slender Coco. But it didn't help her.

Coco jumped over the desk just like her cat had bounded for the soup. "You fucking bastard ! You poisoned my soup!"

Khin Chit fell to her knees. "I'm sorry, she forced me to do this. Su Myat has my son as a hostage. She threatened to kill him." Coco, left handed as she was, grabbed Khin Chit by the throat with her right hand and began punching her across the face with her left. "*Dang fu,*" whore! and "*jian,*" traitor! she screamed in Chinese. The Bulgari diamond wedding ring on Coco's finger ripped into Khin Chit's face. The blood spurted out and dripped down to her already wet longyi. Coco continued to hit her for a good ten minutes. Khin Chit's face became an unrecognizable bloody mess. Part of her nose was hanging from her face, her right cheek was split wide open revealing teeth and her right eye was closed tight. Coco seemed to gain in strength and enthusiasm with each blow she rained on the hapless woman. The veins in her neck grew larger. Her wide open eyes acquired a demonic glow. Finally she took a deep breath. A desire to kill Khin Chit right there surged through her. She would have enjoyed it. She had the same feeling of exhilaration that she had when she hit the captain of the Brown football team over the head with a beer bottle in Providence. He had grabbed her tits without permission and called her a "love coolie". He too deserved it. He had to miss three games.

But Coco's left brain finally took over. Her staff was right outside. What would she do with the body? Still, the betrayal shocked and hurt her.

She pulled Khin Chit to her feet. "Get out of here and never come back!" She spit on her. "You can become a whore. You can fuck fat Australians and Germans. We'll have a lot of them here now in Myanmar. And make sure they are drunk so they don't notice your ugly face. Now get out!" She pointed to a door off to the side.

Khin Chit thanked Madame, grateful to be alive. Then, blood dripping from her face, she managed to walk out of the room.

Coco looked at her own hand, covered with Khin Chit's blood but also her own. It had bruises all over it. "Shit. The bitch hurt my hand with her face," she said aloud in English. But that wasn't all. Her wrist was swelling as well. In fact her whole left arm was in pain. But one good thing. Her griffe platinum Bulgari ring, with its exquisite large diamond, wasn't damaged at all. The diamond just sat happily as it always had, seated in the ring, with just a little blood on it. Not bad considering it had ripped off half of Chit Khim's nose and face. A diamond in this case was *not* Chit Khim's best friend. Coco laughed. Maybe she should write Bulgari and commend them for the quality of their product. Unfortunately, it was unlikely Bulgari would feature her commendation in its advertising. Coco found a tissue and gently wiped off the ring, ignoring the blood all over her hands. With difficulty, she took off the ring and the simple gold wedding ring as well. Then she took off her techie Nike GPS running watch. It had just arrived by Fed Ex a week ago and she was quite taken with it. But her swelling wrist wouldn't tolerate anything on it. "I had to wait a week for that watch. Now I can't wear it. I should have shot the fucking bitch," Coco said aloud. "I've been dying to use my Glock."

Coco then bent down and stroked her dead cat. She spoke to it softly in English. "Sam, my sister. You saved Coco's life. I loved you so much, little baby. You were my only friend." She picked up the dead cat and hugged her. She began to cry just a little. She didn't care that some vomit from the cat was soiling her cute D&G top.

She had had a close call. This outrage could not go unanswered. She would get revenge. And a new cat.

Chapter Eight

BY AUTHORITY OF PRESIDENT BARACK OBAMA
OF THE UNITED STATES

EXECUTIVE ORDER 99876

PROTECTING THE CURRENCY OF THE UNITED
STATES FROM EXCESS SPECULATION

By my authority as President based on the Constitution and the laws of the United States of America and as the Commander in Chief charged with protecting the United States, the following measures are hereby ordered:

1. An Office for Dollar Defense will be created and placed within the Federal Bureau of Investigation. The Office for Dollar Defense will be charged with enforcing the measures summarized below.

2. The promotion or holding of alternative currencies such as gold or bitcoins for use within the United States will be classified as an act of aggression against the United States.

3. A wealth penalty of 5 percent per annum will be levied on all real and financial assets domiciled outside the United States and owned by American citizens, permanent resident (green card holders) and corporations. These assets would include but not be limited to stocks, bonds, precious metals including gold and silver, real estate and plant and equipment.

4. The cases of all Americans with a net worth greater than five million dollars who have renounced their citizenship in the last five years will be reviewed under a special audit conducted by the Office for Dollar Defense. The presumption will be that this renunciation was done for tax purposes.

Unless the renunciator can prove otherwise, the renunciation will be deemed invalid. The renunciator will need to pay all unpaid taxes and penalties assuming he or she had never renounced citizenship.

It was early Saturday morning in Singapore. Ian rubbed his eyes as he stared at the Bloomberg screen in his apartment. The Obama Administration had issued this order at six p.m. Friday evening Washington time.

The Republicans were already screaming that the President had exceeded his authority and that his wealth penalty was really a tax that required the approval of the House of Representatives. They also objected to the promotion and holding of gold, bitcoins and other alternatives as an act of aggression against the United States. Nobody, however, was objecting to the review of the cases of all Americans that had renounced their citizenship over the last five years.

Ian wasn't surprised by the move on gold and bitcoins. He had always predicted that governments everywhere would not just sit by and let the markets and gold take away their monopoly to issue fiat money currency. The Blakely Funds had not been big players in the gold or bitcoin markets. But the wealth penalty and the review of Americans renouncing their citizenship were something else. The political climate in the US had turned very hostile to corporations and individuals who had financial transactions and wealth abroad.

The major corporations would fight the wealth penalty and probably win on constitutional grounds. But individuals might not fare as well. And besides, Obama had gotten away with one Executive Order after the other. At the least Congress would probably finally change the tax code to punish individuals and corporations with foreign assets and income abroad. And now Ian's citizenship renunciation was going to be reviewed yet again. He had literally spent millions on lawyers and accountants for this already. And he had paid over one hundred million in an "exit fee".

One day at a time. He was now a Singaporean. He had no desire to return to the United States. So long as he stayed away from the US, he should be safe. But he knew that in reality he wasn't. Uncle Sam's long arms reached everywhere. They would find some way to screw him. Of that he was sure. One way would be to pressure the Blakely Funds' investors into withdrawing their money. He had deliberately excluded US investors from his funds. Again, his funds were outside U.S. jurisdiction ...maybe. They all had major investments in companies that traded in the US stock markets.

In Ian's view this was a sad day for America and the world. Ian never really wanted to give up his citizenship. America was founded as a land where property was protected by its constitution and its laws. But now its constitution was being ignored and its laws were being changed to confiscate property. The dollar had been strong of late. It didn't need this kind of help. Obama has issued this order to pander to his core anti-capitalist base. Myanmar on the other hand had been a lawless place where only the top government leaders had any real property. Now that was apparently changing. America was getting worse, Myanmar of all places was getting better.

He clicked off Bloomberg.

It was time to go to Yangon.

Chapter Nine

"Even a casual traveler notices that the independence of Burmese women is remarkable. They manage their own affairs, hold stalls in the bazaar with which no one interferes, marry when they choose, and divorce their husbands as soon as they please...They flirt, they dance, and laugh with as many admirers as they choose, and, last of all, they smoke – not dainty little cigarettes – but cigars!"

—*From Major-General A. Ruxton MacMahon,
<u>Far Cathay and Farther India</u>* (1893)

Ian walked hurriedly towards Immigration, his computer bag in one hand and his iPhone in the other. He waited impatiently for it to acquire a signal. No luck. The airport was old. And at that moment crowded. He groaned as he saw a long, snaking line for Immigration . Unhappily, he got on the tail end. A middle aged couple just ahead of him, Australian by their accent, were loudly complaining about the wait time.

Ian was approached by a short, but muscular looking young man dressed in a dark blue military uniform and dark sunglasses. "Dr. Blakely?"

"Yes."

"I am Major Nyan Myint, General Maung Myo's assistant," the young man said in heavily accented but passable English. "I will take you to your hotel. General Maung Myo sends his apologies. He was called to Naypyidaw for an urgent meeting. That's the name of our new capital."

"Yes, I know." Standing erect in the military uniform and dark sunglasses, the Major looked like he had just jumped out of a Graham Greene novel.

"He will return from Naypyidaw to Yangon tomorrow morning. It's a short plane ride. He'll be available for lunch. He wants you to have a pleasant evening tonight."

This was not what Ian wanted to hear.

"Give me your passport and follow me."

That wasn't what the Australian couple wanted to hear. The woman complained loudly about how "it helps to know the right general around here." As they passed the Immigration booth the Major held up Ian's passport. The Immigration officer nodded and waved them through.

"Any baggage?" the Major asked as they headed into the baggage area.

"No baggage," Ian replied. "Just my computer bag carry-on."

"Sorry for all this confusion," the Major said. "Next month a new private aviation terminal will be opened. You won't have to put up with all these people."

Something to look forward to, Ian thought. He couldn't help noticing a small dark woman and her thirty years older, grossly overweight, white boyfriend, husband or perhaps just client. Filipina, maybe Thai. She had a big tattoo on her right arm and she wore a tee shirt that said "Kiss Me I'm Drunk." As she leaned over to pick up her bag on the conveyor belt, Ian got a bird's eye view of her push up black bra and smallish brown breasts. She gave Ian a slight smile. Ian followed the Major outside. A black Mercedes was waiting directly under a NO PARKING sign. Another young man, also in a dark blue military uniform and dark sunglasses, was standing stiffly next to the car. He opened the door, Ian got in the back seat and the Major in the front. The other young man drove.

It was Sunday evening. Seven ten p.m. in Singapore, seven ten a.m. in New York and five forty p. m. in Yangon. The global markets were closed. Ian would do some evening sightseeing. He asked the Major if he wouldn't mind swinging by the Shwedagon Pagoda before going to the Strand Hotel where he was staying. Not seeing the Shwedagon Pagoda when visiting Yangon was like not seeing St Peter's when visiting Rome. Ian didn't have time for more than a drive-by. And actually he had no real interest beyond that, as tramping around Asia looking at religious shrines was not his favorite use of time.

The first thing Ian noticed on his drive-by was that in Myanmar people drive on the right but the steering wheel is also on the right. Easier to remember he guessed.

The Shwedagon pagoda is on a hill and the black Mercedes stopped conveniently in a no parking zone at the base. Ian got out for a moment and stared at the giant 362 foot gilded stupa, a dome- like spire, covered with gold plates,that soared upward into the twilight sky. As he was standing there floodlights came on and illuminated the dome. Ian couldn't help himself. He tried to calculate how much the pagoda was worth in gold, assuming a gold price of $1300 per ounce. A bit of shame then came over him. He felt like Juan Pizarro shaking down the Inca Emperor Atahualpa. He understood why some untutored people didn't like hedge fund managers and their philistine tendencies. He would have to come back and spend more time at the Shwedagon. One day.

He got to his suite at the Strand at about 7 pm Yangon time. The Strand wasn't the newest or the best hotel in Yangon, but it was a colonial jewel and therefore one of Yangon's most expensive hotels. Ian knew all about the hotel and its history and couldn't resist staying there. Known in its heyday for its famous ballroom and whites-only exclusivity, the Strand was opened in 1902 by the Armenian Sarkies brothers. The Sarkies brothers were the same as the ones who also opened the somewhat bigger but equally historic Raffles Hotel in Singapore, and the less well known Eastern and Oriental Hotel in Penang. The whites-only policy at the Strand was ended when the Japanese invaded in 1942 and replaced it with a Japanese-only policy. The whites were all sent to less luxurious, non-racially exclusive, prison camps.

After a string of dismal managements under Burmese socialism, the Strand had been restored to full splendor. Unfortunately, the Strand had no pool. A pool was normally a sine qua non for Ian who religiously adhered to his daily swimming routine. But he was only staying one night and had swum in Singapore that morning. Being six foot three meant that his feet had to hang over the edge of a too short but otherwise charming canopied bed. But Ian liked the ambiance of the teak and marble floors and having a butler right on his floor ready to attend to his needs.

He was a little hungry. Hotel room-service menus, even those of historically interesting hotels, aren't known for their originality. He ordered what were termed "spicy spring rolls". The butler took forever supervising the setting up of Ian's dinner in his room. Finally, he was alone. He turned on his TV while he ate and took in an English news program. The announcer was going on and on about how people in Myanmar loved their government because of all it was doing for them. Ian laughed. *How lucky the people of Myanmar must be*, Ian reflected.

As he was finishing his spicy spring rolls, his room phone rang. It was the Major. "Sir, there is a Miss Kyaw Cho here to see you. She was sent by General Maung Myo."

"Of course, send her to my room."

Thirty seconds later his room bell rang. At the door were the girl and the butler who attended Ian's floor. Miss Kyaw Cho was about five feet four and had beautiful Chinese eyes which Ian instantly appreciated. She was dressed in a purple Burmese longyi with a multicolored plaid-like design. She wore a white ornamental belt and a dark red top that left her shoulders bare. She had orchids in her hair which was tied together in a long single braid that came over her right shoulder and reached her waist. And of course she had thanaka on her cheeks. No stupid tee shirts. She looked like something from a fashion magazine.

The butler bowed. "I beg you, sir, if there is anything that you need do not hesitate to call me." He immediately disappeared down the hall.

I got here a hundred years too late, Ian thought. *Imagine being a white guy surrounded by butlers like that and women like Miss Kyaw Cho.* Actually he wasn't late at all.

Ian motioned for Miss Kyaw Cho to sit down. He wondered why she was there. He assumed she had come to go over some preliminary things on tomorrow's schedule. Although the hour was latish and she wasn't carrying a briefcase or a computer. And she certainly wasn't dressed in a sex-neutral power outfit like an upwardly mobile American female on Wall Street.

"Good evening Dr. Blakely," she began.

"And good evening to you. How can I help you?"

She smiled. "General Maung Myo is sorry he could not be with you tonight." Her English had a British tone. "He wants you to relax and sleep well. He sent me over as a present."

"Present?" This was a new cultural experience for Ian. Nobody had ever given him this kind of present. *A beautiful Burmese sleeping pill.*

"I have been trained in traditional Myanmar massage. Of course I will do whatever you want."

"I see."

"I am your present," she repeated with a coy smile. "I invite you to enjoy me."

Ian reflected. Of course any textbook would say he was supposed to say "no" to this present. Certainly if he worked for a politically correct American bank or had to report to an American regulator he would have to say no. But he was a hedge fund manager and not an American. He could have sex with whomever he fucking pleased. It improved his thinking process. It was in his investors' interest. A horny fund manager who is always thinking about women is a lousy fund manager. Besides, he never made money in the markets doing what he was supposed to do. Plus turning down a present from the General could be construed as an insult. The General would lose face. Asians don't like to lose face. Cultural sensitivity was a requirement for Westerners living in Asia.

It was too late to google "Business Etiquette in Myanmar." The only question was, *was somebody screwing with him*? Were some goons with cameras out in the hall waiting to break in on him just as he was enjoying Miss Kyaw Cho? He got up and checked the hall. Nobody. After all, the Major did deliver the girl. So she did come from the General. He was going invest with the General and his wife. So he was going to have to trust them. Trust had to start somewhere. Did not the great J.P. Morgan once say, "a man I do not trust could not get money from me on all the bonds in Christendom?"

What the hell, he thought. *Never look a gift whore in the mouth.*

Chapter Ten

It was 8:10 a.m. Monday morning in Yangon, 9:40 a.m. Monday morning in Singapore and 9:40 p. m. Sunday night in New York. Ian was reading the Financial Times on line, having slept like a baby after dutifully taking the General's Burmese sleeping pill. He was surprised at the speed of his internet connection. His guidebook said the internet in Myanmar was almost non-existent. The guidebook was only a year old. Guidebooks anyway were so old fashioned, so one step behind. Things in Myanmar were changing at internet speed. Of course, Rudyard Kipling, Burma's colonial chronicler, didn't have internet. *How did he survive*, Ian wondered?

His Skype connection flashed. It was Henry Ashton. "Ian," Henry said. He sounded agitated. "Did you see the news?"

"I'm here in Myanmar, Henry. I'm lucky to be getting your phone call."

"Ian, Wang Qiang is dead. They found his body floating in the Inner Harbour in Macau."

"Jesus."

"The police said he had a lot of gambling debts. They think one of the triads did him in. His studio was torched."

Ian shivered.

"What do you think, Ian?"

"I don't know, Henry. Has anybody approached you about my painting?"

"Nobody."

"I don't know what to say. Have the police called you?"

"No, Ian. Well, I can't see how we are involved. Did you send him his money?"

"No. I could never get a hold of him."

"Neither did I." Henry said. "Well, his estate will come after us in due time. That is, if they know about us. And if he has an estate."

"There may be no record," Ian mused. "Let's wait until then. What do you think?"

"Ian, I think there's more to this than meets the eye. And I think you know more than you are telling."

"I agree there is more to this, Henry. But I swear I don't know any more than you do. We should just sit tight. If somebody contacts you from the authorities, get consult your attorney. I'll do the same. I'm not urging you to withhold any information or do anything dishonest. We'll pay the estate when properly billed. But I think for our own safety we should not volunteer any information to anyone. Least of all the Macau police."

Silence spun down the line. Then Henry said. "I agree." He hung up.

Coco was watching her Bloomberg. Her special satellite on the roof provided her with the full Bloomberg service. It was Sunday morning. Ian Blakely would be arriving at ten thirty. Things had apparently gone well with Kyaw Cho. Coco had done her research. Blakely was a brilliant fund manager but he was a womanizer with an acute case of yellow fever. He had been divorced recently so he didn't have to be faithful to anyone. She guessed correctly the beautiful Kyaw Cho would put him in the right frame of mind. She had taken a gamble. The whole thing might have pissed off another man. But maybe not. All men are the same. Pigs. Still, Blakely was obviously a handsome man, judging by the pictures she had found of him on the internet. She already felt a certain attraction to him. If Blakely put the money in the deal and she got the painting back, one day she would fuck him herself.

Something on the Bloomberg caught her eye.

"CHINESE PAINTER WANG QIANG FOUND DEAD

In what appeared to be a homicide, the body of well-known Chinese contemporary artist, Wang Qiang, was found floating in the Inner Harbour of Macau. Wang was known for his portraits of wealthy Chinese, especially wealthy Chinese women. Police said that Wang's studio near the St. Paul's ruin had also been torched. The entire event had all the earmarks of a triad killing. Wang apparently had large gambling debts. No further details are available at this time."

Coco smiled. Wang was finally gone. Her day was off to a good start. And there was a bonus. Wang's paintings would go up in value now that he was dead. One day, after her husband passed away, she would hang the painting in her bedroom.

Chapter Eleven

Women must tell men always that they are the strong ones. They are the big, the strong, the wonderful. In truth, women are the strong ones. It is just my opinion, I am not a professor.

– *Coco Chanel*

The black Mercedes appeared outside Ian's hotel at exactly 9 a.m. The Major, in the same dark blue uniform and dark sunglasses, opened the door. Ian got in the back seat and began sipping the bottled water that had been thoughtfully provided. He nibbled on spicy cooked Japanese peas from a bowl next to the water. He lowered the back window so he could savor the steamy air, mixed as it was with the smell of car exhaust. July is the middle of the rainy season in Myanmar. It had rained earlier that morning but it wasn't raining now. Heavy traffic and some flooding on the streets slowed them down in the city, although ignoring all traffic lights helped make things go a little faster. Of course, there weren't many traffic lights to ignore. The police directed the traffic. Traffic lights, like cell phone roaming, no doubt would be coming soon. The police saluted and stopped traffic to allow Ian's car to get through. On the way Ian took in some of the old colonial buildings in downtown Yangon. The buildings were architectural gems, monuments to yesterday. Monuments to an Empire that his father's ancestors had built and then abandoned. As the Romans had left Britain, so the British were gone from Rangoon. If time allowed, Ian would take a closer look.

Ian had seen pictures of some of the buildings he was looking at. The Rangoon of old had been an important colonial center in the British Empire. It was a bustling cosmopolitan place with a large Indian population. And it had an infrastructure of streetcars, gaslights and telephone services comparable to those of Europe. Ian would have much preferred the Rangoon of old to the Yangon of today.

Forty minutes later he arrived at the General's house. It was located in a lush green, suburban area, outside of the downtown. Two soldiers, both with automatic rifles slung over their shoulders and dark blue helmets, stood guard in front of a double iron gate. Above the gate on an iron circular arch was an inscription in Burmese. The soldiers saluted and opened the iron gates allowing the car to enter. The Mercedes slowly made its way up a long circular gravel driveway that was lined on both sides by gorgeous pink bougainvillea that alternated with red and white blooming plumeria. Ian had read in his guidebook on the plane ride up from Singapore that in Burma plumeria was supposed to be kept blooming all the time. Otherwise you would have money problems. Parked off to one side was a truck with an antenna on the top and two soldiers inside.

As the Major opened the car door for him, he breathed in the humid non-air-conditioned air. He always enjoyed humid, non-air-conditioned air. Ian marveled at the house, mixture of brick and faded teak. This house had to have had a long history. And like the lush foliage had obviously been rained on a lot. The house looked to be quite large, perhaps 10,000 square feet. It had an air of faded gentility and even mystery. Ian wondered what secrets it held, what grand parties it had hosted back in those days of imperial grandeur. The house had to be at least a hundred years old. It was wrapped in two floors of verandas, the verandas on the second floor being stacked over those on the first which in turn were held up above ground level by wooden stilts. The roof of the house was pitched and Ian counted three gables. On the far side of the house was scaffolding and he could see workmen in longyi and no shirts on the pitched roof. Two more armed soldiers stood at attention at the front of the house.

As Ian emerged from the car, a dark Indian-looking man attired in a plain dark red longyi and sandals rushed out to meet him. He was carrying a large umbrella, which Ian immediately had to get under. Ian knew the drill. It wasn't still raining but why take the chance? Ian was the honored guest. He would not be allowed to risk getting wet in the sixty feet between the car and the house. The much shorter Indian looking man would hold the umbrella over him. If Ian was lucky, the much shorter Indian man would not accidentally poke his eye out with the umbrella.

The Indian looking man escorted Ian into the house. As he walked to the house, he passed through what seemed like an honor guard of stone water jars, several with beds of diamond shaped small green leaves floating on the top. Probably water chestnuts. Other jars hosted what Ian guessed were water lilies. Small fish swam among their roots. Mixed in with the water jars were purple and white orchids in separate pots. Ian looked up. A gaggle of crows was hovering above him, raising a racket with their screeching. The crows like the soldiers added a sinister note to what was otherwise an idyllic scene. But these were Burmese crows. According to his guidebook, crows were good luck for Buddhists at least in Burma. He presumed that was still true.

Ian crossed through one of the first floor verandas. Rattan chairs, that looked like no one had sat in them for a long time, were on forlorn display. Perhaps once upon a time, people with pinkish white skin, who looked like his British ancestors, sat out on this veranda, drinking themselves into peaceful oblivion, surrounded by beautiful flowers and servants who bowed at the slightest provocation. His great grandfather had only been in Burma for six months when he found himself transferred with a promotion to Kampala. No matter. Kampala, Calcutta, Rangoon, maybe Jamaica, there was always a house or a bungalow where the senior servants of the Empire could relax after a hard day's colonial duties of bringing civilization to the grateful natives. That is, when they were not at the Club. This was the world the way it was supposed to be, or so his grandfather had taught him. Except that it hadn't been that way for a long time. Were the crows overhead then?

Ian followed the man into a darkish room that had all the earmarks of a British gentleman's library. The room even had a faint scent of cigars. The man signaled to Ian to sit down in front of a large wooden desk. A large computer screen sat on the desk with an iPad next to it. Incongruously, a large marionette, a mustached miniature brown man dressed in an elegant and colorful longyi, sat out in the middle of the desk.

Ian, ex-professor that he was, couldn't resist getting up to inspect the dark teak bookshelves that lined one wall. He was surprised to find them filled with mathematics and finance texts. And some technical books on drilling for natural gas. He randomly pulled out one of the books, an introductory MBA text written by a friend of his. He opened the book and noticed immediately that someone had underlined with red highlighter all over the book. Except on page sixty seven someone had written in "STUPID" in large capital letters. He scanned the page. The author, his friend, was going on and on about the beauty of the Efficient Market Hypothesis. What his friend wrote *was* stupid. If he believed all that bullshit, he wouldn't spend a day trading. He put the book back.

Then in a far corner he noticed some musty old books that looked like they had been bought in a rare books shop. He went over and examined them. They were no doubt the type of thing his ancestors, in their world without TV and internet, feasted on. At least when they were sober. *The Complete Works of Sir Walter Scott, A Compendium of Poems by William Henry Wordsworth, Percy Bysshe Shelly, the Collected Works*—all stuff written by dead white guys that the world had forgotten. Certainly the Burmese had forgotten them. The books had suffered mildew damage and the pages stuck together.

Opposite the bookshelves was a large painting of a young white woman seated with what must have been her two young children. She had haunting sad blue eyes and no smile and wore an off-white dress. Next to the painting was what looked like a little golden altar and a miniature statue of the Buddha. Placed next to the Buddha were several oranges on the one side and cut flowers that Ian guessed were some kind of lily. Overall, an interesting choice of décor and reading material for a Burmese general.

A heavy set woman, her face plastered with thanaka and wearing a brown longyi, sandals and a brown tee shirt, entered the room and set out a pitcher of tea and two teacups. Five minutes elapsed. Then ten. Then twenty. Ian poured himself several cups of tea. He would have preferred espresso made from his Italian machine back in Singapore. And he would have preferred Coco to have been on time. Was she late on purpose? He didn't like it when people played games with him.

Finally she made her entrance, carrying a large black computer bag. Devan had told him Coco was a young woman. But Ian was still a little surprised at just how young she looked. A search on the internet had revealed little about General Maung Myo's personal life or his new wife. The only thing Ian could find was that the General had two daughters by his first wife and a son. Only one daughter was still alive.

Coco was attired in a blue longyi, sandals and a multicolored traditional Burmese blouse. She wore long jade earrings that matched a bracelet on her right wrist. Myanmar is known for its jade. She was also wearing large dark sunglasses and had a liberal dose of whitish thanaka painted on each cheek on her face. Ian noticed the "G" on the side of the sunglasses. G as in Gucci. Madame looked Chinese, as far as he could tell, but the sunglasses hid her eyes. Anyway to his untutored Caucasian eyes in Myanmar, most people looked Chinese. He was surprised by the sandals but actually they made sense. She appeared to be somewhere around five foot seven. No need for high heels. So many Chinese women he knew in Singapore were quite beautiful and well, quite short. They could barely manage to walk around with pumps and stiletto heels that added at least five inches to their height. Would the women of the new Myanmar ditch their sandals and longyis for slutty miniskirts and heels? Only time would tell. Ian liked slutty miniskirts and heels, but he was already acquiring a taste for the more demure longyi and sandals.

Thanks to the thanaka and the sunglasses, Ian wasn't sure he'd recognize Coco if he saw her again. He didn't know it then but of course that was the idea.

Coco swayed from side to side in a hurried manner as she walked in. She smiled at Ian as she thrust out her hand in an aggressive American style to shake

Ian's. Ian noticed that her left hand looked battered and bruised. And she wasn't wearing a watch or a ring.

"Nice to see you this morning. I'm Ian Blakely."

"Sorry I'm late, Ian," she said. "I was on a conference call with our Indian partners." She extended her hand. "I like to be called Coco." She smiled. There was a smart-alec curve under her lip. It was instantly recognizable as an *I'm trying to decide if you're an asshole* curve.

"Yes, Devan mentioned that," Ian said. "Where did you come up with that name?"

"Coco Chanel. You've heard of her? She's one of my heroes. Since high school." Coco instantly realized it was a mistake to tell Ian this. She was wearing a Chanel bag in the Wang Qiang painting. She hoped the big Gucci sunglasses that she was wearing today would distract him. At least she hadn't told him the real truth. That it was Wang Qiang who had gotten her into Coco Chanel. For Coco, Chanel was a woman who rose up from humble beginnings to become a fashion idol and mogul. Before she was Coco, her fake English name had been Helen, a name chosen by her father. A name that now made her shudder every time she thought of it.

Ian wasn't too interested in why she was Coco. Chinese in Singapore and Hong Kong often chose what he considered to be really strange fake English names. Queenie, Fanny, Lovely, Coco... take your pick. He wasn't surprised by the name Coco. Ian pointed to the painting on the wall. "Who's she? I have an interest in art."

Coco turned to the painting. "She was the young wife of the British general who used to own this house a hundred years ago." There suddenly was a touch of sadness in Coco's voice. "I often wonder what kind of life she had. I found some of her letters. She was very homesick for England. She had an old boyfriend who used to write to her. She loved him." Coco turned back to Ian. "She hated her husband. Stupid military guy. She was an intellectual. She was forced to marry him. Her father was a parson or something poor like that.

Educated but poor. " Coco pointed to the old books at the end of the bookshelves. "Those were her books."

"Did she ever see the old boyfriend again?'

"No. She died here in Myanmar of malaria. In this house. In this room. I had this room totally ripped apart and changed into a study when we took over the house. Fucking Asians are so superstitious. My husband wouldn't have moved here any other way. Somebody dies in your house and down goes the price. I brought in a Buddhist priest to exorcise the house for good measure. It was a big deal. I saved the books. I found the letters when the workmen were pulling the room apart. She had the letters hidden under a floorboard. The painting was stuck in a closet and in bad shape. I had it repaired and reframed. Her name was Charlene. Charlene Bottomley. I wish I had known her." As Coco talked, she held a pen in her hand. The way a woman might hold a cigarette or a small cigar.

"So he was military?"

"Yes, her husband's name was Major General B.S. A.H. Bottomley. I've renamed him Bullshit, Asshole Bottomley. Fucking British. Don't they have real names?"

Ian smiled. He often teased his British relatives for this. Initials were the thing in the days of the Empire. "No, just initials. So changing the room got rid of Charlene's ghost?"

Coco shrugged. "Asian people believe in this shit." She poured herself some tea and took a sip, the cup reflecting in her sunglasses. The curved smile came back. "So. You fucked Kyaw Cho?"

"I did," Ian replied after some hesitation.

"That's good. We don't want do-gooders for a partner. And men, if they are too horny, can't focus their minds on business."

"I've always believed that," Ian replied. "I'm not a do-gooder. And I've never had a problem focusing."

"I picked her out myself," Coco said. "She's a smart girl. Her father ran a jewelry store but he died when she was ten. Chinese. Most of the jewelry people in Yangon are Chinese. Of course she has a Burmese name. For appearances." Coco put her pen in her mouth. Like she was going to smoke it.

"You selected her?" Ian asked.

"I'm going to ask her how good you were." Coco laughed an *I gotcha* laugh.

Ian didn't know what to say. "She seemed like a very intelligent woman."

"Born here but she's got Chinese brains." Coco laughed again. "She's not a regular hooker. I had to pay her extra. I hope she didn't act too innocent." She put her hand under her chin and grinned at him. "I want a full report."

"She did a superlative job." He was dying to remove Coco's sunglasses and see what her eyes were saying. "I used to be a professor by the way. I'd give her an A."

"Harvard, right?"

"Harvard Business School. And let me guess," Ian said. "You got all As at Brown?"

Coco smiled. "Yes, I did. I was a math major. Phi Beta Kappa. But for my MBA I got all Bs."

"Where?"

"Here at the local university. A brand new program. Actually, I just finished the program. It was either the local university or Harvard. I decided to go to school here. I heard most of the professors at Harvard are unbearable."

"They are. Why only Bs?"

"The school here's so easy. I just answered enough of the test questions to get a B. Then I left. I had better things to do than take their stupid tests."

"You mean you deliberately didn't answer questions because you didn't feel like it?" Ian found himself liking Coco.

"I knew all the answers. Actually, Bs were pretty good. I never went to class. I had Kyaw Cho go in my place. I read her notes and the bullshit textbook."

"They let you do that?"

Coco replied in a tone bordering on disbelief. "This is Myanmar. I'm General Maung Myo's wife. I do what I want. I'm thinking about getting a doctorate."

Ian reflected that flunking General Muang Myo's wife in Myanmar might not put a professor on the tenure track.

Suddenly her demeanor changed. "Shall we get down to work? The General will meet you at lunch. We have little time. He's a military man. He likes everything to be on schedule. I'll go over Zafar with you. If you have questions, I'll answer them." She flipped on the computer screen. Ian noticed her fingernails were bitten down.

Ian interrupted her. "I'm pretty familiar with the technical side of this project. But, I do have some personal questions. Perhaps it's impertinent of me to ask them, but I won't be involved with this project unless I get answers."

Coco turned the screen off. "Ask."

"Let's start with this. Devan says you saved the General's life. How did you do that?"

She stared at him for a moment. "Okay. I'll give you a short version of the whole fucking family soap opera. In the late Forties my father was in the Guomindang army. You know. The Chinese Nationalists. The ones that lost to the Communists."

"I know."

"Well, his unit fled to Northern Burma in 1949 when the Communists took over China. He was young and resourceful. He's had various businesses in Burma over the years. He's been a silent partner with the General."

"I see."

"Ian, do you know the Heimlich Maneuver?"

"What?"

"The Heimlich Maneuver."

"I know what it is."

"Well, I took this Women's Empowerment course at Brown. They taught us how to do it. Actually, any moron could learn it."

"I guess they figured liberated women should be ready to alleviate digestive blockages."

"Fuck." Coco laughed. "It was a new course. I'm sure the course is more sophisticated now."

"I'm sure it is."

"Anyway, I was in Myanmar on vacation. I had just been promoted at my job in investment management at one of the bulge bracket banks in New York. I got that promotion without having an MBA at that time by the way. The only person to do that. Anyway, my father and the General are friends. The General invited us for lunch. My father brought me along to introduce me to some young military guy who would be at the lunch. A total asshole. But I figured it was just a lunch, good for laughs."

"This lunch would be a normal thing to do in Burmese society?"

"Well, maybe not. But the General and his daughter are Westernized in certain superficial ways."

She looked at her iPhone. Probably to check the time. Ian was struck by the absence of an expensive Swiss watch. And where was the diamond studded engagement ring? The absence of jewelry must be some Brown snobbism which overrode her Asian default algorithm compelling her to buy high end European brands. There was no way he could know that Coco's hand and wrist were so swollen that she couldn't wear her ring or her watch. Or that her hand and wrist were casualties in her effort to bash the traitor Khin Chit's face into an unrecognizable mass. Or that she wouldn't wear any necklace lest he associate with it with the one that lay between her naked breasts in the painting.

Coco continued. "The General's daughter Su Myat was there with her husband General Sein Soe and the young military guy. Her husband by the way is an idiot who has his job only because of Su Myat's father."

"Your husband?"

"Right. I hope all these Burmese names aren't too much for you."

"I'm keeping up."

"Anyway. They served a chicken curry for lunch. Somehow the General's chicken had a bone. It got stuck in his throat. He couldn't breathe. He was gasping for breath. Everybody started screaming like a bunch of assholes. But nobody did anything. Finally I couldn't take it. I got up, reached around the General from the back, did my woman's empowerment Heimlich Maneuver, picked him up and, pop, the bone flew out of his mouth."

"Flew out of his mouth?"

"Like a fucking bird."

"So you were a hero."

"Naturally the General immediately consulted his astrologer. After all this is Burma or Myanmar or whatever you want to call it. The astrologer said this was a clear sign I was to be the General's wife. The stars just happened to be lined up just right. Then his favorite monks chimed in with the same story."

"So you listened to the astrologer and the monks."

"My father did. He owed the General a great deal of money. Actually, he owed the General his life. But that's another story."

"So you are a good Chinese girl. You obeyed your father."

"If you want to write a novel, you can write it that way. It would fit your Western romantic illusions about the mysterious East. And who knows. Maybe the astrologer and the monks were right." Coco smiled as she said this.

"So which way would you write the novel?"

"That I was on a fast track career path in New York. But I decided to stay here. I thought I had a greater opportunity here in Asia. Here I can make a difference. My husband can open many doors. Even if he can't always see the way I can, the opportunity that's behind them. I was working eighty hour weeks in New York and I had no life. I won't say the work wasn't interesting. The area I was in focused on internet stocks. But there was so much useless bullshit. For example, at the bank along with everyone else I had to attend political correctness seminars. Imagine. I had to waste hours and hours learning how to be nice to women and black people. These New York banks are so fucked up. At least they could have limited the courses to white guys. They're the ones who needed the courses. And I had to follow a stupid dress code that drove me crazy. They wouldn't even let me wear shorts to work on Saturdays. I'm not just a financial machine. I'm a *fashionista*. I'm Coco. My personality is too non-conformist to fit into a large organization. Anyway, I made the choice, not my father. I've always gone to the beat of a different drum."

"So marrying the General was an opportunity?"

"I'll be honest. Yes an incredible one. An opportunity to help this country and make a fortune along the way." She laughed. "This is romance, Asian style."

"So what opportunities do you see behind the doors your husband opens?"

"Project Zafar for one. Anyone with half a brain could see even ten years ago that this country had to change and that it was loaded with natural resources. Burma before the Japanese invasion was one of the most advanced countries in Asia. Okay, a lot of the business was in the hands of the whites, the Indians and the Chinese. The Burmese traditionally were rural, perhaps a little slower. But still. Then after the war and independence came fifty years of fucking looney tunes socialism. Things eventually had to change for the better.

Those with the right connections and with vision would make fortunes. And help the country in the process. My husband may be shrewd and powerful but he's not a businessman. I am. This country is filled with oil and gas. And smart people. If you give them a chance."

"But he's well connected."

Coco's voice turned hard. "But I was the one who developed Project Zafar. In cooperation with Devan and the Indians. With my help the General understood everything. He pulled the strings. He got us the options on the blocks. He's making sure the government lives up to its obligation to sign the PSC. That's Production Sharing Contract. The government has agreed in principle to the PSC."

"I know."

Coco continued. "There will be more projects coming, by the way. Hotels, condos, maybe a bank. And I'm going to promote Burmese fashion. My mind just runs. You've heard of the old snooty whites-only Pegu Club?"

"Actually, my grandfather spoke of it. But really I don't know much."

"Your grandfather? That's right. He was British, wasn't he?"

Ian smiled. "You do your homework, I see."

Coco just stared. Her sunglasses gave up nothing.

Ian added. "He was stationed for a time in Burma, in the Indian army."

"Well your grandfather would know the Pegu Club was the place to be in colonial times. The building's abandoned now but parts of it can be reclaimed. Very beautiful, lots of teak. I might revive the club. We might even let whites in. Whites I choose. Burma was a romantic prosperous place in its day. Myanmar can become that again. We will run the club, not the colonial power. So what's your next question?"

"Tell me about Su Myat."

"Very good. You remembered her name."

"I'm not senile yet."

"I'm not a hero to Su Myat. She hates me. I think she wanted to see her father die right there. She and her idiot husband just sat there. And so did the moron from the army that they expected me to swoon over."

"It must have been quite a lunch. How was the food apart from the occasional chicken bone?"

Coco smiled. "I'm beginning to like you. You really are an asshole."

"Such flattery," Ian replied.

"Devan did explain to you that Su Myat has another group of Chinese investors?"

"Yes."

"It's all on the internet. You can read about them. The whole group is really stupid. They just have money. No expertise in natural gas. They have no way of getting the gas to China. The government won't allow another pipeline across Myanmar into China. Connecting to the existing Chinese pipeline stretches its capacity. And the gas can't go south by tanker. China isn't interested in LNG from Myanmar that has to go down through the Straits of Malacca and under the eyes of the US navy. The Myanmar government wants to balance the Chinese with the Indians." She smiled. "Not the Indians with feathers. The ones with dots."

"I know which Indians you mean," Ian said. "Devan says Su Myat is ruthless."

"I'm no delicate Madama Butterfly. She will be sorry if she fucks with me."

"Do *I* need to worry about her?"

"What can she do to you? Look, if you want a risk free investment, buy a US government bond. We're going to make a fortune on this. You have to expect some competition."

"US government bonds are not so risk free anymore. She hates you because of money? Or because she thinks you stole her father's love?"

Coco shrugged. "I don't give a shit."

"One more question. Why do you want me in Project Zafar?"

"We need one more investor. But this investor must bring more to the table than money. We want somebody who is financially sophisticated. And we need someone to run the SWF. Frankly, your financial expertise is needed by the group. And we could use somebody who is a citizen of an ASEAN country. ASEAN is the Association of South East Asian Nations, of which Myanmar is a member. Which I'm sure you know. ASEAN is a big deal to the government here." Coco handed Ian her memo on the Sovereign Wealth Fund. "I don't know if you've seen this."

"So what happened to your hand?"

Coco hesitated, then managed a smile. "Kickboxing. It's a hobby."

Ian figured out what she was really saying. *Not your fucking business.*

The heavy set Chinese looking woman poked her head in the door. She held her hand up palms out signaling "five."

"Okay," said Coco, looking at the woman. "Ian, we have lunch in five minutes." She turned the computer screen back on. A large ship with four large white domes taking up its entire length flashed onto the screen. She suddenly became very excited. "Look at that. I'm not an engineer. My background is finance and computers. But this is a new LNG carrier. It will carry our liquid natural gas across the Bay of Bengal to India. Isn't it beautiful?" She bit her tongue. She was about to say *like a painting.*

"Yes, it is," Ian replied.

"The carriers' LNG tanks have a spherical design. That's the way most of them are built nowadays." She changed the picture on the screen. "If you want,

I'll arrange a meeting with our Indian partners and have one of their engineers bombard you with details. It's exciting stuff."

"That might be a good idea. But later."

Coco continued. "And here is a floating storage terminal. The gas comes up below the ocean floor, gets liquefied into LNG and shipped across the Bay of Bengal to just below Kolkata. Tsunami comes and everything floats like a cork. No environmental problems."

She flipped the screen again. Her discounted cash flow model came up. "I used to do these models on Wall Street all the time. I can do this shit in my sleep." She rested her chin on her hand and smiled. "Chinese are good at math." There was something about her tone that said, *Ian you may have been a finance professor at Harvard but I'm better at math than you.* "Now look at that. We make 20 percent annual return for ten years. And that's after the government gets its cut. This is a great deal for us and for Myanmar. And for India. The Indians get the LNG at least fifteen percent cheaper than they would pay on the world market."

Ian had already received a version of this model from Devan.

"Ian, you won't get a better project than this. And after this if you are in our group there will be more. Myanmar will be a gold mine. You've got to be here."

Ian replied. "Well, I've suspected Myanmar offers great opportunities. Otherwise I wouldn't be here." *Devan was right about Coco*, Ian thought. *Smart and good looking. Like his ex-wife. A dangerous combination.*

She pointed the way out of the study. "We better get to lunch."

"We're not having chicken curry, I presume."

"You definitely *are* an asshole," she said smiling. "Oh, by the way. Here in Myanmar we squat at a low table and eat with our right hand. No knives and forks. You're okay with that, right?"

"No problem." Ian actually was panicking. He could not imagine his six three frame squatting for lunch. He remembered the time in Inner Mongolia when he fell over backwards taking a shit on a Chinese style hole-in-the-ground squat toilet.

"Good." She pointed again. "Let's go."

Chapter Twelve

When I die I will be a Burman ... and I will always walk about with a pretty almond-coloured girl who shall laugh and jest too, as a young maiden ought. She shall not pull a sari over her head when a man looks at her and glare suggestively from behind it, nor shall she tramp behind me when I walk: for these are the customs of India. She shall look all the world between the eyes, in honesty and good fellowship, and I will teach her not to defile her pretty mouth with chopped tobacco in a cabbage leaf, but to inhale good cigarettes of Egypt's best brand.

— *Rudyard Kipling*

Coco and Ian proceeded down a long dark hall. The floor creaked under Ian's two hundred ten pounds. Finally they arrived at a large dining room.

It was not what Coco had just led Ian to expect. Unlike the rest of the house, the room was very light. A large bay window faced out on what looked like what was normally a small pond and gazebo, making for an idyllic scene. Except for the fact that there was a large bulldozer next to the pond and the pond had been drained. Evidently some kind of work on the pond was underway. In the center of the dining room was a long mahogany dinner table. It was a Western style table, not low along the ground. It had settings with forks, spoons and plates at the one end for three diners. And a pot of tea with three teacups. Ian turned to Coco who was sporting her curved grin.

Before Ian could return the compliment and call Coco an asshole, the General entered. The General walked slowly with a cane but he stood ramrod straight. He was dressed in civilian clothes, a white Lacoste shirt, dark longyi and sandals. Like Coco, he was wearing sunglasses although his were a little less outrageous than his wife's. He and Ian shook hands and introduced themselves. The General motioned to Ian to sit down. The General took the seat at the end of the table, resting his cane against the table.

"My wife designed this room," he said, a bony hand motioning to Coco. "She wanted good *feng shui*. The Chinese have their ways." He spoke with a British accented English.

"I put in the bay window for more light," Coco added while pouring the tea. "It's not in the style of the house but it's in the back so I don't think it compromises anything. When they built the house over hundred years ago, they didn't have the technology for this type of window. Now, the window opens the dining room up to what will be the water of the pond. They are doing some work out there now but the pond will be refilled soon. That's why all the equipment is there."

The bay window actually allowed in considerable sunlight and the room was actually quite bright.

"Good *feng shui,*" Ian said.

"Of course," Coco said.

"Coco is very smart as you can see," the General said. "And good with money. I never met a Chinaman who wasn't. Of course, Coco is a woman but she thinks like a man."

Major Nyan Myint poked his head in and said something in Burmese. He then handed the General a landline phone. The phone with a long cord that must have been connected with the next room. The Major stood at attention.

The General put his hand over the phone. "It's our President. Excuse my rudeness." He took the call and spoke in Burmese in a conversation that would last about five minutes.

Ian looked at Coco. She made a face that said *who do you know that gets a phone call from the President?* Coco said almost in a whisper. "Cell phones' voice quality is crap. He hears better on the landline. He feels it's more secure. Oh, and thank God he's retired. Otherwise we'd have to live in Naypyidaw."

Minutes later the General finished his call. "Our President wants to know when we submit the final documents on Zafar. They need that to approve the PSC. Once the PSC is signed, we will set up an opening ceremony. The Indian President may attend."

Coco commented. "Devan and I have been working on that. We have a meeting coming up in Singapore. The documents should be ready shortly after the meeting. The government's staff has already gone over a draft."

The Major took the phone and left the room. The General spoke. "As I was saying, the Chinese are very good with money. Like the Jews. You are Jewish?"

Ian got this question wherever he went in Asia. He was in finance, and sometimes wore glasses. Somehow in Asia that made him Jewish. "No I'm afraid not. Anglican on my father's side, Catholic on my mother's. My mother was American and my father a Brit."

The General spoke slowly. "I hope one day Myanmar can be like Singapore. Very advanced country. And disciplined. They kept English. We dropped it from our schools. That was a big mistake." He reached for tea. The tremor in his hand was noticeable. The tea slowly made its way up to the General's mouth like a plane on climb-out through some rough clouds. "Of course we are different from Singapore in one important way. In Singapore, the immigrants, that is the Chinese and the Indians, run the place. The native Malays must take a back seat. Here in Myanmar it is the opposite. The natives, the Myanmar people, run things, not the Indians and Chinese. We want to keep it that way."

Ian held his breath. It looked like the tea was about to go over. But somehow it didn't. Ian met the General's gaze. His gaze was still strong, unlike the rest of him. Then Ian looked over at Coco. *LNG promoter. I can believe that. Wife of this elderly man? Absurd.* "I live in Singapore. I really like it there," Ian said. "Yes, everybody speaks English."

111

The General spoke. "Did Coco tell you? I'm a Sandhurst graduate. The Brits are good people. Great legal tradition. A marvel. Even though they did bad things here."

There was something about the General in the slow way he spoke that reminded Ian of Don Corleone. Don Corleone after he had taken a few bullets and slowed down a bit. Physically not the man he used to be. But still The Man who gives the orders. And commands respect.

At that point two women in longyi, sandals and Western style blouses, their faces covered with the usual thanaka, entered the room. They brought platters of various dishes and placed them on the table. Ian was taken aback by the quantity. But the aroma was delicious. No wonder Rudyard Kipling liked Burma so much.

The women were bringing out enough food to feed an entire division of the Army of the Republic of the Union of Myanmar. *This was a good sign*, Ian guessed. Although he would have to swim an extra hour to work this off. The first thing the women did after placing the dishes on the table was to then place a small bowl of rice before a small statue of the Buddha which was off to one side of the table.

But a look of concern came over Ian's face.

Coco with her American education figured out what was wrong. "Don't worry," she said to Ian, "Everything's been peeled and washed. You won't get Delhi Belly here."

The General smiled.

"Funny you should mention," Ian said. "People from the West are gastrointestinal weaklings. Things are too clean. The germs know this. They lined up at the airport when my plane landed in Hyderabad recently. I got really sick in India."

"I got sick when I first went to the U.K," the General said. "You have nothing to worry about. Coco supervises the kitchen."

Coco grinned. "Another one of my talents."

The General commented. "Traditionally in Myanmar we eat with our hands. But I gave that up at Sandhurst. That would never do with the Brits. Oh, and strict Buddhists don't talk when they eat either but that's not my custom. I like to talk." His boney hand shaking slightly, the General pointed to the plethora of dishes that had been placed on the table. "We love mangos and hot chilies here. And of course curries. But our curries are better than the Indian. More subtle." He pointed to one dish. "This is called a mango fish. Very tasty." He reached over and, with some effort, placed a spoonful on Ian's plate. Another miracle. His hand shook all the way but nothing was spilled. He then pointed to another dish with some type of noodles swimming in gravy. "That is monhinga. It's our national dish. We usually eat it for breakfast but I thought you should have some." Fortunately, the monhinga was just a little too far from the General to reach. "What is the national dish in America, Mr. Blakely?"

"Hot dogs," Ian replied immediately.

Coco looked like she was rolling her eyes but Ian really couldn't tell with her sunglasses.

The General nodded and took an extra breath. "I like hot dogs" the General said. "There's a place here in Yangon where you can get them. I have one of my people get me hot dogs once and while. You don't mind hot chilies? We have been eating them here for a thousand years."

"I'm used to hot chilies." Ian wisely decided not to tell the General that there were no chilies of any kind in Asia or Europe until the Portuguese in the sixteenth century brought them from the Americas. At least that's what all the books said.

The General then went on as Devan predicted to tell Ian some stories about his days at Sandhurst. He ate with a fork and spoon in the Southeast Asian style and did manage to spill a good portion of his food on his shirt. Coco actually got up and helped him clean off his shirt on one occasion. Ian was surprised at the tenderness she showed him. It seemed out of character. But

Devan had told him Coco would surprise him. When he was a little kid, his aunt had had a stroke and Ian had found her really disgusting when she ate. Ian suspected that the General had had a stroke. But the General was an affable host and expressed an interest in Ian's British ancestors and their service to the Empire. And he didn't seem embarrassed at all that he required Coco's assistance while eating.

Then towards the end of the meal the General suddenly turned serious. "So why does the Chetty want you in our deal?"

Ian, confused, turned to Coco.

"He means Devan," she said.

"Oh, okay. Devangar Saravanan was a student of mine when I was a professor at the Business School at Harvard. As you know, the Blakely Funds now total some nine billion in US dollars. That gives us size, but we are still small compared to some other funds." Ian didn't want to mention that excluding American investors had limited the growth of his funds. "But that gives us flexibility. We've launched a new energy fund investing in Asia. The price of oil and other hydrocarbons has dropped and now is the perfect time to be investing. Devan and I maintained contact over the years and now of course we both live in Singapore. He's tried to get me interested in Myanmar for some time. It seems also that my Singaporean citizenship adds something. Project Zafar is looking like a good fit for my new fund. And I'm really excited about starting a sovereign wealth fund for Myanmar."

The General nodded. "Your ASEAN connection is important. So you taught at Brown?"

Ian turned to Coco again. She said nothing.

"No, I'm afraid not. Harvard was enough. Actually, I've never even been to Providence or Brown. Boston snobbery I guess."

"So you just met Coco this morning? She seems to have a high opinion of you."

Ian smiled. "Well, I'm happy to hear that. But no, our paths have not crossed until now. I don't know how she arrived at her high opinion."

Ian thought he detected a look of relief on the General's face. Then the General belched loudly. He looked at his watch. "I'm afraid I have to go." He spoke slowly but deliberately. "But I can assure you this deal will go through. The government has negotiated the PSC and will sign it. This deal is very important for Myanmar. We have made many mistakes here to be sure. But we have preserved our country. We have overcome the divide and rule policies of our British colonial masters. We have many minority groups that sometimes have their own ideas. But we have prevented our country from becoming divided. Now we must move forward. We cannot be dependent on any one country. That includes China, India, the US or Britain. " He began to stand. Coco immediately took his arm to assist him. "I hope you will join us. My Chinese wife will make sure you make lots of money. I have never been that interested in money. I only want to serve my country." The General got up slowly and extended his hand to Ian. "I believe people not numbers are what are important in any deal. But I want this to be a gift to my country. Myanmar will get a lot of money from it. The money will come in after I am gone. I know that. But I hope Myanmar and my young wife use the money wisely. That I cannot control. But if you join us and do your job honestly, you will be a great help in that regard."

"Sir," Ian responded. "If I run the Sovereign Wealth Fund I will invest the money in the best global assets I can find. If I am pressured to make stupid investments in somebody's pet company, I will quit. Of course the fund will be at the disposal of the government to invest in Myanmar. Hopefully, it will be for infrastructure, education – things like that."

The General nodded. "Myanmar is opening up. We have huge natural resources. Oil, gas, gems plus agriculture. We can use the money wisely and educate our people. Or we can be like Thailand – hookers, temples and beaches for the tourists."

"Yes." Ian thought the General's assessment of Thailand was a little harsh. But he didn't argue.

"I hope we will get to know one another better. It takes time to get to know a person and how he will react in difficult circumstances. But I have judged you as a man who is trustworthy and honorable."

Ian stood up and shook the General's hand. "Thank you for saying that, sir. I hope this will become a long term relationship. And I've made a decision. I'm in. I'll join Project Zafar. It's an honor to be associated with this project."

"Excellent." The General smiled. "Although at my age long term has a different meaning than for you." The two men continued to shake hands. Then Ian turned to Coco and shook her hand. T "Are you going right back to Singapore?" the General asked.

"Well, I have some phone calls to make. I'm staying at the Strand. After I make my calls, I thought I would walk around downtown just to get a feel for the older colonial Yangon. Then I'll leave."

"Excellent idea. There are many beautiful buildings that your British ancestors built. But not without the help of our people. The city hall which you should see had a Burmese architect. Major Nyan Myint and my car are at your disposal."

"That's not necessary. I thought it would be interesting to just look around a little. It's the professor in me. Just have the Major drop me at the hotel."

"Very well. After your walk, the Major will take you back to the airport. I insist. He is at your disposal, as you wish." Using his cane, the General slowly made his way out of the room. The Indian looking man who had ushered Ian into the house suddenly appeared. Ian shook hands again with Coco.

Coco said. "The entire consortium will be meeting in Singapore at the offices of Calcutta Global Oil Company a week from Thursday. If you can, you should be there. You will get to meet everyone."

"This is really a balancing act for Myanmar, isn't it. The Indians will balance the Chinese. The Chinese have their pipelines in the north."

"Yes." Coco smiled. "Our Indian partners will host the upcoming meeting. They always provide a big Indian lunch. I hope you don't mind the smell of Indian curry."

Good God, more curry! Ian thought. *Why can't these people just drink with their meals like his British ancestors?* "It's the smell of money that's important," Ian said. "I'll be at the meeting in Singapore, of course. I'll have the initial ten million wired to Devan immediately."

Ian took his leave.

Coco didn't like it that Ian would be wandering around Yangon unescorted. He needed protection. Some trick by Su Myat could blow the whole deal. She called Major Nyan Myint. He answered on his cell phone. She spoke in Burmese. "I want nothing to happen to Dr. Blakely. You understand? He is your responsibility while he is in Myanmar. Follow him without his knowing it. We have enemies. They are now his enemies. But he doesn't know them."

"Yes, Coco."

She had no choice on this. But she wondered if she was sending a fox to guard a rabbit. She wanted to call Ian and tell him to be careful what he said in front of the Major. But she knew if she did that, Ian would get cold feet and never put in the ten million.

Chapter Thirteen

In Republics, the great danger is, that the majority may not sufficiently respect the rights of the minority.

—James Madison

The trip back to the Strand took longer than it should have. July is the middle of the rainy season in Myanmar. It seemed like the heavens had opened all the way up for about ten minutes. As usual, a junior soldier did the driving while the Major sat alongside him. The Major sat ramrod straight with an earplug in his left ear which Ian took no notice of. Nowadays almost everyone everywhere nowadays walks around with some kind of earplug, listening to iTunes, talking to their squeeze or whatever.

Ian called Anita in Singapore as soon as he got in the car. He was surprised the call actually went through, especially given the rain and given that he was in Myanmar. A glass partition sealed off the back seat of the car so Ian assumed he had some privacy. "You've already got the documents. I've decided to do the Zafar deal. Call Devan and wire in the ten million."

"Yes sir," Anita said.

"So what about Wang Qiang?" Ian asked.

"Amazing. It's all over the art world. He was up to his neck in gambling debts."

"The police have no idea?"

"Not yet."

"I've received no calls?

"None, Ian."

"What about Cairncross?"

"No word."

"Very strange. Well, the less we say about Wang the better from my point of view."

"I've been treating this as highly confidential," Anita said.

"What about the new Obama Executive Order?"

"There's a chorus of screams from all the major nations of the world," Anita said. "They are worried US investment in their countries will evaporate. It already looks like the US will have to retreat on this. Maybe the Republicans will be more cooperative on tax reform."

"And the order to reexamine the cases of people who renounced their American citizenship?"

"Unfortunately, there seems to be general support for that in the US. The average citizen wants to punish renunciators as these people now being called."

"I would like to avoid publicity on this. Only 'no comment' to the media, if anyone calls. Let's hope they don't." Ian was getting a headache just thinking about all the hours he would have to spend going over this with some thugs from ODD. They would be a bunch of self-righteous cowboys, whom he suspected, unlike the IRS guys, weren't up to speed on the arcana of the American tax code. Government bullshit. The ODD was under the FBI to scare people. Ian was very unhappy. If word got out he was under investigation, this could hurt his business with Asian clients. They would simply avoid investing with him.

He began to deliver a lecture to Anita, which he did from time to time. He had nothing else to do as his car was stuck in traffic and even Major Nyan Myint couldn't do anything about that. "Anita, think about it. The United States was founded as a Republic with a profound respect for property rights and a distrust of autocratic European kings *and* democratic mob rule. Most Americans today still are sympathetic to the fight against the British king. And with popular support, right after the American Revolution the statue of King George was ripped down in lower Manhattan." He paused. "Against my advice of course."

"What advice? You aren't *that* old."

"It's the advice I would have given. Statues teach us history."

"You would have been really popular with that recommendation."

"Like I am now. Anyway, what is less well known is the Founding Fathers' mistrust of what they considered democratic mob rule. Good old Ben Franklin once said that a democratic election was like two wolves and a lamb voting on what they would eat for lunch. The Founding Fathers thought men without property who were in the majority would vote to take the property of men with property."

Anita had heard this lecture before. She didn't always see eye to eye with Ian on this. "Professor Blakely. I agree with you. Except some men really do have a lot of property. Humans have a sense of fairness. It may not be logical. But it's evolutionary. You're a big fan of evolution. The big alpha male shouldn't get everything even if he earned it. It's probably been that way for millions of years. It's in our DNA. After all you were born smarter than most people. Maybe *that's* not fair."

"Ah, Anita. Another one of your left-handed compliments. Or should I say left-winged? I should have a lobotomy?" Ian fidgeted with impatience as he said this. The traffic had picked up a little but things were still pretty slow.

"Not a good idea. My income depends on your being smarter."

"Anita you're such a pragmatic commie. I've worked hard for what I have. I didn't steal anything. My investments are providing jobs and furthering human knowledge."

"It's not logical but some people don't see it that way."

"And that's why America was set up the way it was. You can't find the word *democracy* even once in the American constitution. . The United States was to be different. If you were talented and worked hard and, yes maybe a little lucky, you could succeed and keep your winnings."

"Unless you were black."

"Okay, okay. But no system is perfect. And that defect has been corrected. Blacks no longer suffer legal discrimination of any sort. According to the latest research, three quarters of a million men died in the American Civil War. That War was largely fought to end slavery. America paid a huge price to eliminate this evil."

"Maybe Obama is correcting things just a little bit more."

Ian grimaced. *Imagine a Singaporean Chinese Obama supporter. And she works for me.* Ian sat back and looked out the window. The rain had stopped. The car was moving a little more quickly. A group of monks were walking right outside the car. Buddhist monks, in their dark red robes, and nuns, attired in pink robes—both with their heads shaved -- are everywhere on the streets of Yangon. *A monk in a cloister is not worth an oyster.* A line from Chaucer that Ian remembered from a freshman English course, when dead white authors were still treated with reverence.

He refocused on Anita. "Correcting things at my expense. Look, America was the greatest country in the world. That's why my British father became an American citizen. If my father were he still living would never have approved of my becoming a Singaporean. He would have said stay in America and fight for what you believe in."

"But you became a Singaporean," Anita interrupted.

"My father's world doesn't exist anymore and he didn't have to have a bodyguard in the US like I did. And he didn't have a billion dollars that the government wanted to take. I've become a Huguenot." Ian had a particular interest in the French Protestant Huguenots who fled France after the revocation of the Edict of Nantes by Louis XIV in 1685. Ian believed that the only way for the rich and talented to survive was to leave and place their capital in places where it was respected and welcomed. And where it would do more good being invested around the world rather than being turned over to wasteful governments.

Little Singapore was a haven for modern Huguenots like Ian. It used British law, it respected property rights, had sound money, it spoke English, it was multicultural and it was a meritocracy. It even had left two statues up in honor of its Great White Founder, Sir Stamford Raffles. It had a certain reverence for dead white guys. And, as the General just said, it was a country run by immigrants. Ian never met an immigrant he didn't like.

But he was agitated. "Anita, the American constitution is now viewed with contempt by so many Americans who consider it an outdated decrepit old document written by long dead rich white male slave owners. I remembered being attacked by one African American female radical in my financial history class --of all places-- at for being a white male obsessed with racist history. As a white male I feel more secure in Singapore than in America."

"The PAP will be pleased to hear this," Anita replied. The PAP, standing for Peoples Action Party, is the ruling political party in Singapore.

"We'll conclude this discussion some other time. *Ya basta* as they say in Miami. I've arrived at my hotel. I have to take my walk."

"Let me get the ten million sent off," Anita said.

Ian took a deep breath. He would deal with the ODD, when the time came.

They had arrived. The sun had come out. The Major got out and hurried to open Ian's car door. He grabbed Ian's arm to help him which annoyed Ian. In Asia age commands respect. But in America, where Ian was from, youth commands respect. He wasn't *that* old. Youth doesn't require assistance getting out of a car.

If Major Nyan Myint, who had been sitting in the front seat, understood any of Ian's conversation, he didn't let on. The glass barrier had made it impossible for the Major to hear. Or so Ian thought. Unless of course there was a hidden microphone in the back seat. That broadcast to the earphone in the Major's left ear.

Chapter Fourteen

There must be a few hundred men who are fairly behind the scenes of the Burma War—one of the least known and appreciated of any of our little affairs. The Pegu Club seemed to be full of men on their way up or down, and the conversation was but an echo of the murmur of conquest far away to the north."

—*Rudyard Kipling,*
From Sea to Sea

Ian planned a round trip from the Strand which was located at one end of the grid that was British designed Rangoon. He would pass by one aging imperial building after the other, take photos and then make a stop at the Sule Paya, Yangon's second most famous pagoda. The Sule Paya is located in a circle that is right in the middle of the traditional commercial district. He made one major decision. It wasn't raining so he didn't bring an umbrella. No umbrella is always a risky decision in Myanmar during the rainy season. But with his guidebook and smartphone occupying his two hands, carrying an umbrella was a pain in the ass. He did however spray himself with a good dose of mosquito repellant. Always a good idea for delicate Caucasians exploring exotic Southeast Asia. He would have Major Nyan Myint take him to the airport when he was finished.

The car was actually still waiting outside the hotel with the driver asleep inside. Major Nyan Myint was not inside but Ian paid this no mind. It didn't occur to Ian that the Major might have retreated to a respectable distance where he could watch Ian unnoticed.

The doorman, attired in longyi and sandals of course, greeted him. Ian noted the contrast with the Raffles in Singapore where a large Sikh in a white uniform and turban guarded the front door. The British used Sikhs all over their Empire in a law enforcement capacity including the police. They were bigger than the locals, had their intimidating beards, a fierce overall look and a reputation for being violent. The Chinese in places like the International Quarter in Shanghai reportedly were scared shit of them. But, as the General said, the Chinese and the Indians don't run things in Myanmar.

He headed up Strand Road to Pansodan Street where he made a right turn. Pansodan Street in colonial times was known as Phayre Street, named after Sir Arthur Purves Phayre, First Commissioner of Burma. Among other accomplishments, Phayre discovered two new animal species in Burma, one a monkey and one a squirrel, both named after him and still carrying his name. Ian reflected that in Singapore Phayre's name would still be on the street as well as on the monkey and the squirrel. Pansodan Street offered a true pantheon of interesting but forlorn colonial buildings, all collectively giving the impression of an Atlantis that had been abandoned to an irresistible anti-colonial tidal wave.

Engrossed as he was in the historical buildings, Ian didn't notice the three monks who were about a block behind him. Nor did he notice Major Nyan Myint who seemed to be accompanying the monks. Perhaps if he had seen them, Ian might have been impressed by the piety of the Major. But he never looked back. What Ian had a particular interest in was the old Port Authority building with its square tower and bas relief sculptures of sailing vessels carved on its upper walls. In its heyday British Rangoon was the third largest seaport in the Empire. According to his guidebook, the foundation stone for this building was laid on March 17, 1926 by none other than His Excellency Sir Spencer Harcourt Butler, Governor of Burma. Unfortunately, Ian also did not notice the city's decrepit sidewalks. As he stepped off a curb into a foot deep pothole, he sprawled headlong forward, flat on the dirty broken pavement. Two longyi clad onlookers immediately stopped to help him rise. The three monks a half block behind him did not come to his assistance. Nor did the Major. Luckily he only suffered a few scratches.

Nothing to do but get up and keep going. Any complaints made to Sir Spencer about the condition of the city's streets of course would have been eighty years too late. And there was so much to see. Singapore has some imposing colonial structures that have been preserved. But the Lion City would kill for colonial buildings that the world has forgotten in Yangon.

Ian made his way up Pansodan Street until he reached Mahabandoola Street where he made a left. In colonial times this street was named Dalhousie Street, after one James Broun-Ramsey, aka the 1st Marquess of Dalhousie, Governor General of India . Lord Dalhousie oversaw the second Anglo-Burmese War which resulted in the British capture of Rangoon and lower Burma. General Mahabandoola by contrast was a Burmese hero who died resisting the British in the first Anglo-Burmese War. In the battle of the street names, General Mahabandoola was the ultimate winner.

Ian's historical tour was about to be cut short. Never mess with the rainy season in Myanmar. As he stood reading an inscription on the side of the former General Telegraph Office and admiring its portico and Ionic columns, the heavens opened up. Bereft of umbrella, he was quickly getting soaked. There was no alternative but to head up Mahabandoola Street as fast as he could to the Sule Paya, taking care not to break a leg on the sidewalk. He could have used a MacDonalds or a Starbucks to duck into but in downtown Yangon they didn't as yet have such comforts of modern civilization.

He arrived at the pagoda soaked and headed straight inside. He didn't notice the two street urchins who held baskets of caged tiny birds or the breathtaking mixed colonial/Burmese architecture City Hall that the General had mentioned across the street. He dutifully removed his soaked Nike running shoes. He made a donation of one US dollar to the shoe lady who would zealously guard them. Shoes do not enter Buddhist temples. Relieved to be out of the rain, he headed into the pagoda. Immediately in front of him was the statue of a sitting Buddha who appeared to be surrounded by some kind of flashing neon halo. Several people knelt in front of the Buddha praying.

Ian wasn't big on sightseeing religious shrines but his interest grew when they were the only shelter from pouring rain. Any shrine in a storm.

He turned around to look behind him. As he did so, he noticed three monks standing between him and the entrance. He was dismayed to discover that these were not ordinary monks. At least one of them was way out of the ordinary. He was unmistakably Adrian Cairncross. While their monastic garb hid their physiques, Cairncross' monk companions did not look like fifty pound weaklings. Cairncross himself had the same threatening look on his face that he had had in Ian's office. One of Cairncross' companion monks had a Mikhail Gorbachev red birthmark on the top of his shaved pate, which made him look more menacing.

Ian was in deep trouble. Here he was in stocking feet and soaked in a strange country trapped by three characters who did not have his interest at heart. He spun around looking for some way to escape. Lo and behold standing in front of him was Major Nyan Myint.

"I hope you don't mind," the Major said, "but when I saw you leave the hotel without an umbrella I thought it best to follow you. You were taking a big risk." He handed Ian an umbrella.

Ian took the umbrella. Then he turned around. The three monks had vanished.

The Major continued. "Let me call the car. You are very wet. Perhaps it would be best to go back to the hotel?"

Ian looked again. No monks. He had planned to end his walking tour with a visit to the Secretariat which was down the other way along Mahabandoola Street. The Secretariat was a must-see. It was the former seat of the colonial government and where the Founder of modern Burma, Bogyoke Aun San and six colleagues, were assassinated six months before independence. But Ian was too soaked and he didn't know what Cairncross might be up to.

A chilling thought came over Ian. How did the Major suddenly appear? He couldn't be one hundred percent sure the Major and Cairncross were not somehow connected. Was the Major's fortuitous appearance staged? *But why? Were they trying to scare him?* "Okay," he said to the Major and hoping for the best, "let's go back."

Something was very wrong. Cairncross was connected to Myanmar, not China. This changed everything. He turned to the Major. "Wait a moment, please." It was pouring outside anyway. Even the umbrella would not keep him dry. He moved away from the Major. Then he called Anita. "Has the wire transfer gone through?"

"It's done," Anita said cheerfully. "Just as you ordered."

"Great. You're so efficient."

"It wasn't rocket science," she said, wondering why he had asked. "Is something wrong?"

"No, nothing," Ian lied. "Anita, why do little children stand in front of Buddhist temples with dozens of birds packed into cages?"

"You're supposed to buy a bird and set it free. It's a Buddhist thing. Of course the birds were raised for this. They're not really ready for the wild. They quickly get eaten by cats or some other predator. You don't see this here so much in Singapore. The environmentalists don't like it. I think it's banned now."

"One more reason to love the Lion City," Ian said. "Not that I love environmentalists."

"Burma's a little more traditional. I'll bet you couldn't resist and generously liberated a bird?"

"When in Rome…I'm in a pagoda. I'll do that on the way out," Ian replied. "One time won't hurt. Besides, I don't know if they have any cats here. Maybe the Burmese eat all the cats." *The cats eat the birds, the Burmese eat the cats. Is somebody going to eat him?*

"Maybe they do," Anita said. "What are you doing in a pagoda?" The call dropped. No surprise.

Nothing like Oriental intrigue. Another chilling thought came over Ian. *Was Coco the girl in the painting? Could that be possible?* Either way, he wondered if Coco had some other agenda up her sleeve. His Wall Street trading instincts told him he just stepped in shit. Still, he wasn't angry at Coco. He was happy the money had been sent. He hated to admit it but he was attracted to her. She was smart, beautiful, cool and different. How many women did he run into like that? The image of his ex-wife flashed before him. He laughed. He hoped Coco didn't like girls.

Still, oriental intrigue aside, he thought he had made a good investment. Myanmar was going to be a land of opportunity. Anyway, he never regretted investment decisions even when they turned bad. He wasn't going to start now.

On the way out of the pagoda, he gave the two urchins with the birds five U.S. dollars each. The Major looked shocked and signaled "no" to Ian. The urchins each released five birds. The two, both who may not have had a bath in their entire lives but who had a copious supply of thanaka smeared on their faces, each gave Ian a big, dirty-faced grin. It was worth it. He knew he was playing the Great White Phony Father, but so what. Besides, Ian felt like he should give thanks to somebody for what, on the face of it, might have been a narrow escape. And somewhere out there in the crowded back alleys of Yangon he had made some cats happy.

On the way back Ian also realized that he also had missed seeing the Pegu Club. What a shame. For an unreconstructed born-to-late colonial like Ian, not seeing the Pegu Club in Yangon was like visiting Rome and not seeing the Sistine Chapel.

Project Zafar was definitely not a risk free government bond. Ian realized investing in Zafar implied a risk adjustment not quantifiable in a traditional discounted cash flow framework. Like getting beat up by monks, for example. Or maybe shot. The Efficient Market Hypothesis, so irreverently marked by Coco as "stupid" in his friend's textbook, wasn't robust enough to accommodate the treacheries of Myanmar.

He knew there were more treacheries to come.

Chapter Fifteen

Hide a knife behind a smile

> ***From Thirty-Six Stratagems
> sometimes attributed to Sun Tzu***

Coco sat comfortably in her office, reading the news on her Bloomberg screen and reviewing closing prices in the Hong Kong and Singapore markets. She was wearing her usual tight Cavalli jeans and a tight blue blouse she bought at Guess. She was congratulating herself. Her little maneuver with Kyaw Cho had worked. Ian had taken the bait. She was always attracted to men who let their dicks have a vote in their lives. She had no use for politically correct Wall Street work drones. They would have all turned down Kyaw Cho. Probably have gotten on the next plane in a self-righteous huff. Thank God she didn't wind up working for them. Ian had passed a test. She lit up a cigarillo. She was pretty sure he had not recognized her. She pulled out a hand held mirror she kept in her desk and looked into it. *These Gucci sunglasses don't look half bad,* she thought. *But they are too big and too old.* She took out another newer pair. She had a drawful of Chanels. But the newer pair were made by a German company named ic! berlin. These sunglasses were very light and according to their website all "screwless." *Sort of like my marriage, she thought.* But they would have hidden less of her face. Sexy but not good for disguises. Not that Ian Blakely or any other man would know or give a shit about her sunglasses. But she'd wear the ic! berlin glasses next week in Singapore. The disguise would be off. She was still partial to Chanel but years ago she had grown beyond an all-Chanel look. And, if her plan worked out, as a side benefit she wouldn't be screwless.

Her main objective was to get the painting from Ian. The $10 million was in the bank. The fish was hooked. If her plan worked out, getting the painting back would be enjoyable. Not only that, Ian really did represent value added to Project Zafar. He really was the perfect manager for the Sovereign Wealth Fund.

Then a surprise.

Her husband entered her office. This was something he did rarely. He slowly used his cane to help himself sit down in front of her desk. "I don't know why you wore those huge sunglasses when that fellow Blakely was here," he began. "But I like your thanaka and the longyi. I like it when you look Burmese. That is, after all, part of your heritage. These modern girls? Especially the Chinese girls in their little shorts? They all look like whores."

Coco snuffed out her cigarillo. "People always say that about the new styles. I'll try to be more Burmese. But everybody wears jeans and shorts nowadays. Especially younger girls." Coco usually wore her jeans around the house. Not too Burmese. She only wore shorts that barely covered her tight Chinese ass on those rare trips, when she was in Singapore or Hong Kong shopping, and her husband was back in Myanmar. So many other young Chinese girls dressed the same way. As did Koreans and Japanese. And so did Caucasians even when they were too fat. Maybe they were all whores. But they looked good.

"You are now thirty, after all," the General said. "Time to look more traditional. You are Madame Maung Myo. You don't want to dress like a Thai hooker."

That was an insult. *A Thai hooker? What was lower than that?* Coco maintained a vaneer of calm and replied. "All of my outfits carry designer labels. I really dress quite modestly. You can't expect your young wife to dress like Queen Elizabeth."

The General sighed. They had had versions of this discussion before. They would never agree on this subject. "I guess I'm not going to win this argument. But you look good in a longyi," he conceded with a gentle smile.

"Thanks for the compliment," she said. "I just bought some longyi. They're newer, more modern than the traditional. I'll be happy to wear them more if it pleases you."

"Let me see your left hand," the General said. She had kept it out of sight during the lunch with Ian. She didn't want Ian to become scared off by what happened and she didn't want her husband to comment on it.

Coco smiled. "You don't miss anything, do you?'

The General picked up her hand. Coco instinctively pulled it back due to the pain. The contrast between his withered bony hand and her beat up but obviously younger hand was marked.

"What happened?" the General said. "Why are you not wearing your ring?"

"I was going to tell you but I didn't want to talk about it in front of Ian Blakely." Coco then proceeded to tell the General how, acting on behalf of the General's daughter Su Myat, Coco's assistant Khin Chit had tried to poison her. And how she had beaten Khin Chit to a bloody mess.

"I let her live."

"That was very wise," the General said. Coco could see the sadness in his eyes. His daughter had schemed to kill his wife. The General sighed. "I have some more bad news. When I met with the President yesterday in Naypyidaw, he said that my daughter Su Myat's group is going to make a bid to take over our project. I really cannot believe she is doing this."

"But that's impossible," Coco said. "They don't know anything about LNG. And they don't have the Indians."

"They want to run a pipeline up to the Chinese pipeline in North Myanmar."

"But that's nonsense," Coco said. "The Chinese pipeline doesn't have the capacity to handle the extra load. And there's already so much noise about the Chinese pipeline and the environment and the local people. The country won't stand for another pipeline. We own the options on the blocks. And we've negotiated the PSC. It's ready to be signed."

"Yes, Coco I know. But my daughter and her husband have been passing Chinese money around." He leaned forward on his cane. "And that's not all."

"What else?"

"A new parliamentary committee has been set up just to deal with energy policy. It has representatives from both chambers."

"What? Since when does Myanmar have parliamentary committees?"

"It does now."

"Damn."

"Coco, you will have to testify before them. The PSC won't be approved unless the Committee approves. Of course, I will be there. But you know Zafar best. And it would be a good idea if Mr. Blakely testifies also. And that Indian fellow from Calcutta Oil. Advaita, whatever his name is."

"Advaita Chatterjee."

"But not the Chetty." The General handed Coco a piece of paper with a list of five names on it. "These are the parliamentarians on the Committee."

One of the names had a big checkmark next to it. "Why the checkmark next to this one name?" Coco asked.

The General shrugged. There was a fatigue in it. "That guy's some kind of environmentalist. He's opposed to all development in Myanmar. I don't know him. Dealing with him is a waste of time."

Coco scanned the list again. "I don't know any of them. Do we have to worry about them? We have a legal agreement."

"They can at least delay Project Zafar if they vote against us. It's politics, I know. They are not nice people," the General said. "Those other four – they will want something."

134

"Like a bribe? Wouldn't that be a mistake now?"

"We will need to talk to them. I'll arrange it. Those four are military. They all owe me favors. And listen. I want you to be involved. Maybe there's something we can do for them. We won't talk to the environmentalist. He's just trouble."

"What can we do for them? Don't you think it would be a little risky at this stage to try to bribe them with cash? The media here isn't as dead as it used to be."

The General thought for a moment. "You may be right. But there's always a way. They may have some need or another we can satisfy that nobody could trace." He shrugged again. "Let's listen to what they have to say."

Coco smiled. "On this, Husband, you are the master."

"You will join in on my conversations with them. They must learn to respect you as they do me. You cannot be a demur Burmese lady. Show them your tough side." He looked at her battered hand. "We both know you have one." He managed a small laugh. "And with them, dress like a Western woman. Modest but no longyis."

"You just told me ..."

With a grin, the General raised his hand to cut her off. "I know. But every battle requires its own strategy. I still like longyis. But not for this. I want you to come across like an American woman. Not so ladylike like our local girls."

Coco laughed, surprised at her husband's advice. *He wants me to be an American bitch.* "You can count on me."

"One other thing. I want you to release that information you have on General Sein Soe. Put it out on those internet blogs. Facebook or whatever. And that video you said you were working on. You know what to do."

Finally! She had been aching to do this. Through her husband's connections, they had documents proving that Su Myat's husband, General

Sein Soe, had taken kickbacks on a bridge project up in northern Myanmar. "But the President will know we are the source."

The General nodded. "The President has asked me to do this. He thought I might object because this involves my daughter. But he needs to discredit General Sein Soe to make sure their project goes nowhere. ASEAN, the Americans, the opposition, everybody will be screaming if the Sein Soe project replaces ours. But the President wants a little extra support."

"Understood. We'll give it to him."

"This is Myanmar. A lot of people in the government don't care who screams so long as they get paid." The General sighed. "I never wanted to do this. My daughter is just not a good person."

Coco reached for another cigarillo and then thought better of it. "And what will the President say when this comes out?"

"He himself will say nothing. The government will call the report a lie. But the damage to Sein Soe and their project will have been done."

"I'll get right on this." *A labor of love for Coco.*

The General got up slowly from his chair. "Just make sure nobody can trace this information on General Sein Soe back to us."

Coco went around her desk to help her husband up. Slowly, he made his way out of her office.

His gait that made Coco nervous. He was obviously slowing down. The General already had one stroke. A cerebral hemorrhage. The doctors were worried about another. He looked very pale. His mind was still sharp as ever but he was becoming more frail every day. Project Zafar still needed his help. She hadn't intended to tell her husband about Su Myat's attempt to poison her. She always hid her hatred of Su Myat in front of her husband. She didn't want to upset him. And she didn't want to seem like the evil new wife. And she needed him alive until the PSC was signed.

As he was exiting the room, the General turned back to Coco. "It would be nice if we could get the Americans involved. They are going through a difficult time right now. This Obama fellow seems so weak. But we could use some extra weight if the Chinese government gets involved with this. The Indians are such lightweights compared to the Chinese." With that, he left

Coco was ecstatic. China's five thousand year record of court treachery was about to kick in. It was in her genes. She was ready to go. She knew what to do. She was a minor in computer science at Brown. She followed internet stocks on Wall Street. She had compiled a list of the emails of all media people that might be interested in Myanmar. She had set up anonymous email accounts which would be hard to trace. She had been working on the video herself for the last three months.

The video had an avatar who was half pig, half military man from Myanmar. The avatar had a sign on his shirt that said Sein Soe and he looked like General Sein Soe. The avatar greedily helped himself to money designated to build a bridge in a poor farm area that needed the bridge. It was actually very funny. And not so happy because it showed poor farmers suffering as a result of General Sein Soe's actions.

General Sein Soe and his evil wife were about to get large chunks bitten out of their asses.

Coco would get the incriminating documents into the media and the video on to You Tube. She hoped it would go viral. Nowadays Myanmar had become of interest globally. She had just needed her husband's permission. He had held back because of his daughter. But now he had to act.

Overall, for Coco this was a good day. A great day actually. She had the green light to finish off the General's daughter. And better than that, Ian's ten million was in. That fish was hooked. She was looking forward to reeling him in. And besides, she congratulated herself, he was a big plus for the project. He wouldn't be happy when he found out about the Parliamentary hearing. But the ten million had come in *before* she knew about the hearing. She had been honest with him.

But these parliamentarians? Just life in a third world country. Higher return but higher risk. She lit up a cigarillo. She had to trust the General's instincts on this. The Zafar group, especially Ian, would be pissed. Ian hadn't signed up for this. But Devan had predicted the General's daughter would pull some last minute stunt. Nobody should be surprised.

This Committee would have to be taken seriously. Even if she managed to discredit Su Myat and her project, this committee could still delay Project Zafar for fucking ever. Nowhere was it written that Myanmar would do the rational thing and harvest the oil and gas that was so plentiful off its coast.

One funny thing, though. Her husband had told her to act like an American woman. That was like telling the Pope to say prayers. She was sure she could live up to his expectations.

Chapter Sixteen

Ian was back in his office in Singapore. It was Wednesday morning. While he loved the charm and grandeur of post-colonial Yangon, he preferred the antiseptic buzz and efficiency of first world Singapore. No dirty urchins releasing birds, no army of *e coli* bacteria or hepatitis viruses lurking on unwashed vegetables. He was too old for that shit.

Ian sat reading the *Myanmar News*, a widely read online English language news source originating outside Myanmar and the government's censors. Two articles caught his eye. The first was that a group led by the China Good Fortune Oil Company was proposing to take over the exploration block currently claimed by the Project Zafar Group. He was not happy to say the least. That was the group associated with the General's daughter. His ten million was suddenly at risk. But the second article consoled him somewhat. It seemed the China Good Fortune syndicate had a problem. The *Myanmar News* carried pictures of General Maung Myo's son-in-law General Sein Soe. The accompanying article went on to say how Sein Soe had taken a huge kickback on a bridge project in northern Myanmar and demanded his resignation. It contrasted him with his father-in-law General Maung Myo who was "always known for his honesty." The article referred to a video making fun of General Sein Soe. It took Ian a few minutes to find it but, when he did, he was impressed. General Sein Soe, disguised as a pig, had gone viral.

Ian suspected these two incidents were not a coincidence. He was willing to bet Coco and the General were fighting back, Myanmar style. And the economics were on Project Zafar's side. Ian couldn't believe that Myanmar would allow another overland pipeline to be built. But it smelled to him like Zafar might be getting bogged down in Myanmar politics.

Ian was about to find out that they played rough in other places too. Like along the Potomac.

Anita poked her head in the door. "There's a Mr. Clarence Whittle here to see you."

"Who? Does he have an appointment?"

"He says he's from the Office for Dollar Defense."

"You mean ODD?" Ian had been expecting a visit. "Send him in."

Thirty seconds later Mr. Clarence Whittle entered Ian's office. Whittle was about six feet, African American and with a physique that suggested he might have just come from a couple of rounds of boxing at the gym. One might have guessed that when he smiled women would find him handsome. But at least this day Whittle wasn't smiling and had an intense intimidating stare. Worse than Adrian Cairncross.

Whittle sat down, exchanged cards with Ian and declined Ian's offer of coffee.

"I'll get right to the point," Mr. Whittle said. "I'm sure you are aware of Executive Order 99876, signed by President Obama."

"Yes I am," Ian replied.

"I have been seconded to the Office for Dollar Defense from the Federal Bureau of Investigation. Pursuant to Executive Order 99876, I am hereby ordering you to do three things. First, you must close down your gold fund immediately. Second, you must provide the Office for Dollar Defense a list of all your clients and their holdings. Third, you should also be advised that the Office of Dollar Defense requires all of your tax returns for the last ten years. You gave up your American citizenship. Under Executive Order 99,876 you are defined as a renunciator. All renunciators are being reviewed by the Office for Dollar Defense. You are required to provide all information we may request." Whittle handed Ian a five page document which spelled out the orders he had just articulated verbally. Ian spent about five minutes reviewing the document.

Ian looked up at Whittle with a small smile. "Well, first of all I don't have a gold fund. So we can forget that. But beyond that, Mr. Whittle, by what right does the ODD have to give these orders? The Blakely Funds are not domiciled in the United States and the Blakely Funds only accept investments from non-American financial institutions. We do not accept any investments from private American citizens or institutions. That is a firm rule. And the names of our clients are confidential. We have nothing to hide. No tax evasion. And I am no longer an American citizen. And I paid over $100 million to the IRS when I renounced my American citizenship. That case is closed. My case was thoroughly reviewed by the IRS."

Whittle looked at Ian with a gaze of a prize fighter staring down his opponent just before the bell. "Mr. Blakely I'll be blunt. The integrity of the American dollar is at stake. The Government of the United States will do whatever is necessary to protect the United States dollar. It doesn't matter where you are. Or what deal you cooked up with the IRS. The Office for Dollar Defense is asserting jurisdiction. So let me ask you a question, Mr. Blakely. Have you ever heard of Wegelin &Co?"

"Yes I have. They were the oldest Swiss bank. The US government shut them down even though they had no dealings in the United States."

"You got it right."

"So you think you can shut down the Blakely Funds?"

"Indeed we can." Whittle reached into his briefcase, and pulled out a thick document. "Do your funds have investments in American stocks?"

Ian said nothing. Of course the various Blakely Funds held positions in various American stocks.

Whittle continued. "The Office for Dollar Defense has reason to believe you became a Singaporean to avoid paying your fair share of American taxes.

Under Executive Order 99876 and by the authority vested into the Dollar Defense Division, your renunciation of US citizenship is being reviewed. This document provides a preliminary outline of the charges that may be brought against you." Whittle handed the document to Ian with his right hand. His hand moved quickly, like he was throwing a jab to the head. Ian's head. "You'll find this document makes interesting reading. You will want to cooperate."

Ian managed a phony smile, like the prize fighter who just took a good shot to the head and didn't want his opponent to think he was hurt. "My tax returns have been reviewed and reviewed and reviewed by my lawyers and accountants and by the IRS. What irregularities? And the IRS already has my last ten years' tax returns."

Whittle continued unperturbed. "We require that you provide the Office for Dollar Defense with said tax returns. The Office for Dollar Defense is separate from the IRS. Read the document I just gave you. The Office for Dollar Defense assumes that all renunciators' forfeiture of American citizenship is invalid until proven otherwise. Upon a finding of material irregularities in your past tax returns and based on your failure to pay and file American taxes since your renunciation of citizenship, the Office for Dollar Defense can charge you with a criminal offense."

"So you're telling me that in the ODD's eyes I am still an American citizen and therefore I owe taxes to the US for the last two years?"

"That's correct. And your failure to pay these taxes could be construed as a criminal act. You should be aware, Mr. Blakely, that it's just a simple matter to arrange for your rendition back to the United States for trial. And don't think the government of Singapore will come to your defense. The Singaporean Government will cooperate with us, I can assure you."

"What do you mean, 'rendition'?"

"I mean we can forcibly remove you, have you brought back to the United States for a criminal trial for tax evasion. Actually, we can bring you to wherever we want."

"I can't believe this," Ian replied. He slammed the document Whittle had handed him onto his desk. "This is an abuse. A violation of everything America stands for."

"My, my, aren't we the patriot." Whittle finally managed a slight smile. He appeared to be a man who was enjoying his job. "You have fifteen business days to reply to the demands and irregularities outlined in the documents I've given you." Whittle got up. "Good day Mr. Blakely. I'll find my way out." Whittle stopped just for a second to look at the Boccioni painting. He shook his head disapprovingly and then left.

Ian stared at the documents. They would have to go to his lawyers. What a nightmare. He was a Singaporean now. But they were saying he was still an American. Maybe he would flee to Myanmar. Of course there he would be promptly murdered by Adrian Cairncross.

His phone beeped again. It was Devan. "Congratulations, I'm so happy you're in."

Ian had to hold back a laugh. "Just in time for the Chinese to screw Project Zafar?"

"Ian, it's not all bad news. Off the record, we've gotten released information showing that Su Myat's husband, General Sein Soe, took kickbacks. And a video portraying General Sein Soe as a pig has gone viral."

"You guys have been preparing for this."

"We didn't know this was coming. But yes the General and Coco had some things in reserve."

"The video's great. But don't you think I should have been told about this before I put in my ten million?" It was dawning on Ian as he said this that his image as the Great White Sovereign Wealth Fund manager might be tarnished by the actions of Mr. Clarence Whittle, unfair as they were. *People in glass houses have to be careful.*

"Ian, we didn't know. The parliamentary committee is a total surprise. Of course we are not surprised Su Myat would pull something. You and I discussed that. Anyway, the Chinese project doesn't have a chance."

"So these documents and the video? They didn't just happen overnight."

"Ian, Coco didn't tell me about this. She didn't want anything to get out if it wasn't necessary. After all, the documents and the video put a knife through the career of the General's son-in-law."

"Coco managed all this?" Ian had to admit the video especially was a damn good job.

"Who else?" Devan replied. "It wasn't me."

"So everything's still a 'go'?"

"Not quite, Ian. Su Myat's project is dead. But ours can be delayed indefinitely with all this politics. The Chinese think long term. We hear they are passing out money. If they can delay Zafar now, maybe they can revive their project later. You've seen the bitching about it that's going on in the parliament."

"So what are you not telling me?" Ian said.

"You, the General and Advaita are going to have to testify before a parliamentary committee. It's really important."

"You're joking."

"No, they've just dropped this on us. Are you okay with it?"

"Parliamentary committee? They have parliamentary committees?"

"Apparently so," Devan said. "We need you for this."

"Do I have a choice?"

"Not if you don't want to lose the money you've put in. The ten million."

Ian sighed. "Of course I'll testify."

"Ian, it's in the interest of the United States that Zafar goes forward. China needs a counterbalance in Myanmar. That counterbalance has to be India, screwed up as it is. But the U.S. has a role too."

"Obviously."

"Ian, I know you are no longer an American citizen. But do you have any ideas for getting the Americans to focus on this? The Chinese are trying to hold up Zafar. We hear they are really throwing some money around."

The bullshit just goes on, Ian thought. He picked up his binoculars. He looked down at the street. He immediately spied two really gorgeous Western girls in tiny shorts walking about a block from his building. For a moment, he thought one of them was his ex-wife. But it wasn't. Now that was good news.

"Ian are you there?" Devan asked.

"Yes, yes sorry," Ian replied. "I'll think about it, Devan. My name doesn't exactly open doors in the corridors of power along the Potomac. I'm a hedge fund guy who made a fortune shorting, renounced his citizenship and who now lives in Singapore." *And now about to be hassled by the US government.*

"Well, maybe you have some ideas. People that could help us. You'll be at the meeting Thursday?" Devan asked. "It's in the Calcutta Global offices not too far from the Fullerton Hotel."

"I know where it is. I can walk from my office." Ian clicked on an old file that had some media articles. He reread a Rolling Stone article of several years ago, following up their earlier one calling him evil. "Goodbye Hedgie and Good Riddance," was the title. He flipped through some old emails threatening his life for shorting in 2008. "We wil shov all your stolen gold up your ass and set you sinking in Biscane Bay," read one epistle.

Ian was always afraid of people who couldn't spell. And why did everybody think he owned gold? The professor in him had gotten him in trouble. He just had to write that article in *Wired* arguing how shorting stocks and, mortgages in this case, improved economic efficiency. That might not have been so bad but he couldn't resist throwing in some zingers like "the Occupy Wall Streeters were a bunch of losers that should spend their time smoking pot and having sex with their dogs." He just couldn't keep quiet like some of the other money managers who had made fortunes in the crisis. Or like Warren Buffet who went around shedding crocodile tears that he didn't pay enough taxes. Ian's father would have advised "stay and fight" for America, the greatest country in the world. But his father had left England because of high taxes and more opportunity in the US. Once upon a time, England had been the greatest country in the world.

Ian buzzed Anita. "I want you to go with me over to Standard Commercial Bank to have a look at my painting. We'll take a car."

"Ian, the doctor said limited exercise is good for me." Anita was actually having a fairly easy pregnancy. "But why do you want to see the painting now?"

"Because maybe I'm missing something. You've been trained in art. You have a better eye than I do."

Twenty minutes later they were in the vault at Standard Commercial. Henry Ashton was out of town, which Ian thought was just as well. Ian carefully unwrapped *Bad Girl* and spread it out on the floor.

Anita spoke. "You should be ashamed of yourself. But this is really beautiful. Wang has a way with texture. It's almost Impressionist. And it's obvious he's into women. Look at how delicate the eyes are. That's a Chanel bag. Timeless. Those pink nipples are an exaggeration. I'll bet he had her use some kind of cream. And her skin – so beautiful. And those heels she's wearing – they look like Jimmy Choos."

"That *is* a Chanel bag," Ian said.

"Yes. It's got the inverted double CC logo on it. You didn't notice that before? If you had looked at more than her boobs, you might have noticed." Anita put her hand to her mouth. "Oh dear."

Ian stood staring at the painting. COCO CHANEL. A chill came over him. It was staring him in the face. Were Coco's outlandish sunglasses and white paste smeared all over her face some kind of disguise? *How could he have missed this?* "Is Coco the girl in the painting?" Ian asked.

"I haven't seen her in person but it's possible," Anita said. "Ian, in the painting she's a little darker than the typical Chinese."

"Maybe Wang just shaded things that way. Maybe she was at the beach."

"Most Chinese don't like to go to the beach," Anita said. "They think only peasants have suntans. But there's something just a little different about her eyes."

"What's that?"

"They're not quite Han," Anita said. "They're just a little rounder. Almond shaped."

"Her eyes are beautiful. What are you getting at?"

"Yes, they are beautiful. But that's not the point. The Bamans are the predominant ethnic group in Myanmar. But there are a lot of minority groups, especially up in northeast Myanmar. Some of them look more Thai than Chinese. Not that a *gweilo* like you could tell the difference."

"So what does all this have to do with anything?"

"We're looking for clues to identify the lady in the painting. Right?"

"Right". Ian pulled out his iPhone. He called Devan. "Answer a quick question for me if you can."

"Sure," Devan said.

"Is Coco pure Chinese?"

"I suppose so. She told me she was raised by her father's sister, her aunt."

"But what about the mother?" Ian asked.

"Who knows?" Devan said. "It's my understanding her mother died when she was young and her aunt raised her. That's all I know."

"So the mother might not be Chinese?"

"I really don't know," Devan said. "These young Guomindang guys like her father often took Burmese wives or mistresses. Actually, there are a lot of minority people up north where I believe Coco was from. They're really ethnically Chinese."

"Thanks anyway," Ian said, turning to Anita. "Devan doesn't know."

"Coco's mother could have been Burmese," Anita mused. "Maybe a minority group like the Shan."

"So?'

"The girl in the painting does not look one hundred percent Han Chinese to me. You met Coco. Did she look one hundred percent Han Chinese to you?"

"What?"

"Come on, Ian. You know what Han means. It's the dominant ethnic group in China. When most people say Chinese, they mean Han."

Ian shrugged. "I don't know. This is all too subtle for me. Anyway, Coco's face was all covered up with huge sunglasses and that whitish thanaka stuff all the women use in Myanmar. And she had on a longyi like everyone wears in Myanmar. She could have been Russian, for all I know."

"She obviously didn't want you to connect her to the painting."

"Obviously."

"Coco Chanel. She's a female fashion hero."

"I know that," Ian said.

"Coco went to Brown, correct?" Anita asked.

"Yes."

"And Wang Qiang was a professor at RISD, right?"

"Oh fuck," Ian said. *It was all so clear.*

"The Rhode Island School of Design in Providence, or RISD as it's called, is a pretty serious art school. I have friends who went there and I've been to parties there. It's really almost physically part of Brown. Brown students can take classes at RISD. Our girl just might have picked up on the Coco thing there. Or maybe from Wang Qiang. He probably advertised for models when he was teaching at RISD."

"Makes sense," Ian said.

"If she wanted you not to recognize her, she couldn't have done a better job. You'll find out at the meeting at Calcutta Global. I guarantee you she's not going to come dressed as a Burmese princess. Or naked either."

"She's got my ten million."

"She knows you will be a friend. You won't embarrass her with the painting. That painting is a liability for her now that she's the wife of the ex-head of the army."

"It could get her killed. Shit. And I bought it."

She's a very smart lady. She hooked you like a fish. But lucky you." Anita gave Ian a fake smile. "Such a good looking fisherman."

"I'm so lucky."

"You are. Really. This does seem like a smart investment. The painting, I mean. It could go for a U.S. half million, especially with Wang Qiang dead. And the LNG investment? It could turn out to be a home run despite all the political intrigue."

"So I've made two good investments. Anyway, I never regret any investment decision."

"And you're not angry with Bad Girl?"

"What do you mean," Ian asked smiling. Actually, he knew exactly what Anita meant.

"You get turned on with the whole thing. Beautiful naked Asian girl, exotic Burma, you make lots of money. It adds some spice to all those dry investment reports you read all day."

"But it might not be worth the trouble," Ian said. "Not if Wang Qiang was murdered for this painting."

"Don't get carried away. He did have gambling debts to the Macau triads, right? Those are his most likely killers."

"Murder is not so exotic. These people are not playing a game. I'll have to be careful."

"You'll have to be careful," Anita said. She looked back at the painting. "But you like adventure, Ian. And you are on the threshold of a big one."

"I think I'd rather jump out of an airplane. With a parachute of course."

"You gave up being a professor. You hedgies lust for adventure."

"I'm just the quiet guy next door."

Anita held her enlarged belly and grinned. "Right."

"Next time I'll buy a landscape," Ian said.

"NFW." Now Anita was laughing.

Chapter Seventeen

A very troubled Ian was attending the Calcutta Global meeting. He was supposed to be the Mr. Clean financial guy. But he would lose that distinction immediately if it became known that the US government – rightly or wrongly—was after him for tax evasion. He would have to tell all. But not today. He would have to learn more about where he stood on the tax matter.

The Calcutta Global Oil Company was located in an older building not too far from Ian's office in the new business district on Marina Bay. No doubt the rent there was a little lower. As Devan had eloquently explained, "We Indians are not really that poor. We're just cheap." When he reached the company's offices, Ian was greeted by Devan, who in turn introduced him to Advaita Chatterjee, Calcutta Global's CEO. Chatterjee was a tall but portly man of around fifty five. He was lighter in complexion than the South Indian Devangar Saravanan. Dressed in a neat, Italian cut double breasted Armani suite and with a small mustache, he presented a polished look.

The three men walked into a small conference room with a round table. Perhaps a minute later Coco arrived, escorted by Chatterjee's secretary. All eyes were on Coco as she entered, briefcase in hand, into the room. Especially Ian's eyes. He wondered if she would sport her Burmese disguise with thanaka, longyi, sandals and supersized sunglasses.

Of course she did not. Anita had it right. No disguise this time. True, Coco was wearing sunglasses. But they were much smaller than the oversized Guccis that she had on the last time and they were not as opaque. Sunglasses are the norm in equatorial Singapore. Ian could see her eyes and he knew right away they were the eyes in the painting. And this day she wasn't trying to look Burmese. She was wearing an elegant light purple suit with a skirt that came to just above her knee. A multicolored necklace – no diamonds, just some

Burmese jade --was just barely visible around her neck. The top of her suit just barely separated and moved up her shoulders in a V neck fashion. Not your Brooks Brothers pinstriped Wall Street power pants suit for ladies. She looked like someone out of the *Myanmar Tattler*. Except there is no *Myanmar Tattler*. Not yet, anyway. Coco looked like an owner, not like a female Wall Street workaholic who worked for the owner. She sat next to Ian. A distant image of none other than the young Jackie Kennedy flashed through Ian's mind.

Coco took off her sunglasses and looked directly at Ian, her famous curved grin in evidence for just a moment. What she was really saying was *I'm Coco, deal with it.*

For Ian there was no doubt. Madame Maung Myo, a k a Coco, was the girl in the painting. He should not have been surprised but he was. He didn't know what to say. "What color is your outfit?" he asked, instantly regretting he had just asked such a stupid question.

"Lilac," Coco replied, her curved grin confirming he had just asked a stupid question.

Chatterjee cleared his throat, signaling the meeting was to begin. He stood up and began speaking. Presumably *he* didn't give a shit about Coco's outfit. As he began to talk, Coco's eyes momentarily found Ian's. This time there was no mocking curved grin. Her eyes projected hunger. Ian instinctively knew what would come next between them.

Chatterjee first welcomed all his guests. Amiably he pointed to two small paintings hanging off to one side of the conference table. The paintings both portrayed the face of a beautiful dark young woman, her blue headscarf only partially covering her head. "Those paintings I recently found in an old shop in Kolkata, as we now call it. I think they are quite a find. They were in bad shape but I had them restored. They are in the tradition of the Mughal courts at which such miniature paintings were very popular. The shopkeeper told me that the woman was actually Hindu and in the harem of the Emperor Akbar

Shah, the predecessor of Shah Zafar. The painter was a young artist who supposedly was in love with the woman. Unfortunately, the Emperor found out and both the artist and the woman were executed." Chatterjee shrugged. "Well, it's an interesting story. Maybe even true. But the paintings survived. I've had them authenticated."

Strange coincidence of sorts. Paintings could be dangerous. Ian looked again at Coco but this time she just looked straight ahead. She slipped a piece of paper towards him. Ian opened it up. *Meet me at my apartment in Ion Residences at seven p.m.*

Chatterjee moved on. "Enough about art. I only have good news. Everything from our side is going forward. We have just placed an order for five LNG tankers. The Indian National Development Bank will finance ninety percent of the purchase with a ten year dollar denominated loan. On the political front, the President of India has agreed to come to the official signing inaugurating the project. His schedule has a window in early August. They want to hold the signing at the memorial tomb for Bahador Shah Zafar in Yangon. That's the good news. Now the bad news, and I hope, Coco, you will be able to tell us things are not so bad. But we hear the project is stalled in the Myanmar Parliament. We hear that your husband's daughter's rival project is under consideration. This sounds like a disaster. Coco, I turn the floor over to you. I hope you have some answers." Chatterjee sat down.

Coco stood up, tall and straight. "What I say in this room stays in this room, right?" She looked each participant in the eye. Each nodded yes. This Coco was no twenty year old Bad Girl or even a demure young Jackie Kennedy. The tremendous self-confidence that was a fundamental part of her character was in full evidence. She projected power and a kind of sex that comes with power.

She continued. "Advaita, I'm not going to lie to you. My husband's daughter Su Myat is doing her best to sabotage our project. Her own project makes no sense and will go nowhere. But it is our impression her Chinese backers are spreading money around in the Parliament. Money talks, people listen. " She paused momentarily. No one interrupted.

Coco continued. "My husband had some information showing that Su Myat's husband, General Sein Soe, had taken kickbacks on a deal purchasing tanks from Russia. With his permission I saw to it that this information, discrediting Su Myat's husband, was disseminated. Su Myat's husband is now in disgrace and so is she. He was supposed to become CEO of their project. I repeat. Their project is dead."

"So we can thank you for these articles?" Advaita interrupted. "And that amusing video?"

"Yes. Advaita."

"That was amazing. So you had this stuff in reserve, just in case?"

"That's correct. My husband had to give permission to use it. But discrediting General Sein Soe was only step one."

"What's step two?" Advaita asked.

"As we are all aware, a new Parliamentary Oil and Gas Committee has just been formed and we must testify before it. Five MPs sit on this committee. They will recommend to the President whether or not to go forward with our PSC. They want to hold hearings in two weeks. Let me be blunt. We will have to do something for four of them. The fifth is a problem but I doubt we can do anything about him."

"I don't like the way I think this is going," Advaita interrupted again, glancing around the table. He was agitated. "My company has not gotten where it is by bribing people. God knows in India we've been asked for bribes more times than I can count. We've said no every time. If you are thinking of bribing these people, count Calcutta Global out."

"Calm down, Advaita. I'm not suggesting we bribe anyone," Coco replied, smiling her distinctive grin. "At least not with cash. Not because of any moral qualms. Passing money to these guys would too dangerous now. It could blow up in our faces." Her eyes turned towards Ian. "I have a better plan. We will need some help from the Americans."

"I'm not exactly a welcome insider in Washington," Ian said.

"Skip the excuses," Coco said. There was something about her tone which said *if you are a man and you want to fuck me, you will figure out a way to do this.* "This project is in the interest of the United States. The Americans don't want the Chinese to take over Myanmar. Since the embargo was loosened up the place has opened up. The Chinese are on the defensive. India is the big counterweight to China. The Americans need the Indians to counterbalance the Chinese. The Indians just need a little help from time to time." She glanced across at Chatterjee. "Sorry, Advaita. But your government just can't seem to go for the jugular on these matters."

"Do you expect the Americans to bribe these Myanmar guys?" Advaita asked.

"Not with money." Coco smiled. "But the Americans can do them some little favors." She glanced at Ian as she reached into her briefcase. She pulled out five sheets of paper with the names of the five MPs and their bios. She handed out copies of four of them. "These are the four we need to get to. All are banned from entering the United States as are their wives and children. We need to find somebody in the US State Department fast. If we can get these bans lifted so that at least their idiot children can attend school in the US, I think it will go a long way. One of them also has a sick wife who has some rare disease that only the doctors in the US know how to treat."

"What did these guys do to get banned?" Ian asked.

Coco answered. "It's in the bios. It's the usual crap." Her eyes darkened as she returned Ian's gaze. "Raping village women. Burning down minority peoples' villages filled with innocent women and children. Torturing people. Shooting student demonstrators. These are all Army guys. They are unelected and appointed by the government, of course."

"And why would the Americans do anything for these bastards," Ian asked, conscious of Chatterjee's eyes on him.

"Because it's the only way to get fucking Project Zafar going and to counterbalance the fucking Chinese," Coco replied.

"Doing favors for these guys doesn't bother you?" Ian asked. He felt uncomfortable. He wasn't accustomed to be on the bleeding heart side of the argument.

Coco's voice was hard. "Ian, when I was five the Myanmar Army came into our village. My father was in Yangon actually working with the army. The army came and took my mother. I was hidden in the back of our small house. They raped and shot her. My father cried but he continued to work for the army. We didn't have a choice. Look, I don't have time for this moralistic, sentimentality crap. Myanmar is not a dinner party, to borrow Chairman Mao's expression." She turned and, going around the table, looked at each participant in the eye. "Are you all on board or not?"

Everyone in their turn nodded yes.

Coco momentarily removed her sunglasses and played with them. Ian stared. He was having an adjustment problem. This woman had gone from sex queen to his boss.

Coco continued. "We have a lot to do. Ian, besides getting some help from the Americans, you have a second assignment. Two weeks from now there are going to be hearings in front of the Committee. They will decide whether to let Zafar go forward or not. Ian, you and I will have to testify in front of that Committee. Advaita I would like you to testify also."

Ian and Advaita dutifully nodded yes.

"We are going to come armed with irrefutable economic arguments for the project. My husband, General Maung Myo, will introduce us. Then I will summarize the project in some detail. Ian, I need you to prepare written version of your testimony on how the Sovereign Wealth Fund will operate. You should emphasize how you will train Burmese to eventually take over. Advaita, I need a written version of your testimony describing things on the Indian side and how your government is supporting this project. Devan you won't be testifying but it would be helpful if you could be available to assist Ian and Advaita in preparing their testimony."

Devan interrupted. "Chettys never get invited to the party."

Coco made a face. A face that said *Devan we don't need any more stupid comments.* Coco continued. "I need the written tesimonies in the next three days. We will have to get them translated into Burmese and distributed to the M.P.s with enough time so they can read them before the hearing."

"Yes ma'am," Advaita said. Ian nodded. Of course it was the last thing he wanted to do.

"But all of our logical arguments won't mean anything if we don't get to these four MPs offline." She waved an inviting hand. "Ian, do you have any suggestions?"

Ian responded. "Actually there is something I can do." *Besides not being charged for tax evasion by the US Government.* "The American Ambassador to Myanmar is sick. I don't think he can help at this time. But I have another idea. I cannot be directly approaching people in Washington myself. I'm persona non grata, as it were, an evil hedgie who made a fortune in 2008 shorting while everyone else was losing their shirt. Let me make a suggestion. Project Zafar or the Calcutta Global Oil company – I don't care which – should employ the top Washington international lobbying firm, Soames Associates, headed up by former Secretary of State Addison Soames. I know him personally. I actually helped one of his kids get into Harvard. Men like Soames get paid to open doors and get things like this done."

"Soames Associates has had dealings with the Indian government," Advaita added. "Addison Soames is considered a friend of India. And he's a good Democrat."

"Anyway, I'm sure he'll do this if I ask him," said Ian. "But this may take more time than you would like. Advaita, you may have to go to Washington. And Soames and Associates isn't cheap."

"I will go to Washington if necessary and we will pay what is necessary," Advaita said.

"What about mystery MP number five?" Ian asked. "Why can't we do something for him?" Ian asked. He glanced back at Coco.

"He's a member of the opposition," Coco said. "He spent five years in a Burmese prison. He's a green and a devout Buddhist. He opposes economic growth of all sorts including our project. He's got a degree in sociology from some Indian university."

"Good grief, a sociologist," Ian said.

"Even worse. From an Indian university," Advaita said.

"There's nothing we can do for him," Coco said. "We won't get his vote. He's a total asshole Hopefully he will do nothing obnoxious at the hearing."

"Like what?" Ian asked.

Coco shrugged. "Maybe he'll throw his sandals at you. Or throw green paint on you. The Parliament in Myanmar isn't Westminster or Washington. Sometimes they behave like children."

"I guess I shouldn't wear my best suit," Ian said.

"Probably not," Coco said. "Advaita, is there anything you can do now on the Indian side?"

"I was just thinking about that. I'll get our ambassador to remind the Myanmar government of the virtues of Project Zafar. And perhaps Soames will have a task for us. But the Indian government doesn't want to play hardball on this."

Coco shook her head. "Does anybody have any balls in India?'

Advaita's head jerked back in surprise. "Apparently not."

Coco reached into her briefcase and pulled out four booklets. "These are the supporting documents for the PSC agreement," she said. "You all have seen and commented on this but here's the final report. We can discuss it over lunch but things are pretty well finalized at this point."

Advaita stood up and spoke, his elegant manner offsetting Coco's "no balls" comment. "Since it's lunchtime we've got something prepared. A little buffet. Plain old North Indian food, lamb curry, Kashmiri naan, okra, raita and the like. Follow me and just help yourself. We can discuss the PSC over lunch."

Ian looked at Coco, who now determinedly avoided his glaze. What trap was she springing on him now? He would find out at seven p.m. on her turf. Now it was curry time.

Chapter Eighteen

Ian was back in his office, his stomach stuffed with North Indian food. He really didn't need this problem with Mr. Clarence Whittle. With Project Zafar he was suddenly up to his neck in international intrigue. That was enough. It was two thirty in the morning in Washington. He couldn't call Addison Soames until the evening in Singapore. After his meeting with Coco at seven p.m.

Anita poked her head in the door of his office. "The American Ambassador is on the line. She wants to talk to you."

The American Ambassador, Kimberly Walsh, was an attractive, divorced, forty five year old white woman with a Johns Hopkins Ph.d. in International Affairs. She had risen quickly in the Foreign Service ranks and many felt she was destined for bigger and better things. Ian had met her at a function at the American Club. She had come up to Ian and introduced herself. She had fixed her cold, lovely blue eyes on him and saying, "Officially I should stay away from you. But you have a reputation for being irresistible." Ian was surprised. He had replied, "I would be bad for your career." "You're right," she said. And walked away, just like that.

"Ambassador, how are you?" Ian said, picking up the phone.

"Ian, I'm here at a function at the Fullerton. Let me get to the point. Something has come up which I believe you are involved with. I'm just about finished. I wonder if I could drop by your office."

"Now?"

"In about twenty minutes."

"I'll be here," Ian replied. "What's this about?"

"I'll explain when I get there. Let's just say we are about to find out if you are still a patriot."

Ian didn't like what he was hearing. This sounded like a follow up to Mr. Clarence Whittle. First ODD, then State.

Exactly twenty minutes later Kimberly Walsh was sitting in Ian's office. He was a little surprised. A blond woman in her mid-forties, she looked younger than he remembered her from the American Club function. She was wearing a blue skirt that came down to just above her knee and conservative white blouse. He had been under the impression that all American female foreign service personnel were required to wear Hillary Clinton pantsuits.

The Ambassador wasn't smiling. She had brought her distinctive but cold, blue eyes. "Let me get right to the point. Our Ambassador to Myanmar has come down with a bad case of malaria. I'm doing double duty, as it were, and taking care of US interests in Myanmar as well. It's our understanding that you have just invested in a Myanmar natural gas consortium led by the China Good Fortune Oil Company. Is that correct?"

"No, Kim, that's completely wrong. I have just invested in a rival group called Project Zafar. Where did you get this false information from? "

The Ambassador looked surprised. "I can't tell you. You're telling me the truth?"

"Of course. Why would I lie?"

The Ambassador smiled. "It looks like we are on the same side."

"I should hope so."

She reached into her briefcase and pulled out a pen and paper. She proceeded to write something on the paper. She then handed it to Ian.

It said. "Can we move this conversation to the toilet?"

"Sure," Ian replied. "It's this way." He pointed. " The two walked silently out of Ian's office. Anita stared at them but kept silent. All the while Ian wondered why the Ambassador was doing this. *Am I really supposed to fuck her in my own bathroom?* That couldn't possibly be it.

There were actually two identical toilets, both unisex, located out in the hall. Ian did not want a grandiose corporate office with bathroom. They were small rooms, with a toilet and sink, not exactly designed for high level meetings or impromptu fucking. The Ambassador turned the latch to lock the door. She half sat on the sink, leaving Ian to stand. She had on a light dose of some kind of perfume which fortuitously offset the smell of cleaners and the floor polish. Ian wasn't all that turned on by ladies' perfumes – he thought they were a relic of an age when nobody had internal plumbing and the fairer sex had to cover up unfortunate body odors-- but he wasn't a fan of floor polish and cleaner smells either. He waited, not understanding what was happening. He did think the Ambassador looked really slutty sitting on the sink. In his younger days, Ian had fucked several ladies in bathrooms. He had one girlfriend, a Boston University English professor and avowed feminist, who liked to sit on the toilet and urinate while sucking his dick at the same time. He fought to flush those memories out of his head.

The Ambassador spoke in a whisper, her lovely, cold blue eyes staring into Ian's. "We had to come in here. Your office is bugged. The phone lines, the office, everything. This is not a joke. The ODD people, led by Mr. Clarence Whittle, are going in secret to a court in Singapore. They are putting the heat on the Singaporeans. They're going to make an example of you. They are going to subject you to rendition and ship you to Guantanamo."

"Shit," Ian said. "Mr. Whittle doesn't play games."

"And he's no dummy either. I'll get right to the point. It is in the interests of the United States Government that Zafar emerges the winner in this contest. Ian, why don't you start by telling me all you know."

Kimberly Walsh had this direct, authoritative way about her. She was giving him an order which he thought she had no right to give. And sitting on a sink in a bathroom in no way undermined her authority. But it was in his interest to follow the order. And it was completely obvious that Zafar was in the interest of the United States. India had to counterbalance China. The Chinese couldn't be allowed to take over Myanmar. So he spent the next twenty minutes updating the Ambassador with pretty much all that he knew. Almost all.

"So how can we help," the Ambassador asked. "We can't rely on the Indian government for anything even though they may mean well."

"Wait here a moment. I need to get some documents from my briefcase." Ian left the toilet and then quickly returned with his briefcase. Anita just stared as he came back from his office. He took care to lock the bathroom door. He pulled from his briefcase the bios of the five Myanmar MPs who might delay Project Zafar. "Take a look at these." He handed the bios to the Ambassador. "The Myanmar government has set up a parliamentary committee to review oil and gas exploration in the country. These are the MPs on the committee. These guys can delay or stop Zafar. I'm going to be testifying before them in two weeks. Supposedly the Chinese are handing out money to stall Zafar even though their own pet project with Su Myat and China Good Fortune Oil Company is dead."

The Ambassador read through the bios. "Nice bunch of guys," she said. "But we don't bribe people, Ian. Especially thugs. Although this last guy looks unbribable. Where did they get him from?"

"He's from the Opposition. A devout Buddhist and a card carrying green. He comes from the moon."

"Four thugs and a wacko."

Ian suddenly realized he had been given a gift. He may not need Soames and Company. "Kim," he said leaning forward in the cramped space, maybe you can help. These four guys are all on the US shit list. They and their families can't enter the US. They've indicated to us that getting those restrictions lifted would make them more receptive to Zafar. Could you at least get the restrictions lifted on their wives and kids so the kids can attend school in the

US? And one of the wives needs medical treatment. Most of the kids are high school and college age. Coco, that is Madame Maung Myo, along with her husband has talked with the four thugs. They'll settle for their wives and kids."

"Madame goes by the name Coco?"

"She prefers that name."

"Okay. Their wives and kids get into the US and Zafar goes forward?" The Ambassador laughed. "Typical Asian guys. We help them send off their wives so they can spend more time with their girlfriends. And their kids can parade around in their BMWs on American campuses."

"The wives and kids didn't commit any crimes, Kim. Who cares about their girlfriends or the kids' BMWs?"

Kim smiled. "At least they've committed no crimes that we know of. This Coco. We know a little bit about her. We think she's a citizen of Myanmar, although at one time she had a US Green Card. But she's the original Dragon Lady. Did you know she went to Brown? A Phi Beta Kappa. And everyone in Brown was scared of her? That she hit the captain of the Brown football team over the head with a beer bottle and put him out of commission for three weeks? That she's a dead shot and acquired a marksman's certificate? She's an ace with a handgun."

"Of course. I know all of this." Actually, Ian didn't know Coco was an ace with a handgun. But

It didn't surprise him."

"Is this someone we can trust?" Kim asked.

"Let me put it this way. You can trust her so long as your and her interests coincide. She's certainly very competent. But I don't think she's really loyal to any country."

"Ian, she's only thirty years old. How does she get to be a promoter of a LNG project?"

"How old is Mark Zuckerberg?"

The Ambassador laughed. "You got me. And how did she wind up being married to General Maung Myo? She's almost one third his age."

Ian hadn't gone into those details. He related the story.

"The Heimlich Maneuver," the Ambassador mused. "She saved his life?"

"That's right."

"That's what I need to learn to move my own career along." She laughed. "Maybe the Secretary of State will get a bone stuck in her throat. My big chance."

"Kim, you never know."

The Ambassador got more comfortable on the sink.

Ian found himself distracted as she slithered into a different position. Actually, he was bordering on a sexual emergency.

"Okay," the Ambassador said, " so we get the entry bans lifted and Dragon Lady, aka Coco, brings the good news to the four thugs who then don't hold up Zafar. What about the Opposition wacko?"

Ian managed to retrieve his attention back from his dick. "The Committee votes four to one. We win. Look Kim, the General's the one who really will get this done. Of course the U.S. should register its concern that Zafar go forward with the Myanmar government. But getting the four thugs' wives and kids off the shit list, and having Coco and the General negotiate the whole thing behind the scenes, is the only way to really get the job done. We don't have much time."

"I can get it done. But I don't like having to rely on Coco and the General. He was no boy scout in his day."

"No choice. And the General by Myanmar standards was a good guy."

"Yeah, right. Okay, we'll live with it." Her blue eyes hardened. "This bitch better not betray us. She is Chinese after all. How do we know she won't switch to the other side?"

"Believe me, she has no loyalties to China. Your interests and hers are one hundred percent aligned. That's what counts. And she did go to high school and college in the US. I think she actually feels a little American."

"Like you, I suppose." The Ambassador smiled, enjoying her little patriotic poke into Ian's groin. "I want to meet your Dragon lady. Can you arrange that?"

"Sure. Now what about my problem? I'm supposed to be Mr. Clean. If it becomes known that the US government is after me for tax evasion – right or wrong – I'm not Mr. Clean any more. When our group hears about this, they'll want to kick me out."

"It's too late for that," the Ambassador replied. "We have to keep this quiet until the Parliamentary Hearing is over. Don't tell your partners. Not yet."

"From what you tell me, Whittle is planning to fuck me over good. It's not fair. My taxes have all been audited backwards and forwards by the IRS and everything was settled."

The Ambassador sighed. "They want to make you an example. You are a prominent renunciator. An evil hedge fund guy who made fortunes shorting mortgages, profiting from the misery of others and then rubbing their noses in it in that *Wired* article. Whittle's been assigned the job of bringing you down."

"That makes my day."

"If Zafar goes through and you and Coco are playing straight with me, I'll make sure the powers that be know you are a patriot. And I will do my best to keep you out of the news until the Parliamentary Hearing is over. I can't do more than that. That's all I can promise."

"Thank you," Ian replied. "Off the record, how did the FBI get involved in this?"

"The FBI scares people even more than the IRS. That's what they want. And believe it or not, the IRS didn't want it. They think the whole dollar defense thing is unconstitutional."

"So the IRS now has a conscience?"

"Stranger things have happened."

"Kim. Am I not furthering the interests of the United States? Zafar isn't going to happen without me."

"Right now ODD has a deaf ear on that subject. They have insisted they have secret information that puts you on the Chinese side. I see now that's bullshit. That was a lie they made up. I'll make sure State is on your side but the ODD guys have the big dicks right now."

"What should I do?"

"Get very public on this Zafar project."

"I'll be testifying in two weeks."

"Keep moving. You've got your own plane. Keep flying. Spend a week in China. They wouldn't dare touch you there. They really might try to grab you here."

"They'd really kidnap me?"

"That may be their plan. The word is 'rendition,' not kidnap."

Ian leaned forward, like he was trying to seduce her. "Kim, I really appreciate your telling me this. I owe you."

The Ambassador smiled and moved off the sink, adjusting her skirt as she did so. Ian did notice her stomach wasn't bandage dress flat like a twenty year old model's. Still, he found her very attractive. Maybe he let it show.

"You thought you were going to get a quick fuck in the toilet?" the Ambassador said.

"I've always been an optimist," Ian replied.

"I'm sticking my neck out for you. That's better than a quick fuck." She opened the door and signaled for Ian to exit. "One more thing. Maybe you should leave the bugs in place."

"No," Ian replied. "I know what you're saying. But I can't run a business that way."

The Ambassador shrugged. Then she and Ian shook hands.

"What a shame," she said looking Ian straight in the eye and drawing close to his face. "You wouldn't be good for my career." Her voice was soft. Her ambassadorial tone was gone.

"You could come visit me in Guantanamo. Maybe we could get conjugal rights."

The Ambassador smiled. "I always fall for men with a sense of humor."

"Good," Ian replied.

"I have to go," the Ambassador said. "I left my bag in your office."

As they returned to the office, Ian noticed the very strange look he was getting from Anita. She was going to be disappointed when he would have to tell her that he didn't fuck the Ambassador in the bathroom. His reputation would suffer grave damage.

When they got back to the office, the Ambassador stopped to look at Ian's Boccioni painting. "This is really unusual," she said. "Who did this?"

"Umberto Boccioni. He was an Italian futurist. Italian futurists were infatuated with technology and excited by what it could do for humanity. Kim, the painting just exudes energy, don't you think?"

"That it does. I like it. What's it called?" the Ambassador asked.

"*Dynamism of a Soccer Player II*. There's a more famous version in the Museum of Modern Art in New York. Nobody knew this one existed until recently. The energy, the love of technology and its role in helping humanity, those are my values, things I admire."

"My, my, so you're not a total philistine after all."

"Maybe ninety nine percent," Ian said.

"So all that greed is really to help the world?"

"That's how I plan to get into heaven," Ian said.

"So, the road to heaven is paved with bad intentions?" Kim turned to look at the painting again. "But where's the soccer player?"

"You have to look. It's an IQ test."

"I imagine you paid a pretty penny for this. You one percenters are driving up art prices all around the world."

"I bought it for pennies at a garage sale. In Zurich. "

She laughed. "I'm sure you did." She leaned over and whispered into his ear. "Be careful." With that, she turned and left.

Anita's smirk begged for an explanation of what had just happened in the bathroom. Ian was not going to satisfy her prurient curiosity. Instead, he spent five minutes writing her a note telling her the office was bugged and she should get it debugged immediately. Then he left early to go for a swim.

Chapter Nineteen

To take an Annamite to bed with you is like taking a bird: they twitter and sing on your pillow.

—From Graham Greene,
The Quiet American

Refreshed by his swim, a troubled Ian went back to his apartment. He wasn't sure what to do. His apartment might be bugged as well. He'd have that checked. Should he flee Singapore? But where to? And his business would collapse if it became known he was fleeing US authorities. All the institutions would pull their money out of his funds.

The hell with it. He would decide tomorrow. Tonight it was time to see Coco. One attractive woman had invited him by secret message to spend time with her in the bathroom. Too bad he had come away empty handed. Well not really. Now a second attractive woman had sent him a secret message to visit her apartment. Interesting times.

Coco's apartment was within walking distance of his. The Ion Residences jut high into the sky just off Orchard Road and offer some of the tonier flats in Singapore. Ian looked around him as he walked. But then he realized the futility of it all. Nobody could hide in Singapore. It was too small. Still, he would make a trip to Beijing as soon as possible. ODD wouldn't touch him there. Besides. Beijing was having one of its smog weeks. Nobody could see him anyway. Or anybody else. As he crossed Orchard Road it was crowded with people. If American agents were following him the crowd would work in his favor. But as he arrived at Coco's building, he thought he saw Major Nyan Myint in the distance. Was the Major a US agent?

Time to see Coco. And tell her the good news about the Ambassador. And walk into another trap?

The door was slightly ajar. The smell of cigar smoke wafted through the air conditioned air.

"Come in, Ian," Coco said from inside.

Ian entered. Coco stood before him, dressed only in shorts like the ones she had on in the painting, high heel cage shoes and no less than two bejeweled necklaces. She stood in front of Ian, the shorts partially open, her naked breasts pointing straight at Ian and a lit cigarillo in her hand. And a smile curled her lower lip. "Make sure the door is closed," she said. "Bad girl is here in person."

Ian pushed the door shut behind him. It was clear he was going to fuck somebody today. If not the Ambassador, well, it looked like Coco .

As Ian closed the door, Coco in an instant dropped the cigarillo into an ash tray and picked up a jeweled dagger that was next to it. She grabbed Ian by the belt of his pants with one hand and pressed the point of the dagger against his crotch. She moved close to him, her breasts leaning onto his chest and her mouth about an inch from his. The two necklaces and what were very hard nipples pressed against Ian's chest. "I'll give you two scenarios," Coco began. "Scenario One is that you don't sell me the painting and I cut your balls off. And your dick. And I will do it."

"What's Scenario Two?" Ian asked.

"Scenario Two is you sell me the painting and you can fuck my brains out. You sell it to me at cost." She gave the knife a little shove against his pants for emphasis.

Ian felt her breasts and the necklaces against him and the inadequate barrier of his pants barely protecting his very vulnerable private parts. Her breasts felt hard but the dagger felt really hard. "I choose Scenario Two," he said.

Coco and Ian, in a typical coital intermission, were relaxing together in bed. Coco had just lit up a cigarillo. The smoke had already taken over the room.

Ian didn't approve. "You're going to give us both a headache with that. Don't you know how bad that is for you?"

"I'm going to give up smoking after Chinese New Year."

"That's six months from now," Ian said.

"Don't spoil things, Ian. This is the first fuck I've had since I got married." She reached over and kissed the spot where just a few minutes before she had sunk her teeth into his neck.

Ian rubbed the same spot with his own hand. His neck was sore but he could feel she hadn't broken the skin. That was good. Human bites can be infection prone. "Are you a vampire or what?"

"Darling," Coco said. "Just a little love bite. You know. Like in high school."

"What high school was that?"

"I went to a prep school in Massachusetts for rich kids. My father had started to make a lot of money. I had time to 'explore' in the countryside."

Ian looked at Coco's left breast. There was a small red mark around her nipple. During their lovemaking, she had encouraged him to bite her hard. He had obliged. He hadn't minded biting her. Just so long as she didn't bite him. "I seemed to have left a mark on you," he said, kissing the mark.

"I enjoyed it. Look, the shrink I went to at Brown said I probably have a hormonal imbalance. I like a little pain now and then. You didn't enjoy biting me?"

Ian replied. "I did. But when it comes to pain I definitely feel it's better to give than receive."

"Okay. I'm cool with that." Suddenly Coco put her hand to her face. "You are bringing up a very bad memory. The shrink said that might have something to do with my need for pain."

"What was that?"

"About my mother."

"Yes of course." Ian remembered what she had said about her mother being raped and murdered. People tend not to forget things like that.

A smile returned to Coco's face. "I don't want to talk about it now. I just want to fuck and talk during intermissions about business and pleasant things. This is an intermission. Can we change the subject?"

"Sure. How many intermissions have you planned?"

She caressed his hair. "Dude, that depends on you."

"Dude? You've spent too much time in the U.S. We have to turn you back into a delicate Burmese princess."

"NFW." She took another drag on the cigarillo. "I see. You are fifty nine? Too much fucking may not be good for your heart."

"I'm in great shape. I'm more worried about your heart." Ian then rearranged the two necklaces which had slid off to one side of Coco's chest. "Coco, Wang Qiang told me himself. He borrowed the necklace and it was a Cartier. There was only one necklace in the painting."

"Ian, you just got a great fuck. Now it has to be one hundred percent authentic and be like the painting?"

Ian let his hand gently caress the necklaces. "These are lovely." He laid the outer necklace down between her breasts. "And they are in such a lovely neighborhood."

"Ian, be careful. The outer necklace is from the Tiffany Sprinkler series. They sell it by the yard. The price goes up depending on how many diamonds you want to load into it."

"And the other necklace?"

"That *is* a Cartier. You just didn't recognize it. You men will always be amateurs when it comes to women's jewelry."

Ian smiled. "Sorry." He momentarily fingered the second necklace. "But I am always eager to learn more." He gently laid his hand on her breast. "Besides, I was distracted by some of your other jewels."

She grabbed his hand and pushed it away. A serious look came over her face. "That prick Wang was sucking me dry."

"He was blackmailing you."

"Yes. It would be a great shame for my husband if the painting became public. Myanmar isn't France. It's a conservative, Buddhist country."

"Are there any other paintings?'

"No. I was only stupid once."

"So tell me, Coco. Why did you leave your shoes on when we were making love?"

She turned to Ian. "Don't you ever watch porn movies? A true slut always wears her heels when fucking. The shoes pointing at the ceiling offer a certain perspective. A certain balance." She lifted up her right leg and pointed towards the ceiling. "These are Jimmy Choos. I love them."

"So you are a slut?"

"The best," Coco replied.

"You really would have cut my gonads off?"

"I have always done what I had to do," she said without the slightest smile.

Ian knew she wasn't kidding.

"Where did you get that dagger?"

"Devan gave it to me. He said he got it in an old shop in Mumbai. He thought it fit my personality. I think he had the hots for me."

"Really. So it's from India?"

"No," Coco said. "It's from Yemen. Supposedly it was owned by a tribal chief."

"Always a bullshit story with these artifacts. Raises the price."

"Correct. The men carry these around. These daggers are expensive."

"Devan really knows how to please a lady. Perfume and flowers are for sissies."

"That depends on the lady."

"He picked the right lady, in this case," Ian said, putting his hand on his gonads.

"Well, Devan's getting married now." Coco smiled. "So I need to find someone else to supply me with a dagger."

"Good luck. I'd rather buy you some jewelry," Ian said.

She turned serious. "No, I just want you to give a good presentation two weeks from now."

"So you never slept with Devan?"

"NFW. He is after all an Indian. And so dark. I'm a Chinese woman. Give me a break. I don't want to smell like curry."

"Another question. Are your nipples really that pink?"

"Darling, you noticed. I've been using something called Finale Pink Nipple Cream. Wang Qiang, pervert that he was, made me use it for the painting."

"Pink Nipple Cream?"

"It's a chemical that turns your nipples pink. Pink nipples were quite the rage ten years ago." She rolled over and pushed her right breast up to Ian's mouth. "I opted for authenticity on this."

"I can't indulge," Ian said, playfully pushing her breast away. "Your tits may be carcinogenic."

"Shit. Wang Qiang said it gave the painting something extra. He said it was art. I was young and stupid. I believed everything he said."

"You were his girlfriend? He was your professor? That's something I never did. Have sex with a student."

"Yes, for a time I was madly in love with him. And no he wasn't my professor. He taught at RISD, I was a Brown student."

"So you've been using this pink nipple stuff ever since?"

"Of course not. You're right. This shit is carcinogenic. But I did it again just one time for old times' sake. Like the painting. So you wouldn't be confused when you saw me in the flesh."

"I think I would have recognized you. But does this stuff work right away?"

"It's better if you use it for several days."

"So you've been planning to have sex with me for several days?"

"I plan everything, darling. I decided to fuck you when I saw your picture." Her hand moved slowly down his body to his penis. "Intermission is over."

"But I have something to tell you. Some good news."

"It can wait," she said, as her mouth followed her hand down to his now rising penis. "The only good news I need now is that I can put your cock in my mouth."

"Don't bite me," Ian said, not sure if he should be alarmed.

"Don't worry. Nobody's lost a penis yet."

Their next intermission had begun.

"You were pretty good," Coco said. "You almost bounced me onto the floor. You don't take pills?"

"Hell, no."

"I'm impressed. A lot of younger guys take pills. Well, you white guys grew up eating eggs and steaks and all kinds of protein." She felt the bicep in his right arm. "That's where you got big muscles." She lowered her voice, affecting a tone of fake sadness. "Us poor Chinese coolies had to eat rice."

"That's how you got such beautiful eyes," Ian said.

"You're so full of shit," Coco replied. She lit up a cigarillo. Ian groaned. "Okay, so what's your good news?"

"I've had a visit from the American Ambassador to Singapore. She's handling things up in Myanmar while the American Ambassador up there recovers from a bout of malaria. She's going to help us."

Coco tensed. "Are you fucking her too? She's very good looking. I've seen her picture."

Ian laughed. "What? Are you jealous? No Coco, I am not fucking her. It seems that Project Zafar is in the interests of the United States. She thinks she can get our four thugs' wives and children entry visas into the United States."

Coco sat up. The businesswoman in her momentarily overcame all jealousy. "Really. That would be so great. Why didn't you tell me before? Now we win."

"I didn't tell you before because you distracted me. With your dagger, your mouth and your vagina. And your lousy cigar."

"You're so easily distracted."

Ian was distracted again. Coco didn't cover her body when she sat up like women often do in the movies after their sex scene. He thought her skinny naked body was so sensuous. But she didn't have any bikini lines. It was his experience that while most Western women like his ex-wife worked at having a tan and bikini lines, Chinese women avoided the practice. Cultural difference. He tried to pull his mind back to business. "The Ambassador would like to meet with you."

"No problem. I could see her tomorrow. But the last flight to Yangon is three o'clock."

"I'll lend you my plane." Ian would have to delay his trip to Beijing by a day. Actually, he wasn't ready to leave that quickly anyway.

Coco smiled her curled lower lip smile. "Are you sure you're not fucking her? I know you would if you could."

"You women are such jealous animals. No, I am not fucking her and stop asking. And behave yourself when you talk to her."

"Of course. I'm not stupid." She lay back down.

"By the way, Coco, are you a Chinese citizen?"

"I am a citizen of Myanmar. I had a U.S. green card but my husband made me give it up when we got married. I grew up in Myanmar. Actually, not counting Hong Kong and Macau for shopping, I've never been to China."

"Really. Make sure you tell the Ambassador that."

"I'm loyal only to Myanmar. I am not a Chinese surrogate. And I am part Burmese, after all. And besides. I like the United States. I spent half my life there. It's a great place. But I belong here."

"Make that point clear with the Ambassador."

Coco leaned over and starting nibbling on Ian's ear.

"On another subject."

"Yes, darling." She stopped nibbling.

"I happened to notice on the way over here that Major Nyan Myant was outside your apartment. I'm not one hundred percent sure it was him but I think so. He sort of ducked away when I saw him."

Coco moved up onto to her elbow. "He provides protection for me, wherever I go," Coco said. "He is loyal to us."

"You're not worried he'll report this meeting to your husband?"

"We are having a business meeting. Why should he think differently? I repeat. He is very loyal to me and my husband." Coco took out another cigarillo and lit it. She watched the smoke drift around the room as she lay on her back.

"I'm getting a headache," Ian said.

"Stop complaining. You got a free piece of ass. You have to put up with a few inconveniences. At least I didn't cut your balls off." Coco stroked Ian's hair with her free hand. "You've still got your hair but you have some gray ones. You're getting old. The Ambassador I read is in her forties. Maybe she's easier to keep up with. The animal desires start to diminish as we get older."

Ian rolled his eyes. "Coco. Will you stop the bullshit?"

She leaned over onto Ian, putting both elbows on his chest, still holding the cigarillo in her hand. "I propose a test. To see if you are too old. I'm half your age."

"Too old for what? I can choke to death on your damn cigar at any age."

"Too old to do me again," she replied. "In the States what do they call three goals in hockey? A trifecta? I want a trifecta."

"That's actually a horse racing term."

"Don't you wish you had pink nipples like me? We could go to Europe and go topless together. With matching nipples. I want to go to Greece. One of the islands. I hear lots of girls don't wear tops there."

"You have a vivid imagination. But it's a nice idea."

She reached over to the bedroom nightstand and put out the cigarillo in the ashtray. Then she got back on top of Ian and started rubbing his chest. "You see darling if you fuck me I can't be smoking at the same time. Doing me is good for the environment. And for my body. Now, can you do it one more time for a better world? And for my body?"

Ian rolled on top of Coco. *Maybe he should have taken a pill.*

Ian was getting dressed. "It's almost nine o'clock." He smiled. "You got your painting. And your trifecta. I hope you are satisfied."

"You did struggle a bit on the last shot."

"Do I hear a complaint?"

"The struggle just added to the pleasure. Ian, trifecta is nice but do they have an expression for four?"

Ian smiled. "You *are* a horny bitch."

"By the way Ian, where's the painting?"

Ian sat on the edge of the bed, his hand holding hers. "It's in the vault of Standard Commercial in here in Singapore. I don't know whether you know Henry Ashton, the Vice Chairman, but he placed it there for me personally."

"I don't know him but I attended a speech he gave one time in Yangon. Little Jewish guy with a stuffy British accent."

"We can trust him. Coco, I'd advise you to leave the painting right where it is at least until things are more settled."

"Wang Qiang was blackmailing me with the painting," Coco said, as Ian buttoned his shirt. " Its release would embarrass my husband and jeopardize Project Zafar. For some reason he went and sold it to you."

Ian had finished dressing. He looked down at Coco who was still naked and smoking yet another cigarillo while lying on the bed. "So that's why you lured me into this? To get the painting back?"

"Look darling. You're going to make a fortune. Besides, I looked at your photo and checked out your reputation. As I told you. I guessed you would make a good fuck. Women can be picky about who they lose their virginity to."

"Virginity?"

"So to speak. You are the first man I've ever had – since I got married."

Ian bowed slightly. "I am indeed honored. You never had sex with your husband?"

"I gave him a couple of handjobs. Or tried to. He couldn't achieve penetration. Ask Bill Clinton. Handjobs don't count. And that was before my husband's stroke."

"I think that was blowjobs in Clinton's case," Ian said. "So maybe your marriage has not been consummated. Well, I guess this is one for the lawyers."

"Where are you going with this?" Coco asked.

"Nowhere." Actually, that wasn't quite true. Ian had a self-imposed rule. No affairs with married women. But traditionally, if a marriage wasn't consummated, then it could be annulled. It was like it didn't really happen. Did an attempted hand job count as consummation? Of course, in this case he could always plead duress since a dagger was held to his crotch. "So Coco, what really happened to Wang Qiang? Who did him in? And how did they know I had the painting?"

"Wang called me and told me he sold the painting to you. Somehow I think the call got intercepted. I'm pretty sure Su Myat found out."

"So who killed Wang Qiang?"

"Don't know. Maybe the triads in Macau. He owed a fortune. Or maybe Su Myat's people. I really don't know. I wish it had been me."

Ian was relieved. He didn't want to think Coco was a murderer. "But all this puts me in danger."

Coco shrugged. She snuffed out her cigarillo, stood up, walked to the mirror and, still naked, began combing her hair. "Next time don't buy a nude. Buy a landscape."

Ian laughed. *Where had he heard that?*

Coco turned to Ian. "Darling, you were in danger from the moment you bought that painting. Not my fault. Please don't be angry with me."

Ian knew he should have been angry but he wasn't. Maybe he liked the adventure. And the sex with a beautiful younger woman. Anita had it right. "I'm not angry," he said.

Coco took a few steps towards Ian and put her arms around him. "Sex with you is very special. One day we will make love under the painting. You can look up at the painting and fuck me at the same time."

"That's a wonderful idea," Ian said, while trying to push her away. "Oh, one thing."

"What's that?"

"Your naked body would look even better with a little tan and some bikini lines."

"Chinese women don't want to be darker. I'm dark enough."

"You'd look great."

"Well, maybe some day. You can take me to the beach at some swanky spa. I will shamelessly expose my body in a tiny bikini and you can get your tan lines."

"Some day," he said, suddenly regretting that she really was married. "It's better I go now." He tried to give her a quick kiss but she opened her mouth and trapped his tongue with hers.

"A lot of Asian women don't like to French kiss," Coco said. "Maybe that's because until recently they all had such shitty teeth. But I had an American education. And all new crowns."

This time Ian had to put more effort into pushing her away. "You're too much," he said. He finally extricated himself and turned and headed for the door.

As soon as the door closed behind Ian, Coco, still naked, ran to the window. She looked down, searching in vain for a face she could not see in the darkness on Orchard Road.

She swore. "That fucking Burman traitor fucking mother scum turtle! I will take care of him."

Chapter Twenty

China, by the standards of every other country, is a most peculiar animal. Apart from size, it possesses two other exceptional, even unique, characteristics. China is not just a nation-state; it is also a civilization and a continent.

—From Martin Jacques,
When China Rules the World

Coco had agreed to a meeting with Ambassador Kimberly Walsh at 2 pm at the American Embassy. Coco the businesswoman was taking this meeting very seriously. The Ambassador had to feel she and her husband could be trusted. But she had to deal with certain conflicts. Her sixth sense told her that Ian Blakely had a romantic interest in the Ambassador. Coco was always the competitor. At some level she regarded Ian as belonging to her.

Coco had checked out the American Ambassador on the internet. B.A. Vassar, Ph.D. in international relations from Johns Hopkins. Age 42, entire career spent in the American Foreign Service, divorced, no children. Coco found a nice color picture of her. Attractive, blond, slim but maybe a slight middle aged bulge. Coco had to zoom in to see that. Coco stood up before the mirror. She had bought a really sexy Herves bandage dress that morning in the Ion mall. A classic. You can't wear a bandage dress unless you have a flat stomach which indeed Coco had. Part of Coco wanted to wear that dress to the meeting. She held the dress up to the mirror. "Mirror, mirror on the wall," she said out loud, "who's the got the flattest stomach of all. She's forty two and American. I'll bet she can't wear this. Too many French fries and pizza." Then she laughed. "I'm not that stupid." She went over to her closet, put the Herves dress back and took out a silk floral colored Burmese longyi with a matching floral colored top. She went back to the mirror. "Exotic is the better approach," she said, still talking to the mirror.

Some Asian American women in the United States hate the word exotic. A fellow student of Chinese extraction used to rant about the word in Coco's Women's Empowerment Course at Brown. Coco thought that woman was stupid. *If you've got it, flaunt it. Always play every card in your deck. Especially around stupid men who only think with their dicks regardless of all the feminist bullshit that the smarter men pretend to embrace.*

But she wasn't dressing for a man on this occasion. Following Ian's advice, Coco needed to emphasize her Burmese heritage to the Ambassador. After all, she was a Myanmar patriot despite her Chinese face. Besides, her personality would never allow her to look too frumpy or like a boring Wall Street MBA. The longyi would create an impression that no pants-suited Hilary Clinton or Wall Street MBA clone could ever aspire to. Longyis were exotic even in Singapore. And Western women looked stupid in them. *Perfect.*

They sat facing one another at a small conference table. Only a large photo of a smiling Obama provided any life to what otherwise was a pretty standard government-issue conference room. Coco sat self – confident, erect in her all-Burmese longyi and sandals. Although she couldn't resist wearing an exquisite Burmese jade pendant that had been a wedding present.

But the Ambassador surprised her. No pants suit. Instead the Ambassador wore stylish slacks and a light blouse which Coco instantly recognized as Ralph Lauren. She did indeed however have a slight stomach paunch, much to Coco's satisfaction. Still, Coco was impressed and wondered, when she herself reached forty two, would her own perfectly flat stomach have gone the way of all stomachs. And would she have given up Calvin Klein, Cavalli and Guess for Ralph Lauren. She laughed to herself. *No way!*

"Your whole outfit is so beautiful," the Ambassador graciously said before even introducing herself. "Your pendant is exquisite. Is it jade?"

"Yes, jade and a little gold. All from Myanmar."

"I'm always surprised in Myanmar. Men and women wearing longyi even on formal occasions."

"It's our national dress," Coco said. "I'm very comfortable in it. It's what I grew up in."

"I see. Well, allow me to introduce myself. I'm Ambassador Kim Walsh. And you are Madame Maung Myo."

"Yes, that's correct."

"But everybody calls you Coco?"

"That's right."

"Is that a legal name?"

"No. I picked the name in college. We Asians pick Western names to make things easier for you Westerners."

The Ambassador laughed. "So, in Asia you get to choose your own name. You don't mind if I call you Coco?"

"Everybody calls me Coco."

"Good. Well, I'm Kim." The Ambassador smiled. "So, Coco. I have a few questions I would like to ask you."

"Fire away, Kim."

"For starters, are you a citizen of China?"

"No, Myanmar. I grew up in Myanmar. And the US. I've never been to China. Well, except for Hong Kong and Macau. But just for shopping. My country is Myanmar. My loyalties are to Myanmar."

"Really." The Ambassador seemed surprised at Coco's answer and wrote something in her notebook. "So you no longer have a Chinese passport?"

"No, I do not. I never had a Chinese passport. Where did you get that from? I am a proud citizen of Myanmar."

The Ambassador wrote something on the file that was open on her desk. "You know we can check on this."

"Why would I lie," Coco said. She pulled out her Myanmar passport. "See for yourself."

The Ambassador took the passport, examined closely for about five minutes, and then handed it back. "You've spent a lot of time in the US, I see."

"High school, college and several years working on Wall Street."

"Did you ever think of becoming a US citizen?"

"I love the United States and I'm grateful for my education there. I considered becoming a citizen but the tax burden is too much. And I think I can make a major contribution in my own country. On Wall Street I'm just another Asian drone working a hundred hours a week."

The Ambassador nodded. "Yes, I know several Asian American women like that."

Coco continued. "My husband is a man of influence. I have a financial background and an aptitude for financial matters. Don't let my interest in fashion or my name fool you. My husband and I make a good team. Together we can make a difference in Myanmar." Coco waited politely, fiddling with her diamond ring that had so effectively destroyed Khin Chit's face. An evil thought momentarily insinuated itself. *What if the ring rendered the same service on the Ambassador? Those blue eyes would go first.*

Kim put down the file she was holding. "Coco, I'll get right to the point. I've stuck my neck way out in granting the families of these four MPs visas to enter the US. I'm putting my career on the line with this. But I've determined Zafar is a major US priority. If it goes through, frankly I look good. If these MPs screw us in some way and you are playing some kind of game, I look bad. I can assure you I will find some way to make you regret it. You will never enter the US again and that's for starters. And I'll make sure you do have some kind of US tax problem." Kim smiled. "Our tax laws cast a wide net nowadays. You've spent enough time in the US that the IRS could define you as a U.S. Person. One of their pet names."

Coco was dying for a cigarillo. But there were no ashtrays in sight. *Fucking Americans,* she thought, *their companies get the whole world hooked on smoking and then they give it up. Just like Prince Charles and the Brits are such great protectors of the environment. In their Empire days the Brits shot every tiger that breathed.* Coco cleared her throat. "I don't like being threatened."

"Fair enough. Just understand my position here. Why should I trust these MPs to carry out their side of the bargain?"

"Kim, four of these M.P.s are military guys. I'll call them what they are, thugs. All four owe my husband favors from when he was head of the army. I don't know why. I don't ask my husband these questions, and he doesn't tell. You can't be certain of anything in Myanmar but I think with your help we've got their vote. I'm sure the Chinese and Su Myat, my husband's daughter, will offer them money. We are not offering them money. That's too dangerous, with the hearing coming up so soon, and the whole country watching. We've taken the high road."

The Ambassador laughed. "Not that high."

"If they don't vote the way we want, you can withdraw your offer."

"And we will," the Ambassador said.

Coco continued. "I'm happy to hear Project Zafar has become an American priority. The prior American Ambassador expressed no interest. We did approach him."

"Yes, well, he's still officially Ambassador to Myanmar. But he's very sick. I'll be running things for the foreseeable future both here in Singapore and in Myanmar as well."

"I see."

Ambassador Walsh tapped her notebook with a manicured nail. Coco, when she wasn't punching people, bit her nails. She had to admit the Ambassador's nails looked pretty good.

"All these dependents," Kim began, "will have to fill out forms and go through the normal interview process at our embassy."

"Kim, you've got no risk. Getting through your bureaucracy will extend beyond the hearings. If these thugs don't vote our way, you can stop the visa process."

"That we will do."

Coco nodded. "I'll make sure they do as we want. Kim, we are happy to have your support. We need your support. But it must be behind the scenes. We don't want the world to know that we've had the Americans do little favors for these thugs."

"Neither do the Americans," the Ambassador said. "This must remain confidential."

"If all goes well at this hearing," Coco said, "we are planning that the President of India, the President of Myanmar and descendants of both the Moghul Indian and Burmese royal families, will attend an inaugural ceremony at the tomb of Bahador Shah Zafar in downtown Yangon. Perhaps, you know he was the last Moghul Emperor of India? The British exiled him to Yangon. Just like they exiled the last Burmese emperor to India."

"I know the histories," the Ambassador said. "Your Project Zafar plays on this Indian/Burmese connection. Remember, the British and the Americans are separate. We're not responsible for the sins of the British Empire."

"I'll make sure they invite you to the ceremony. I'm a businesswoman, Kim. I don't do geopolitical stuff. But it's in Project Zafar's interest that the world knows we have the Americans on our side. Along with the Indians, of course."

"I agree," said the Ambassador. "Nobody's invited me yet. But I think I should go. Maybe the Chinese would like me to stay home."

"Fuck the Chinese. I'll make sure you are invited. Count on it."

The Ambassador set her notebook aside and smiled.

Coco continued. "The ceremony, on the surface in part, is going to be an anti-colonial love-in. And hopefully a Myanmar-India love in. Burma was part of British India until 1937. Nothing like a little old fashion Brit bashing. But all the anti-colonial stuff is just bullshit. Everybody in Southeast Asia likes the Brits today."

"The issue today," Kim said, emphasizing each word, "is keeping China from dominating Myanmar. Do you yourself think keeping China from dominating Myanmar is a good idea?"

Coco's hand made a dismissive gesture. "Anybody in Myanmar with half a brain thinks that's a good idea. True, there are lots of people in Myanmar who would just take Chinese money, no questions asked. But in my opinion they are stupid. Look, I'm not anti – Chinese. We just need balance. Like in Singapore. I'm Chinese by ancestry. So what. The Chinese who run Singapore don't kiss China's ass every day of the week. " Coco grinned. "They spread their smooches around. The US, India, Indonesia, Malaysia and China. Balance."

"A smooch for India and the US on this one?"

"Yes. I think it's in American interest that the world does view this as an American priority. Even if it is not an 'American Project'. It's an Indian project."

"Agreed," Kim said.

Coco smiled. Overall, surprise, surprise, she found herself liking the Ambassador. Kim was an ambitious woman, like herself. Coco liked ambitious women. *So long as she didn't fuck Ian Blakely.* "Look, we Burmese are a prickly bunch. We want to maintain our independence. You know that Burmese armies defeated the Chinese in the late seventeen hundreds? Their crack Imperial Manchu troops went down in flames in our jungles."

The Ambassador smiled. "But the Qianlong emperor considered it a Chinese victory. After the wars were over, the Burmese came with tribute for the Mandate of Heaven, as the Chinese emperor was called."

Coco smiled. "Really. I see you know your history, Kim. I didn't take any history courses at Brown. The only liberal arts course I took was on gay and lesbian literature. I was a math major with a minor in computer science. I do know the Qianlong emperor was a Manchu with his head up his butt. That's what I learned in second grade here in Myanmar."

The Ambassador smoothed her Ralph Lauren blouse. "Coco, are you familiar with the tributary system?"

"No."

"Well, when the emperors ruled China, all the neighboring countries – including Vietnam, Korea, Burma – brought tribute to the Chinese emperor and were considered under Chinese suzerainty. In other words within China's sphere of influence. The Chinese government of today, although they deny it, still views their neighbors through the lens of the tributary system. They expect Myanmar to offer tribute, whatever that may be. I'll be blunt. We don't think this is in Myanmar's interest. Or any of the neighboring countries."

"Or in America's interest," Coco said with her curled smile. "You want these countries to be under American suzerainty, to use your word."

The Ambassador smiled. "Right."

Coco shrugged. "I'll leave the geopolitical stuff to you, Kim. I just want to get Project Zafar approved. There our interests coincide."

"Agreed. That's the important thing. I do have some personal questions."

"Personal?"

"Yes," the Ambassador replied. "We can't have some scandal come and bite us in the ass."

"Ask."

"Do you have any romantic involvement with Ian Blakely?"

"None whatsoever." *Not counting last night's fucking frenzy.*

"Do you have any other romantic attachments in Myanmar or elsewhere?"

"None whatsoever." These questions pissed Coco off. "You think because my husband is much older that I must be fucking some younger man?"

"Coco, calm down. If you've got any skeletons I have a right to know about them. My career will be on the line with this."

"Ian Blakely isn't that young anyway." Coco smiled her curled smile.

"So, no skeletons?"

"None."

"It's my understanding you saved your husband's life?"

"Yes."

"Do you mind telling me how this happened?"

Coco related the story. "This is not public information," she added.

"They really taught you the Heimlich Maneuver in a Women's Empowerment Course?"

"They wanted us girls to develop confidence so we could handle any situation."

"Well, I guess you did," the Ambassador said. "What about your hitting the captain of the Brown football team with a beer bottle?"

"He molested me. He won't do it again."

"Nowadays the universities have instituted rules to protect women. You wouldn't have to do that today."

"That's nice. But I prefer more direct action. I grew up in Burma where direct action is preferred to reliance on institutions."

"Okay. Now tell me about Su Myat. Your group has two offshore blocks. Your geological survey shows massive reserves of natural gas and possibly oil. Correct?"

"You are well informed, Kim."

"Not as well informed as we'd like to be, Coco. Su Myat has a group backed by the Chinese. She wants to take these blocks away from you?

"That's right."

"Her group. Are they a front for the Chinese government?"

Coco shrugged. "You never know with the Chinese government. They have their fingers in everything. But they have two pipelines and a superhighway running from the Bay of Bengal to Yunnan Province in China. For all practical purposes they have taken over Northern Myanmar. There's a lot of resentment about this now in Myanmar so the Chinese government is trying to avoid too much publicity. But yes, I think the Chinese government is behind this. They would like to take over all of Myanmar's oil and gas. They don't want the Indians getting a share." Coco leaned forward. "They have two goals here. One, screw the Indians. Two, get more oil and gas under their direct control."

"And Su Myat? She's pro Chinese?"

"She's pro Su Myat. Pure opportunist. She would sell out the Chinese in a heartbeat if it suited her. Just as she's selling out Myanmar."

"So there's no real loyalty to China with her."

"None. And her proposal is dead in the water anyway. You are aware of the publicity surrounding her husband taking kickbacks?"

"But she's not giving up?"

"No, and neither are the Chinese."

"That video was quite a good job. Who put this out?"

Coco managed a big smile. "I have no idea."

"You were a computer science minor. And you followed internet stocks on Wall Street?"

Coco continued to smile. "Pure coincidence." She had broken a few laws in getting the information on General Sein Soe and the video out. She didn't want the Ambassador to have to report her for something. She leaned forward and spoke softly. "Kim, we all want Project Zafar to succeed. Whoever did this might have done one or two illegal things. Technicalities probably. This is how things get done in Myanmar. Better to break a beer bottle over somebody's head then go to the courts."

The Ambassador thought for a minute. "I guess I don't need to know. But it was a pretty good job. How about Su Myat's loyalty to her father?"

"None. It breaks his heart."

"And she hates you?"

"This is confidential. I shouldn't tell you this but she tried to kill me."

"How did she do that?"

"She had one of my staff try to poison my soup. She kidnapped the woman's son and held him hostage. Luckily my cat ate the soup first." Coco found herself looking at her ring.

"So what happened?" Kim asked, jotting down a note.

"The cat died. And I beat the shit out of the staff member. Of course I fired her."

"You beat..."

"I let her live. She was lucky." Coco raised her left hand. "My hand's still a little bruised. She hurt my hand with her face."

The Ambassador looked at Coco's hand. Most of the swelling had cleared up but there was still a slight discoloration. "You didn't report this to the police?"

"Again. I prefer more direct action. Laws in Myanmar are optional. Perhaps I shouldn't have told you this. You don't really need to know. Reporting it to the police would make this public information. We don't want that. This is my husband's daughter."

The Ambassador leaned back, her steady gaze on Coco. "You are an interesting person," she said.

"I don't take shit from anyone," Coco said.

"Do you think Su Myat will try to kill you again?"

"She might. She's crazy." Coco grinned. "She might even try to kill you. Don't bother to learn the Heimlich Maneuver. It won't help."

"I'll keep that in mind." The Ambassador took a deep breath. "It's in America's interest that the Indians and Zafar win on this one. That will help keep Myanmar independent. But the Indians, shall we say, will need a little help from time to time."

Coco smiled. "The Indian government could use a set of balls. At least the old government. We'll see about this new one. Look, Kim, our interests are one hundred percent aligned. Don't worry about my Chinese face. I was born in Burma, my father fled China and the communists. I'm nobody's tributary. I am loyal to Myanmar. I'm proud of my Chinese heritage but I don't give a shit about the communist Peoples Republic of China."

"I hope not." The Ambassador stood up and offered her hand. "We are partners here in a manner of speaking. Just make sure our four thugs vote for Zafar."

"They will," Coco said.

The two shook hands. Coco felt good about the meeting. It wasn't something she expected but she felt a kind of bond had developed between her and Ambassador Kimberly Walsh.

It was time to go to the airport. Awaiting her in Myanmar was the traitor Major Nyan Myint. His elimination, in one form or another, was next.

Chapter Twenty-One

A mantis is catching a cicada but a finch is hunting right behind the mantis.

— Chinese proverb

Coco carefully loaded her Glock G29 with new ammunition. Always a good idea with a gun that hasn't been used for a while. She had no idea if she would need the pistol but just holding it made her feel better. Her bruised left hand had almost completely healed so she could easily control it. She had last practiced with it in the States three years before at a shooting range up in Ardsley, a New York suburb north of Manhattan. Maybe she was a little rusty but she felt confident. It was just the right size, a subcompact, a fine pistol for a lady. She placed it in her blue Chanel bag where it fit comfortably. A big package of sanitary pads was in the bottom of the bag. She placed the package over the Glock so it wouldn't be obvious if someone opened the bag. The bag itself had the word "Chanel" on the side, along with the Chanel logo and the address, 31 Rue Gambon, Paris. Coco liked the bag because it was so gauche it was edgy. She wouldn't dream of carrying this particular bag in New York. But people in Myanmar were behind China and just learning about all the glorious European brands. They needed instructions, that is, the bag had to say "Chanel" right on the side. In Myanmar, even the famous Chanel double C logo wasn't enough.

The house was quiet. All the staff were gone. The Opposition leader, Aung San Suu Kyi, was holding a rally in downtown Yangon that night. The staff had collectively asked Madame if they could be excused for four hours to attend. Coco, a product of a U.S. liberal education, had of course granted permission. She and her husband were alone in the big house.

Coco had had a routine meeting three days before with her husband and Major Nyan Myint. The Major was especially cordial towards her and the meeting went smoothly. The Major had requested a week off to go hunting in Northern Myanmar. This was something he did once or twice a year on an estate owned by a former military guy. He claimed he was hunting deer but Coco assumed he was hunting tigers or some other "protected" species. The local Chinese actually ran some local restaurants in the area that specialized in serving illegal game. Coco felt bad for the tigers – you can't go to Brown and not come out wanting to save tigers -- but she had other things to worry about. The Major had always been correct but not really warm in his dealing with her. She didn't know where his real loyalties lay.

She was suspicious of the Major's cordiality at their last meeting. The Chinese have an expression, *When the weasel says happy new year to the chicken, it's not good news.* The Major had been spying on her in Singapore. Of that she was almost certain. And she suspected he had been working with Adrian Cairncross when Ian Blakely had taken his little history tour of Yangon. The Major was a military man, given to simple solutions. Just like Su Myat. Getting rid of her might be one of those solutions. Let him try. She was not going to be this weasel's fucking chicken.

Coco got up and walked over to the window and looked out towards the gazebo and the pond. It was dark and she couldn't see much. Only the bare outline of the bulldozer that was being used for the pond's reconstruction. She opened the window to catch a breath of the night air. Normally she kept it closed, keeping in the air conditioning and keeping out the mosquitos which brought dengue and malaria. But in Myanmar mosquitos were not the only potential invaders. A friend of hers had almost died from a bite in her own bedroom by a snake called Russell's Viper that had apparently crawled right through an open window. Coco never went walking outside the house at night. She was afraid of the jungle. The gazebo and the pond were cutsie human artifacts carved out of the jungle behind it. They were to be looked at from the safety of the house. The jungle was a dangerous place, with its own weird cacophony of insect and animal sounds that went on all night long. And the whole property, like all of Southeast Asia, was crawling with snakes. She listened to the noises, wondering if there was some hidden message, some warning. A bullfrog croaked. That made her feel a little better. He was not a threat. He was telling her things would be okay. She would find out in a few minutes that the bullfrog was indeed her friend.

Suddenly she heard footsteps. They were clearly not those of her husband and his cane. She immediately hurried back to the desk and her Chanel bag. The door to her office opened, making a creaking sound. She instinctively knew a snake was entering. Major Nyan Myint. Dressed in the distinct maroon colored robes of a Burmese Buddhist monk.

"Do you always dress like a monk when you're shooting tigers?" Coco asked. "And does shaving your head improve your aim?"

The Major pulled out a large government-issue pistol and got right to the point. "You are a traitorous whore. You have betrayed Myanmar and your husband. You are selling out our nation's resources. You have committed adultery with the foreigner, Ian Blakely. In the name of the people of Myanmar, I am sentencing you to death." He rendered this verdict in English. A colonial throwback? In days gone by in Burma many a verdict had been handed out in English.

"Your holiness." Coco asked, looking at the Major's eye, not at his pistol. "How much did Su Myat pay you for this?"

The big pistol waggled a dismissal. "I'm not doing this for the money."

Coco grinned. "Bullshit. You're being paid and you know it." She looked at the big pistol's muzzle. A .45, *a big fucking gun.*

"You Chinks only think about money."

"You Burmese don't think at all," Coco replied.

The Major became angry. "Come with me," the Major said, pointing with his pistol towards the door. "Any false move and I'll shoot you on the spot."

"If you're going to shoot me, I have to look good." Coco stood up and slipped into the six inch heels that lay under her desk. They were cheap no name shoes that she had picked up in Singapore. But in the dead of night who was going to know the difference? And they would serve a purpose. This day had not been a longyi day for Coco. Rather she was wearing tight Calvin jeans and a blue Guess tank top. She put on the light jacket that was hung over the back of her chair. That too she had just picked up in Singapore at a little shop called *bebe* that was part of a US chain and wasn't pronounced *bebe* like it was in Spanish but rather *bibi*. It was a little chilly that night. She eased the Chanel bag over her shoulder. She stood up and, with the help of her six inch heels, towered over the five foot sixish Major Nyan Myant. She knew it pissed him off. She smiled down at him.

"You won't be needing that bag," the Major said.

"Major, I'm an Asian woman and I'm always going to look good. I will die with my Chanel. I'm not going without the bag. Shoot me here if you don't like it."

The Major grabbed the bag and opened it without pulling it from Coco's shoulder. Maybe the sight of a woman's sanitary pads embarrassed him. Or maybe he was just careless. But he didn't see the Glock and he didn't notice that the Chanel bag weighed a bit more than if it just held a few sanitary pads. He let go of the bag. "Keep your stupid Chanel. Now let's go. We're headed for the construction area next to the gazebo. Right next to the bulldozer. Make a sound or call for help and you will die instantly. I will then have to tell the world what a traitorous whore you were. This way you will just disappear. But you will have honor. I'm giving you that. I will say nothing but nice things about you after you disappear."

"Oh thank you. How honorable of you."

"Nobody's going to hear you if you scream. Because you are such a generous, liberal person." The Major laughed. "You let your staff go to hear that stupid woman. Very convenient. Oh, and just for your information.

Nobody knows I'm here either. I walked over. My wife and children are up-delta visiting her mother. And I'm in North Myanmar shooting deer. And there are plenty of monks on the streets of Yangon. Nobody will remember me. Nobody will know I was here."

"You are so fucking smart," Coco said.

"As a monk I'm going to do a good deed. I'm going to release you from the cares of this life. We Buddhists believe in doing these good deeds. With animals, with birds… with whores." He motioned with his gun. "Move."

They headed out the door. There were no noises in the empty house other than Coco's heels on the old wooden floors. Coco had to hand it to the Major. He knew the servants would be gone. When they were outside Coco momentarily was overwhelmed by the darkness and the noise from the jungle. Her hands were shaking. In the darkness Coco couldn't see potted red bromeliads lining the passageway out to the back of the house. She had put them there herself. She was startled for a second by a lizard that she almost stepped on. She had to walk slowly in her heels.

She had to get a hold of her fears. In her Women's Empowerment Course she had been taught to calm her fears by visualizing intimidating people in demeaning positions like sitting on the toilet. She visualized the Major in a Brown football uniform. This time she had a Glock, not a beer bottle.

The visualization worked. She felt an adrenalin rush. The dark side of her nature kicked in. Sometimes hormonal imbalances had value. She would enjoy killing the Major. Her hands stopped shaking. She was under control. She had to outthink the Major. She stepped gingerly through the grass, hoping no snake was underfoot and making sure not to trip with her exaggerated heels. No visualization would cure her fear of snakes. With her left hand, she unbuttoned her Chanel bag, guessing that in the darkness the Major wouldn't notice. Finally they arrived at the gazebo and the bulldozer. Coco's mouth dropped. She could just make it out in the darkness. But right in front of them was a large pile of dirt and a freshly dug ditch. A very deep ditch. There was a shovel lying against the dirt pile. The Major had done his planning well. This was going to be Coco's grave. The ditch would be covered by the pond when it was refilled. That was actually scheduled for tomorrow. She was going to be compost for waterlilies. *Bullshit on that.*

"Stop," the Major commanded.

Coco stopped, positioning herself with the moonlight coming behind her. It wasn't a full moon. What there was of the moonlight shone on the Major. She would be harder to see. Her hand reach into the Chanel bag past the sanitary pads and grasped the Glock.

"So you will shoot me here," Coco said, distracting him. "You are the traitor. I realized that when Blakely told me you showed up in the Sule Paya temple right when Cairncross was there."

The Major laughed. "You're a clever Chink. I'll give you that."

Unlike other brands, the Glock does not have a safety that has to be disengaged. Rather the Glock has what his called the Safe Action Trigger in which your finger is the safety. No dangerous delays in disengaging a safety. You only had to know how to squeeze the trigger properly. Coco knew -- her finger had been well trained on the use of this Glock trigger.

Coco knew in the darkness the Major could barely see her. But she could see him well enough. Suddenly a nearby bullfrog let loose with a massive croak. Presumably he was trying to impress some female. He must have been really horny. The Major momentarily looked over at the direction where the sound came from and cursed in Burmese.

One little distraction was all Coco needed. She dropped to one knee and aimed the Glock, still in the Chanel bag, at the Major. The Major saw the Chanel bag aimed at him but no Glock. He was momentarily confused. The bag was upside down and some of the sanitary pads had fallen out. As a military man he had been trained to respond to people aiming guns at him, not ladies handbags. How could he know that he was in mortal danger from a French fashion icon? Or maybe, he did perceive the danger. Coco after all was holding the bag so it was horizontal – the proper way to shoot someone with a pistol. But perhaps the Major had seen too many old Hollywood movies where the little lady holds the gun but doesn't seem to have the balls to shoot the bad guy. Of course he thought he was the good guy. He hesitated just for a second. Just long enough. In this situation he who hesitates is dead. Maybe he thought the little lady couldn't do it. He was wrong.

Coco had been taught to aim for the heart. It was too easy to miss somebody's head. She pumped two bullets into the Major's chest. He went straight down on his back, never getting to fire a shot. Blood was spurting all over his chest. Coco went over to him and put another bullet right between his eyes. Just in case he was faking it or wearing a bullet proof vest with maybe some ketchup for blood. Like in the movies.

Now Coco had a problem. What to with the body? Conveniently the Major had solved the problem for her. She would just execute his plan for her. Teetering on her heels, she took the nearby shovel and rolled his body into the ditch. "These cheap shit heels are a real pain," she said aloud. Her Calvin jeans and Guess top could be washed but the heels were probably going to be toast. Good riddance. And the Chanel bag, ripped open with bullet holes, was useless. What a waste! She couldn't even give it away to one of the servants. She left the Glock in the bag. She took off her bebe jacket and got to work. She spent the better part of two hours shoveling the dirt. And rolling rocks down over the body. The Major, ever methodical, had placed rocks next to the dirt pile. The rocks were an extra precaution. Coco had watched enough American gangster programs to know that dead bodies fill with gas and have a tendency to rise. The rocks would prevent this although they probably would not be necessary since the body would lie buried beneath the liner for the pond. She tossed in the Chanel bag with the Glock and the sanitary pads. Tomorrow under her direction the workmen would install the liner for the pond. She would make sure thee workmen didn't do any extra exploring. The Major had it all planned. The pond would be refilled leaving behind only the sound of bullfrogs, insects and perhaps the quiet slither of snakes. And the Major, the Chanel bag and the Glock would be gone.

She walked slowly back to the house, exhausted and still worried about snakes. Her whole body ached. She had some bites, probably mosquito, on her arms. She should have left the jacket on. All that shoveling. Ladies could shoot Glocks all day long but grave digging was a man's job.

She headed back to her office. She took off her heels. They were covered with mud and the heel on the right shoe was coming off. She tossed the shoes into the trash basket. Part of her had enjoyed this evening. The Dean at Brown made her see a psychiatrist after she had bashed in their star athlete's head. The shrink had told her she had a dark side she had to control. She had tried. She really did stop going to bars and looking for fights. But as with the traitorous Khin Chit, when someone threatened her, her dark side took over. At least she didn't go around killing innocent people for fun. She went into her bathroom and looked at the mirror. She had an animal like look on her face. Her eyes seemed to belong to some feral beast that she didn't recognize. And her hair stood out like she had placed her hand in an electric socket. This scared her. She had mud all over her. She tried to clean herself up. She would bathe when she got back to her bedroom.

A pang of guilt came over her. She knew the Major had two young children and a wife. She remembered how she felt when her own mother was killed and raped. She would see that his family was well taken care of. Her immediate problem was what she would tell her husband. That, it would turn out, wasn't going to be a problem.

Coco went to her bedroom, which adjoined that of her husband. The General was lying in bed. The TV was on, some English football match. He was a big Man U fan. But the General seemed to be asleep, his mouth open. The older people get, the more they resemble one another, mouths open, drooling, shadows of the vibrant beings that they used to be.

She looked at her husband with both admiration and sadness. He was so smart, so wise. Once he had been energetic and handsome. Often she truly wished she had known him then. She studied him closely. Usually, when she came into the bedroom and he was asleep, he would wake up enough to say something to her. This time he wasn't moving or talking. Something was different. Something was wrong. She came over and held his hand. He didn't respond. Then she shook his hand. His eyes opened just slightly. He just moaned a little, but he didn't talk. Coco knew what had happened.

The General had had another stroke.

Chapter Twenty-Two

I didn't kill the princes.

—*Former Burmese Queen Supayalat,
in response to a reporter's question in 1924*

After Coco had called the doctor, she sat on the bed for a few minutes holding her husband's hand. She knew she had a really big problem. How to explain Major Nyan Myint's disappearance? No one, least of all the Myanmar military, was going to believe that she had killed an officer in the Myanmar army in self-defense. The truth in this case was not going to set her free.

Coco waited ten days to alert the military authorities after the Major had disappeared. Supposedly he was on a week's leave in north Myanmar hunting so her delay was quite appropriate. That left plenty of time to finish the pond and eliminate all traces of construction. Another good break. Her husband's daughter and her enemy, Su Myat, was conveniently out of the country at the time of her father's stroke. Coco had some time. Step by step she maneuvered. She wanted the workmen on the pond to be gone before anyone came poking around.

When she did finally speak with his commanding officer, Coco told him that the Major had been entrusted by her husband, General Maung Myo, with a delicate mission to negotiate with his daughter, Su Myat, and her husband. She told the Major's commanding officer that only her husband, General Maung Myo, knew the exact reason for Major Nyan Myint's mission. She left the definite impression that Su Myat had something to do with the Major's disappearance and that the Major had been a victim of foul play.

Finally, well after a week and a half had gone by, Su Myat came to visit to see her father. Coco of course had to receive her. A servant ushered her into Coco's study. Coco was wearing a blue longyi and matching top and no jewelry, the image of a demur Burmese maiden. Su Myat was conservatively dressed in Western style slacks, a blue jacket and a Louis Vuitton bag on her arm. Su Myat was a woman of about sixty who had maintained her figure and was still good looking for her age.

This was an awkward moment. Of course there were no hugs. Unlike Latins, who hug one another at the slightest provocation, Asian people aren't big on this practice. Especially when they hate one another. Su Myat and Coco started out by not doing the traditional Burmese slight bow cum handclasp. Coco motioned to Su Myat to sit down but she refused. Su Myat could not contain the fury in her eyes. She was glaring at the much younger and somewhat taller Coco who stood behind her desk. She had to know Coco was the source of the video that disgraced her husband. But on one level this was an old story. Older daughter from a first marriage, younger beautiful wife from a second marriage. The older daughter hates the younger wife and the threat she poses to the father's assets. As all estate lawyers know, *she who holds his dick last, gets all the money.*

It had been a week and a half since her father's stroke and the Major's disappearance. Su Myat told people she was out of town shopping in London although Coco suspected she was in Beijing plotting her next move with her Chinese backers. Or perhaps she was doing both. Now she had returned and was finally getting to visit her sick father.

Coco offered Su Myat tea which she declined with a rude wave. Coco, keeping her cool, poured herself a cup and sat down.

"You are a whore with no shame," Su Myat began, speaking in English. "You told the military and the police that Major Nyan Myant had been visiting us!"

Coco blew gently on her teacup. "Yes I did. Because it's absolutely true. The Major was totally loyal to your father and to me as his wife. The General sent him over to negotiate with you. Perhaps to find some way to cover your shame on account of your criminal husband and his kickbacks? I don't know what went on in your house but I do know the Major has been dealing with you. We will not rest – I will not rest, even if your father is no longer able— until we get to the truth of what has become of this wonderful, loyal man. Major Nyan Myant is a hero as far as I'm concerned. I will not rest until his disappearance is solved. And if there is foul play, I will track down those responsible unto the ends of the earth."

"You are a whore," Su Myat spat out.

"My husband has held back with you because you are his daughter," Coco said quietly. "When he passes, I will not be so kind. For now, I will not respond to your insults."

Su Myat could not hide her rage. Her face was practically purple with a large vein pulsing in her neck. She couldn't say that the Major was really plotting with her against her own father. Or that she had asked him to kill Coco. *Coco had her by the balls.* "I don't know what kind of game you are playing. But we had nothing to do with Major Nyan Myant's disappearance. Coco, you know that and so do the military. You, Coco bitch, are an adulterous whore. I know you were fucking that older white financial guy down in Singapore. I have a witness."

Su Myat in her rage had slipped. "Really," Coco said cooly. "And just who is this witness."

Su Myat did not respond.

"You have no witness," Coco said, knowing Su Myat could not say the witness was the Major and that he was spying on her behalf. "Where is this witness? What is his name?"

Su Myat was silent, her hand gripping her Louis Vuitton bag.

"Because there is no witness. You, Madame, are a fucking liar."

"You are despicable," Su Myat replied.

Coco watched her, letting seconds tick by. "I have been one hundred percent faithful to your father," she said quietly. "Your father, whether you like it or not, is my husband as long as he lives. I have always loved and respected him."

Su Myat, now shaking with rage, replied. "You are a traitorous whore."

Coco responded. "And by the way, it is you who are the criminal, not just your husband. You forced my assistant to try to poison me. I could have gone to the authorities with that. But I didn't. To spare your family the shame."

"That's a lie. I never tried to poison you. Don't blame me because one of your chink assistants betrayed you. Anyway, you deserved to be poisoned."

"So you're fully familiar with the incident." In her rage, Su Myat was committing one "gotcha" slip after the other. Coco slowly sipped her tea, then stood up and put on her sincerest phony smile. "Shall we go visit your father now? That is why you came here, I presume."

Su Myat nodded. She couldn't talk.

They headed for the General's bedroom. He was lying with his eyes closed, with a supplementary oxygen hose attached to his nose. A second tube was attached to his arm. This provided water and sustenance. It so happened the doctor, a Charles Farnsworth, was there at that moment. He was British, a cardiologist, trained in the UK. He had treated the General after his first stroke and had continued to treat him on a regular basis. A short, overweight man with a slight stoop, he had a lucrative practice in Yangon treating rich locals and foreigners. He had met Su Myat on previous occasions and bowed slightly.

"I'm so sorry about your father," The doctor began, moving out of earshot lest the General might comprehend what he was saying. "The General has had another cerebral hemorrhage, I'm afraid. There's not much we can do. I've had him on some medications but I'm afraid he'd been slipping in the last few months. The oxygen helps his breathing."

"How long does he have?" Su Myat asked.

"No way to know. He could die tonight, he could last for another month or two. We just don't know. It's very doubtful that he will recover in any significant way."

"Shouldn't he be in a hospital?" Su Myat asked.

Farnsworth shook his head. "I think he's better off here, given the state of hospitals in the country right now. We've got the necessary equipment here. Just make him comfortable. There's not much anybody can do." The Doctor turned to Coco. "Madame, with my encouragement, reads to him every day."

"I read him the local news," Coco said quietly, with an air of reverence.

"And he understands?" Su Myat asked, unable to hide the anger on her face.

The doctor nodded. "Patients in his state do apparently have some limited powers of comprehension. And the reading may be very comforting to him. We really just don't know. But I think reading to him is a good idea. You both may wish to read to him. You could take turns."

Su Myat went over and held her father's hand. There was no reaction. She turned back to the doctor. "You can let her do the reading," she said as she gave Coco a nasty glance." I have another question, Dr. Farnsworth."

"What's that?"

"Are we going to do an autopsy?" Su Myat asked.

The doctor seemed perplexed. "Your father is still alive. We don't do autopsies on living people."

"I know that," Su Myat responded, annoyed.

The doctor continued. "Of course when he passes we will do an autopsy if the family so requests." He turned to Coco. "His wife would normally make that decision."

"I have no objection," Coco said.

"But why would you ask such a question now?" the doctor asked.

"How do we know he's not a victim of foul play?" Su Myat said.

"What do you mean foul play?" the doctor replied. His eyes sharpened. "This is an elderly sick man who has had a second, totally debilitating stroke. I have been treating him on a regular basis and I can assure you there has been no foul play. I don't know what you are implying but I deeply resent your question."

Coco could see where Su Myat was going. She was going to spread a rumor that Coco had done in the General. And maybe had an affair with the doctor.

"I have no objection to an autopsy and nothing to hide," Coco said. She looked over at her husband who was white as a sheet and still as stone. He always looked like this since his stroke, like he was already dead. Coco hoped he was not hearing what was being discussed. She then looked at Su Myat. "There's no depth to which you will not stoop, is there? Go ahead. Make up some story about how Dr. Farnsworth and I poisoned my husband. You are such a bitch."

With that, Su Myat left the room without saying a word and departed from the house.

Dr. Farnsworth studied Coco. "This is one angry and insulting woman. My reputation is one hundred percent beyond reproach. But she has some power. Her husband is a big military guy. This is Myanmar. Should I be worried?"

"It's hard to say what she will do, Doctor, but she's under some pressure now along with her husband. Just make sure you've got good records for everything you've done. And please keep treating my husband. You have my full support.

Coco returned to her office. She would read to the General later. She was nervous. Things had gone well with Su Myat. The bitch had committed one blunder after the other. But Coco knew she was taking a huge gamble. But there was no choice. Who would believe that she shot and killed a Myanmar army officer in self-defense? Would the military police stumble onto some clue that was somehow left in the backyard by the pond? She had spent some time inspecting the pond. She had been out every morning supervising the workers. Nobody ever saw any body. She didn't think there were any incriminating clues. The body was covered with rocks and was buried well below the pond, not in it. It wasn't going to fill with gas and float up into the pond. But she wasn't a forensic expert.

But neither were the military police who were conducting the investigation. Any expertise they might have in torturing suspects would be of little help in this crime scene investigation. Attributing the blame to Su Myat just might work. General Sein Soe, her husband, was already under great pressure because of the information Coco had released. This was Myanmar. The Army especially might want to use this as an opportunity to get rid of an embarrassment. She could see them assuming Su Myat and her husband were somehow guilty. Still, a senior officer disappearing without a trace?

Coco walked over to the dining room where she had a clear view of the pond. It looked so serene. There wasn't a hint of the prior construction to the casual observer. She had hired a consultant and hadn't gone cheap on constructing the pond. It would last for years before needing repairs. Coco laughed to herself. Asians didn't like to buy houses where people had died. If it became known that the Major had been killed on the grounds and was buried in the back, then the house's value would plummet. Probably it would have to be torn down. Another gem of Burmese colonial architecture lost. She had planned to commission a statue of her husband and have it placed by the pond. Not now. Her husband would be horrified if he knew his statue was set near the Major's bullet ridden corpse.

Any thorough investigation would involving draining and then tearing up the pond. But they wouldn't do that unless they had a reason. She wondered if Su Myat knew how the Major had planned to kill her. That would be a problem. She might have put the pond idea in his head. Hopefully Su Myat had told the Major to kill Coco and he had cooperatively said "leave it to me." As any manly military man would say.

So far so good. The military police had already inspected the house and the grounds. Apparently they had found nothing. Nobody had asked about construction in the backyard. As far as she knew, the military police didn't even know about it. So they probably didn't interview the construction firm or the workmen.

Coco knew Sherlock Holmes or even Inspector Clouseau could crack this case. And she would be toast. But this was Myanmar. Holmes and Clouseau wouldn't be working on this case. Backward Burma just might save her ass.

There was a knock on the door. Her assistant poked her head in. "Lieutenant Hantha Min is here to see you."

Lieutenant Hantha Min was in charge of the investigation of Major Nyan Myint's disappearance. He entered the room and executed the traditional Burmese slight bow and handclasp which Coco returned. The Lieutenant sat down.

"Madam," he began in Burmese, "I'm terribly sorry to be bothering you. But I have my duty."

"Of course," Coco said.

"This investigation would be greatly helped if your husband could speak," the Lieutenant said.

"He can't talk. But don't take my word for this. You should speak to Dr. Farnsworth. He is treating my husband."

"He's English?"

"Yes, and he's here now."

The Lieutenant seemed strangely flustered for the moment. But then he nodded.

"Follow me," Coco said. She escorted the Lieutenant to her husband's bedroom. Dr. Farnsworth was standing outside the bedroom talking with the nurse assistant, a plump Burmese woman of about thirty. Coco had wondered if the good doctor was banging the nurse. Coco hoped he was. That would help take the burden of suspicion off of her if Su Myat spread some nasty rumor that Coco and Dr. Farnsworth were lovers and had conspired to murder her husband. *Fucking Burmese intrigues.*

"Dr. Farnsworth, this is Lieutenant Hantha Min."

"Pleased meet you," responded the Lieutenant, while shaking hands.

Coco felt relieved already. The former regime had pulled English out of the schools during the darkest days of the dictatorship. *The Lieutenant, judging by his greeting, couldn't fucking speak English.* That's why he was flustered a moment ago. He didn't want to reveal his ignorance in front of the English doctor. Coco felt confident that, if he couldn't speak English, then he he'd never watched Dr. House or gone to Harvard Medical School and wouldn't be looking around the backyard for DNA samples.

The Lieutenant began asking the doctor a series of questions, all in Burmese. The first concerned his interviewing the General. Coco found herself acting as translator.

"I absolutely forbid your speaking with my patient," Dr. Farnsworth pronounced with a full high end British accent right out of the movies. "First of all, he probably won't understand a word you say. Secondly, if he does, what you say may upset him. He could die from this stress. I assume you don't want your name in my report on his death."

"What is the cause of the General's condition?"

"The General suffered a massive cerebral hemorrhage, the second in his life. The first was two years ago and was far less threatening." Coco translated.

"You are his regular doctor?"

"Yes. I took over that function after his first stroke. I've been seeing him on a regular basis. Although I'm sure he has been seeing a traditional doctor." All Asians, even educated ones, resort to traditional medicine, even as they see doctors trained in Western medicine. JIC – just in case.

"Is there any evidence of foul play?"

"None whatsoever. This is an eighty five year old man who had a prior stroke and who had blood pressure issues. Why would you ask such a question?"

As Coco translated she wondered the same thing.

The Lieutenant did not answer. He simply thanked Dr. Farnsworth and he and Coco returned to Coco's office.

"Well, thank you for assisting me," he said. "We are pursuing all avenues in this investigation. Major Nyan Myint had been hunting in North Myanmar. We are questioning several local people up there. Perhaps he had an accident or was the victim of foul play. There are a lot of dangerous minority people up there. Not so safe."

Oh shit, Coco thought, *they are going to torture some poor minority people into confessing to Major Nyan Myint's murder.*

"Why did you ask if my husband's stroke was possibly the result of foul play?"

"It's an obvious question, Madame. The stroke occurred at the same time as Major Nyan Myint's disappearance. That's all I will say. Except if I were you, I would be careful. If there is foul play here, you might be a target as well."

"Thank you for the warning," Coco said. "I appreciate your concern."

"Madame, you stated in your original report that the last time you saw Major Nyan Myint was two weeks ago in a meeting with your husband?"

"Yes sir, that is correct. We haven't seen him since."

"And you think he was on some secret negotiation with General Sein Soe, and his wife, Su Myat?"

"My husband was very secretive about that," Coco began. Even though he had differences with his daughter, this was family and in this case he didn't want me involved. And he didn't want publicity. But I want every lead investigated. Major Nyan Myint did have some dealings with General Sein Soe and his wife Su Myat on behalf of my husband. They must know something. It's public knowledge that I don't get along with Su Myat and she and her husband have a rival natural gas project. A hunting accident? That's possible too, I suppose. But the Major is a military man. He knows guns. And I want to say this. The Major has been very loyal to my husband and is someone we have totally trusted. My husband does not know he has disappeared. I am not going to tell him even if he comes out of his coma. I must be clear about that, Lieutenant."

"I understand. Do you think Su Myat could arrange the murder of Major Nyan Myint?"

"I think she's capable of anything. Her brother and sister died under mysterious circumstances. But I'm the wrong person to ask. She hates me. That's a family secret that everybody knows."

"Yes, we do know that. Well, I will have to talk with your husband if he does recover."

"Of course." Coco lowered her head. "But I'm afraid he won't."

"One more thing, Madame. There are some questions I have to ask. Please do not be offended. What is your relationship with Major Nyan Myint?"

"I am not offended. Lieutenant, you are doing your job. Our relationship is very formal and very correct. The Major's loyalty is really to my husband. He extended this loyalty to me. He is a model husband and father as far as I can tell. That's all I can say."

The Lieutenant sighed. He had to ask the question but he was glad it was over with. "Let me know if you are going to travel outside of Myanmar. I am sorry to have to ask you these questions."

"I have to testify before Parliament in Naypyidaw next week regarding Project Zafar which I presume you know about. My husband was supposed to be there supporting me but obviously now he cannot. I'm not going anywhere in the next two weeks. Business does normally require me to travel. My husband delegated business matters to me. But with my husband like this, I'll be staying in Yangon except for the testimony when I go to the capital." She put her head in her hands. "Forgive me, but I have to deal with three things at once. My testimony, my husband and now Major Nyan Myint. It's too much."

"I understand. Do you want a temporary replacement for Major Nyan Myint? To be of assistance?"

"No. Thank you very much, but not at this time. I want to believe the Major is alive. There must be some simple explanation. My husband and I want you to find him. We will need a driver here and in Naypyidaw next week. But that's all."

"I will arrange that. Thank you for your time." The Lieutenant got up, executed another clasped hand bow and left.

As soon as the Lieutenant had left, Coco went to the dining room and looked back out at the pond. The pond was now her coconspirator, hiding a secret she wished never to be revealed in her lifetime. She never wanted to go out there again with the Major buried under the pond. Maybe his ghost would surface in the pond and take his revenge. She was ashamed of herself. She had some Asian superstitions after all.

Somewhat depressed, she went back to her office. Thinking about the Major under the pond and her husband lying near death weighed on her.

When she got to her office, she looked in the mirror. She suddenly laughed out loud. *An affair with Major Nyan Myint? Ambassador Walsh and Su Myat suspect I'm fucking Ian. Ian thought I might be fucking Devan. People might believe I'm fucking Dr. Farnsworth Everybody thinks I'm the young second wife slut.* She turned to the mirror and asked out loud. "Mirror, mirror on the wall, who is the biggest slut of all?" She listened to the silence. "You gave the correct answer." Her mood had improved.

Chapter Twenty-Three

You can design and create, and build the most wonderful place in the world. But it takes people to make the dream a reality.

—*Walt Disney*

Naypyidaw --according to the guidebooks -- *royal capital, abode of the kings.* Napyidaw International Airport, *Ian's kind of airport.* A brand new 12,000 foot runway, very few planes, no ATC delays, no lines or hassles at Customs, no angry Australian woman like his last visit to Yangon. The airport seemed almost abandoned. Actually, Ian was met by a Mynamar military officer who escorted him right through Customs and would serve as his driver. The officer introduced himself to Ian but Ian didn't catch the name. Ian wondered what had become of Major Nyan Myint.

The plan was that Ian would check into his hotel, then immediately go to Coco's hotel. Coco had insisted on this arrangement for "appearances". He thought she was overdoing things, but it was her call. As far as he knew, Coco was unaware of his American rendition problem. Informing her of this was not going to make her day. He had spent part of the last two weeks inhaling the polluted air of Beijing. He felt a certain irony in hiding out in authoritarian China to escape kidnapping from agents of the so-called "land of the free." But he had to spend some time in Singapore for some important meetings. In Singapore he was nervous but he couldn't bring himself to hire a bodyguard. He had had one in Miami and he thought the guy was a pain in the ass. And what would a bodyguard do against a gaggle of American agents seeking his rendition, possibly armed with a Singaporean court order? In Singapore the bodyguard would probably be a Sikh. The British had used Sikhs throughout the Empire in police work in places like Shanghai and Rangoon. They were tall, bearded and scary looking. Many of their descendants still did security work. The Chinese used to be scared shit of them. Ian doubted the ODD people would be similarly intimidated.

Anyway, Ian didn't want a scary Sikh or any other kind of bodyguard in his life. He tried to alter his daily schedule while in Singapore. He couldn't spend all of his time in Beijing. Ambassador Walsh had told him that, if he managed to successfully testify before the Myanmar Parliamentary committee, it would give him some stature against ODD. The more publicity the better. She also told him ODD might try to prevent him from testifying and snatch him before the event. That he should be careful. The ODD boys didn't care about American interests in Myanmar. A full behind the scenes war had broken out between ODD and State over Ian's possible rendition. ODD wanted to bring back someone of Ian's stature to parade as a "prisoner of war" in front of the American people in the war on expatriate tax evaders. Apparently they had other targets as well. Poor bastards. The Department of State on the other hand was fully behind Ian. They wanted him to look good before the Myanmar Parliament and media. They didn't want any hint that he had allegedly engaged in some kind of disreputable tax dealings in the US.

Ian and Coco would go over their testimony this evening. Their testimony before the Parliamentary Committee would be tomorrow morning.

His hotel was really a resort, a little ways from downtown in what was called the *hotel zone*. He had time and he asked his driver to swing as close as he could by the new Parliament and the other government buildings. He gaped out the window at what he saw. Of course he didn't see too much since it was pouring rain. But basically what he saw was a series of low rise monument style buildings with identical Buddhist style pointed spires rising from their roofs. The spires were a sort of hat. They all had a sameness that suggested *government*. The Myanmar government certainly didn't do this on the cheap. He tried to compare this with New Delhi and Brasilia, the two other government capitals dropped from outer space on a virgin environment. Ian was familiar with both. He decided he preferred the originality of Brasilia. The

220

architect of Brasilia, Oscar Neimeyer, was certainly an original thinker. But all three capitals gave Ian the impression that they belonged somewhere else. Ian preferred the colonial district of old Rangoon and its dilapidated sidewalks. Of course he was part Brit and partial to the old colonial masters.

As he headed for his hotel, Ian noted a huge pagoda that was a Shwedagon look-alike. No need or time to stop for a drive by on this one. One day he would spend more time visiting the original in Yangon.

The rain was coming down hard and visibility out the windshield was limited. It was the kind of rain that resulted in fifty car pile ups on I-95 in Florida. Ian had narrowly avoided being in such a pile up in his days in Miami. The road he was on would put I-95 to shame. Twenty lanes to be exact. But no cars. Naypyidaw is a brand new city. Build it and they will come. Someday.

Finally he arrived at his hotel. He only had a carryon bag with his computer and a set of underwear and a new shirt for tomorrow. Of course his plane carried a more ample wardrobe. Another nice thing about having your own plane. It can serve as a convenient back up closet while you are traveling. Ian ran for the lobby in the rain, ignoring two doormen, one who chased after him with an umbrella, and the other who wanted to carry the luggage Ian didn't have. So he said nothing to the eager hotel staff that wanted to carry his bags nor did he tell them his name. This would prove fortuitous.

As he entered the lobby his phone beeped. Two text messages. The first was from Coco. "Call when u arrive." The second was from Ambassador Walsh, equally short. "Dont go to ur hotel."

Too late. He was already in the lobby. He looked to his left. *Shit.* There was Adrian Cairncross and two burly companions heading straight for him. They weren't dressed like monks although they both had bald pates like monks. One of them had the same red birthmark on the top of his head like the monk in the Sule Paya. Ian looked to his right. There was Clarence Whittle and two burly companions heading straight for him.

Cairncross reached him first by a split second, grabbed his left arm and shoved what felt like a gun into his left side. The barest split second later Whittle grabbed his right arm and shoved what felt like a gun into his right side. "You're coming with me," both Cairncross and Whittle said simultaneously. They then looked at one another, astonished. "Who the fuck are you," they both said again simultaneously, while letting go of Ian. Cairncross and Whittle were standing face to face, guns in hand, staring at one another.

Ian ran out of the lobby and jumped back into his waiting car, leaving an astonished and angry Adrian Cairncross and Clarence Whittle in his wake. Nobody offered to carry his bags or hold an umbrella. "Let's get out of here," he yelled at the driver, who probably didn't understand the English but being a good army man figured out the command.

He called Coco. "I've just had a really scary experience," he began.

Coco seemed to not hear him and interrupted him. "I'm not actually staying in the hotel where I'm registered," she said. "For security purposes I've checked into another hotel. Your driver has the information."

"What fucking security?" Ian was almost screaming. "Why didn't you tell me about a security problem?"

"What do you mean?"

"I just escaped from a security problem."

"Are you okay?" Coco asked.

"I'm fine. I'm in the car you sent."

"Then we'll discuss this when you arrive at my hotel. Your driver will take you here." Coco hung up.

Ten minutes later Ian was sitting in Coco's hotel room's living room suite. Devan and Advaita Chatterjee would be arriving shortly. The four of them would be reviewing the presentation for tomorrow's testimony. Coco would do the bulk of the presentation but Ian and Advaita would also be testifying.

Ian would talk on the Sovereign Wealth Fund and Advaita on technical details and the Indian side of the project. Devan the evil Chetty would be nowhere in sight.

Ian was working on a tall glass of rum to calm his nerves. The Chinese everywhere know that when a Caucasian gets agitated, alcohol is required. Coco herself was sipping juice from a freshly opened coconut. And smoking a cigarillo which stunk up the room and drove Ian crazy. Coco was sporting a Burmese look with an off white longyi with a reddish floral pattern and sandals. But with a sexy white tank top from Zara's. She just couldn't resist. "So what was your big problem," she began. There was something about her tone and the curl on her lip which seemed to say *I hope you're not making a big fucking deal over nothing.*

Ian related his experience at the hotel. "I'm lucky to be here. Two groups intercepted me simultaneously in the hotel lobby. They shoved guns into me at the same time. One group was led by an American. I know who the Americans were. A bastard named Clarence Whittle and two of his sidekicks from the new American Dollar Defense Division."

"What would they want?" Coco asked, sipping from her coconut.

The cat was about to jump out of the bag. Ian had to fess up. "They wanted to kidnap me and bring me back to the US for tax evasion. It's under a new US regulation that Obama's cooked up to punish people who gave up their American citizenship."

"Fuck." Coco flicked some ashes onto the tile hotel room floor. "They can do that? I remember learning about something called an ex post facto law. It's in the US Constitution. You've already fulfilled all their requirements and paid your exit fee."

"Ex post schmacto. America does what it wants. And Obama thinks the Constitution was written by dead white slaveholders and is something to be ignored."

"And how can the US be kidnapping people in Myanmar?"

Ian tried to wave away the smoke from Coco's cigarillo. It always seemed that the smoke headed straight for his head every time she took a puff. "They do what they want. Uncle Sam thinks he rules the world."

"You didn't tell me about this," Coco said with rising annoyance. "We're presenting you as Mr. Clean. This will wreck your image if it becomes public."

"It's something that just happened. Ambassador Walsh and the American State Department are trying to protect me. They insisted I not talk about this."

"And who was in the other group that attacked you?"

"A thug I know as Adrian Cairncross and two Burmese apes he brought with him. I've seen them all before. Cairncross was on my left and Whittle on my right. Both had guns poked in my ribs, like bookends. Anyway, they started cursing at each another and let me go. I got the hell out of there."

Coco began to laugh, more from astonishment than anything else. "So, two groups of goons were trying to kidnap you and they cancelled each other out. This sounds like a fucking Chevy Chase movie." She squinted her eyes and took another puff on the cigarillo. "Did anybody in the hotel recognize you?"

"I don't think so. It was pouring rain and I had run into the lobby."

"Suddenly you are a problem," Coco said.

"I'm not the only problem. Now, you tell me who is this Eurasian who calls himself Adrian Cairncross? I know you know."

"Yes, I know. Adrian Cairncross is his real name. He took the name of his father, a Lieutenant Cairncross in the British army. His mother is none other than Su Myat. She had an affair with Lieutenant Cairncross when she was in London at school. I don't know why she didn't have an abortion. The world would be a better place without Adrian Cairncross. They had a quickie marriage, followed by a divorce. My husband supported Adrian since he was an infant. Paid for his education at Oxford. Adrian was kept out of Myanmar and grew up mostly in the UK. A little family secret that not everybody knows."

"Including me," Ian said, finishing his rum. "You have so many secrets, Coco. Why didn't you tell me?"

"I didn't think Cairncross would bother you. And I had Major Nyan Myint to protect you when you were in Myanmar."

"And where was he today, by the way?"

Coco shifted in her seat and looked away. "Don't ask me that question again."

"What?"

"We have a replacement driver. That's all you need to know."

"Don't ask? So more Burmese bullshit. I'll bet you know where he is."

Anger swept across Coco' face. "Can we move on? We have a lot to do tonight. You are supposed to be Mr. Integrity. Now the Americans want to kidnap you for tax evasion? Does anybody know this?"

"So far, no. This just happened. Obama and the American government are persecuting Americans who gave up their citizenship. I've done nothing wrong."

"Big fucking deal," Coco said. "As if our enemies are going to care when they find out."

"Don't complain. You sucked me into this with your porn painting."

Coco sighed. "It was your horny dick that got you into this." Coco was smiling, her anger evidently abated.

Ian poured himself another rum. Straight up, no ice. "The Department of State is on my side. They want Project Zafar to go through. For them I'm a good guy. I'm counting on them to stop this ODD witch-hunt."

Coco rolled her eyes. "So, we have two branches of the American government fighting it out. At least the British weren't that fucking stupid.

They always acted in their own interest. So, what happened after you left the hotel?"

"How the hell should I know," Ian said. "Maybe they all killed each another."

"Let's hope they didn't," Coco replied. "We're presenting you to the Parliament and the people of Myanmar as a financial man above reproach. The last thing we need is a bunch of dead bodies in your hotel."

"Look, Coco. This isn't my fault. The American government has gone crazy."

"I don't give a shit." Coco was getting agitated again. "I have to find out what happened after you left the hotel. Will this make the newspapers?"

"I have no idea. I think I better call my office and have them cancel the hotel reservation. They can say I can't make it because of a canceled plane flight because of the rain. So no one will know I was ever there."

"Good idea but probably a waste of time," Coco said.

Ian called Anita and instructed her to cancel the reservation.

Ian's phone beeped.

It was Ambassador Walsh. "Ian, did you get my message?"

"Kim, it arrived a split second too late. But I got lucky."

"What do you mean?"

Ian explained.

The Ambassador broke into laughter. "This isn't funny, I know."

"But you are laughing."

"Sorry. The question is, will this make the newspapers?"

"If it does, I'm a liability. Coco is sitting right here by the way. She's worried I may become a liability."

"Put her on speaker," the Ambassador said. "I want to keep her on board."

Ian put his phone on speaker. "She wants to keep you on board," he said quietly.

The Ambassador continued. "Coco, I share your concern. Public knowledge that Ian is being pursued by the U.S. government will torpedo your project. It won't matter if he is innocent or guilty. But Project Zafar is in the interest of the United States. I want to help it to succeed any way I can. As I told you. I'm sure Clarence Whittle will not want to bring to the world's attention that he was in a foreign country on a kidnapping mission. And that he failed. Whittle knows if Ian's testimony is a success the US Department of State can force the Dollar Defense people to withdraw the case against Ian. He wanted to prevent Ian from testifying. That's why the rendition attempt now. It failed. As for the other group, I don't know. But I doubt they want to admit carrying guns around in hotel lobbies in Myanmar."

Coco spoke. "So Ian is like the man who fell out of the plane without a parachute, and landed in fifty feet of shit. And then walked away."

"An apt analogy," the Ambassador said.

Ian spoke. "Kim, could the other group – Adrian Cairncross and Su Myat – have learned something critical? Something they could use against us? Like the American government being after me?"

"I doubt it. It's unlikely the ODD guys did any talking. My guess is they left that hotel as fast as they could. They are probably on a plane right now out of Myanmar. Whittle is a bit of an innocent abroad. He's in over his head. It wouldn't occur to him that Cairncross might be useful to him. And he was probably scared shitless that Cairncross was somehow connected with the police in Myanmar. The police might detain him. His career would be ruined if that happened. He could easily spend some non-quality time in a Burmese jail. And I would think the other group didn't hang around either. They don't want that kind of publicity. They too could be thrown in jail."

"I hope you're right," Ian said.

"I'll find out what I can on this. Let's cross our fingers. Once you give that testimony, and if it goes over well, I think I can get the ODD people off your back."

"So, Ian's not a liability?" Coco asked.

"We have a good shot at this if you guys do well tomorrow. That's all I can say," the Ambassador said.

Ian looked at Coco who seemed a little more calm. "Thanks, Kim."

The Ambassador spoke again. "One more thing. Do you think this Su Myat and Cairncross have any more tricks? They must be desperate."

"Su Myat is a very determined person," Coco said. She won't give up until she's dead. Their project is dead and her husband is under a cloud. But just screwing Project Zafar may be enough for her. And her Chinese backers. I'm sure she's offered the MPs money."

"Well, if your testimony goes well, Zafar goes through. And we'll get visas for all these guys' family members. Thugs that they are. I just had the chance to read over their files. One of these guys ordered an entire village to be burned down. With everyone in it."

Coco spoke. "I'm sure he did it with the best of intentions." Coco bit her lip, the cynicism perhaps even too much for her. "They are all bastards. What can I say, Kim. Myanmar is changing. That's the good news."

"Let's hope so," the Ambassador replied.

Ian spoke. "You made this hearing possible, Kim. Mission accomplished. Only the families go to the US. We didn't break any US laws. "

"I hope not," Kim replied. "By the way Coco, how is your husband?"

"Thank you for asking. I have to say he could die any time. I must rush back to Yangon right after the hearing tomorrow."

"I'm sorry."

Coco was sad. "He had a good life. And, by Burmese military standards anyway, he was a good man."

"I would agree with that," said the Ambassador. "Ian, let me know how the hearing goes." She clicked off.

Ian noted the flexibility of Coco's character. She could be fucking him with wild abandon one moment and crying for her husband the next.

"We do have another problem," Coco said. "I'm not sure who's behind it. That's got me worried."

"What's that," Ian said.

"At our hearing tomorrow," Coco said quietly, "My sources have informed me that some monk is going to show up at the hearing and burn himself to death in opposition to Project Zafar. Right in front of us."

Chapter Twenty-Four

People want economic development first and foremost. The leaders may talk something else. You take a poll of any people. What is it they want? The right to write an editorial as you like? They want homes, medicine, jobs, schools.

Lee Kuan Yew,
former Prime Minister of Singapore

They were in what amounted to a small auditorium. In the front sat the five parliamentarians. Facing them at a long table were Ian, Coco and Advaita Chatterjee. Coco's attire was fastidiously demur and Burmese, with a blue floral pattern longyi, sandals and a simple necklace with a Burmese jade pendant. Not the extravagant necklace she had recently worn for her meeting with Ambassador Walsh. Ian was wearing a standard Brooks Brothers light Wall Street blue pinstriped suit, which he actually hated and normally wore as little as possible. And a striped tie. Advaita Chatterjee sported a more European look with a double breasted Armani sport jacket that must have been really hot outside of air conditioning. Ian thought he looked great but Coco had argued with him the night before. She thought he should wear more traditional Indian attire. He wasn't a Chetty, and Coco wanted to emphasize the Indian side of Project Zafar. But Chatterjee insisted he never dressed that way and wasn't going to start now. Ian couldn't understand the argument. He just assumed Chatterjee's darkish Bengali face would make him look Indian enough. The original plan was for the General to sit with them but of course now that was not possible. In his stead, Coco brought a large framed photo of her husband in his full military uniform, handsome and standing erect, taken when he was head of the armed forces. She placed this photo prominently on the empty chair next to her.

Behind Coco, Ian and Advaita, on both sides were seated gaggles of reporters, both foreign and from Myanmar. A large portrait of Myanmar's President graced the back wall, along with an even larger portrait of Bogyoke Aung San, the country's Founding Father. In one corner of the room, was a large seated statue of the Buddha, accompanied by flowers and a plate of fresh mangos and oranges.

Coco, Ian and Avaita had prepared written testimonies, accompanied by PowerPoint presentations. Coco had the testimonies translated into Burmese for the five parliamentarians, all of whom had recently put up websites partly in English. But, in at least three cases, Coco knew they really could not function in English. Piles of English and Burmese copies were available at the door for the media.

The plan was for Coco to open the presentation and then be followed by Ian and Advaita. Using PowerPoint, she would show the listeners pictures of gleaming LNG tankers and floating LNG platforms. She would emphasize the benefits to Myanmar and the absence of major environmental concerns, since unlike the Chinese pipelines in the north, Zafar would not require overland pipelines. She would also emphasized that, based on their study, there was probably such a large quantity of gas and oil available not only in the Zafar block but in other promising nearby blocks that there would be a surfeit of oil and gas for the country for the foreseeable future. She would emphasize that Myanmar would get a hefty percent of the revenues off the top. Coco would paint a picture of Myanmar becoming a rich Persian Gulf state, more advanced in thirty years than Singapore. *Ian had to admit Coco had a gift for bullshit.*

Ian's major task in the presentation was twofold. The first was to give his listeners a global perspective and convince them that Myanmar would be making a mistake by leaving its gas and oil in the ground now. As an investment manager and former Harvard finance professor, he would draw on his expertise to argue that Myanmar would be better off monetizing at least some of its energy assets now rather than later. The future price of hydrocarbon assets was uncertain in the long run. Technology breakthroughs such as horizontal drilling and fracking could actually drive the price of natural gas down in real terms over time. LNG prices and natural gas prices in general were not the same around the world at the present time. But advances in LNG transport were likely to equalize them in the long run. The law of one price was an iron law of economics that was being enforced by globalization and technology. Better for Myanmar to diversify with vast storehouses of gas, oil and monetary reserves. His Sovereign Wealth Fund would be the proper vehicle for the monetization of some of Myanmar's hydrocarbon assets and creating those monetary reserves for the future.

His second point was to emphasize his integrity. All investments by the Sovereign Wealth Fund would be outside of Myanmar in major global corporations. There would be no investing in domestic entities of politically favored Myanmar cronies. Completely transparent financial reports would be prepared on a quarterly basis. At this point he was totally dependent on the US State Department to keep the trace of a Dollar Defense scandal away from him. Of course he wouldn't be mentioning that in his presentation.

Advaita's major task was to emphasize the financial commitment that his company and the Indian government were making to Project Zafar. And the big technological breakthroughs that his company had made lowering the cost of floating liquid natural gas. But he had a third mission. Some of the listeners might be suspicious of Coco because she was ethnically Chinese. Some Burmese were already unhappy with the Chinese influence in their country. Chatterjee embodied the Indian connection to this project.

The hearing began with an introduction by the head of the Committee. He gave a twenty minute speech about how the future prosperity of Myanmar was his only concern. The speech of course was in Burmese. Coco turned to Ian and Advaita, who of course couldn't understand and whispered. "So far so good, just political crap."

Ian sat nervously looking around. He did not relish the prospect of a burning monk. Coco had concluded that the monk might be another trick from Su Myat. If so, the monk would be "rescued" before lighting himself up.

If not, and the monk was genuine and really went up in flames, Project Zafar would at best be delayed significantly and at worst canceled. And maybe everyone in the room would go up in flames. Myanmar was a Buddhist country and the monks were a political force to be reckoned with. In her presentation, Coco was going to include a special contribution for the repair of some pagodas in North Myanmar that were right near the Chinese pipelines.

It was the Project Zafar's team's turn to begin its presentation. Coco began. But she didn't get far. A scream let loose from the back of the room. A monk, in a dark purple robe, had entered. A second monk was dousing him with some kind of fluid which had to be gasoline. Its smell was filling up the room. The monk began shouting in Burmese. The media turned their attention to him, snapping photos and surrounding him. Burning monks sold more newspapers than lectures about hydrocarbons.

Ian grabbed Coco's arm. "That monk is one of the men who chased me into the Sule Pagoda. And was with Cairncross yesterday. He's got that red birthmark on his forehead. And the other monk looks familiar too."

"You're sure?" Coco asked.

"Completely sure."

"So he's a fake. He doesn't plan to burn."

Coco stood up and started walking slowly towards the monk. She pulled out the cigarette lighter that she always had with her, lit it up and held it high in the air. Then she screamed, first in Burmese, then in English for the benefit of the foreign media. "Project Zafar has been sent by the Buddha for Myanmar! I am prepared to sacrifice my life for it. My dear reverend, we can die together." She walked slowly, staring intently at the 'monk.' She repeated, "Let us die together!" The monk's eyes opened wide and he began shaking. Coco took another step. She was getting dangerously close to him. The smell of gasoline permeated the air. The monk and Coco could go up at any time. The reporters began edging back, still snapping Coco, but not wishing to be part of the barbecue. All eyes were on her. Then the monk suddenly turned and ploughed into the crowd of reporters that had formed behind him. He didn't want to be part of the barbecue either. The reporters pushed him down. Coco screamed, again first in Burmese, then in English. "Arrest this man and that other man as well. They are not a monks! They have insulted our country and our religion!" Suddenly Security officers appeared and dragged away the two monk imposters. Coco returned to her chair.

"You have the balls of an elephant," Ian murmured.

Her hands were shaking. "I need a cigarillo."

"There's no smoking in here," Ian said, putting his hand on her arm. "There's still a gasoline smell."

"I don't give a fuck. Women in Burma smoke cigars. You said so yourself. I need one now."

Ian looked up. The doors to the conference room had been opened. The gasoline fumes were going.

"Okay, smoke," Ian said, after a slight hesitation.

Coco pulled out a cigarillo from her briefcase and lit up, ignoring the "NO SMOKING" sign in English at the back of the room. Her hands settled down.

"How did those fake monks get in here in the first place?' Ian asked.

"They bribed the guards no doubt," Coco said.

Advaita had been watching all this with a cool detachment. "This beats anything in India for drama," he said. "I thought we were all going up there for a moment. Coco, you were amazing."

The Committee Chairman asked Coco if she wished to continue or delay the presentation. Coco said she was ready as soon as she finished her cigarillo. The Chairman announced a fifteen minute recess.

The presentation once it resumed could not have gone more smoothly. The Zafar team had expected tough questions that might interrupt the presentation, but the Parliamentarians sat obediently like good students and had no questions. After the fake monks' threatened incineration and exposure for fraud, nobody had it in them for further histrionics.

Just as the presentation reached the scheduled Q&A section, an urgent message lit up on Coco's iPhone. It was from Doctor Farnsworth. "Your husband only has a few hours."

Coco then relayed this message to the Chairman and asked him if she could take leave before the hearing ended. The Chairman polled his fellow Parliamentarians, inquiring if all their concerns had been answered. All the Parliamentarians replied affirmatively . The committee then took a vote and unanimously agreed to recommend to the President that final approval be given to Project Zafar and that the President sign the PSC at his earliest convenience. Zafar was going to happen.

Coco stood up with her hand on her husband's portrait. The effect was quite dramatic and the reporters snapped away with their cameras. Ian picked it up and carried it out of the room as they left. Ian couldn't believe how well things had turned out for Project Zafar, if not for the General. The Project Zafar team then flew back to Yangon in Ian's private jet.

Coco got back in time to hold her husband's hand just before he passed away.

Chapter Twenty-Five

And, for an instant, she stared directly into those soft blue eyes and knew, with an instinctive mammalian certainty, that the exceedingly rich were no longer even remotely human.

— William Gibson,
Count Zero

Ian and Ambassador Walsh were sitting together in the ground floor restaurant at the Fullerton Hotel right off Singapore's Marina Bay. They were waiting the arrival of Clarence Whittle. The Ambassador had arranged the meeting.

"Whittle told me he would be a little late and to go ahead and order a club sandwich for him," the Ambassador said.

"This guy thinks he's so important," Ian said. "Well, order a club sandwich for me too." The Ambassador called the waitress over, a brown Malay woman with a green headscarf. She ordered three club sandwiches.

Kim had preferred to meet in the American Embassy, but Ian would have none of it. He didn't want to be in what he now regarded as enemy territory. Even now he couldn't be sure the Ambassador could really protect him. The Fullerton, which sits between the Singapore River and Marina Bay, was a favorite of Ian's and a Singapore landmark. The original building was built in the 1920s and included neo-classical features such as fluted Doric colonnades. Its original primary user was the post office. Ian often marveled at how the colonials, in what was a tiny outpost at that time, could write so many letters as to require such a large and magnificent post office. The Fullerton has had its admirers over the years. The occupying Japanese during WWII – certainly discriminating users – took over the Fullerton as their general headquarters.

More recent restorations had turned the building into one of Singapore's iconic buildings.

Ian felt more comfortable sitting out in plain view. It turned out that just as Ian and Ambassador Walsh sat waiting, the middle aged couple next to them had a little dispute which got quite loud for a few moments. It seemed that the man received a call on his iPhone from someone who might have been his girlfriend. His wife, who was sitting opposite him, registered her disapproval, screaming curses in English and what sounded to Ian like some Chinese dialect he couldn't place. Finally, the man got up and left, followed by his wife who didn't stop screaming at him.

"She was yelling in Fukienese," the Ambassador said. "I speak Mandarin but I understand some Fukienese. That's a regional dialect. I think she was threatening to cut off the gentleman's gonads."

"At least she didn't shove a gun in his ribs," Ian added. He looked at his iPhone. Whittle was already ten minutes late. "Are you sure Whittle won't show up with a gaggle of goons?"

"If he does, they'll have to take me with them. No, I'm sure he won't do that."

Ten minutes later Whittle arrived. He offered a cursory "sorry I'm late." Whittle glared at Ian as he sat down. His opening remarks were not friendly. "Don't think you're so smart. It's just a matter of how and when with you. We're going to get you one way another."

Ian smiled. "Nice seeing you again, Clarence. How'd you like Yangon?"

"You call me Mr. Whittle, or I'll break your head right here." That was a threat that the muscular Whittle could undoubtedly make good on.

The Ambassador spoke. "Let's start this meeting on a civilized basis. Mr. Whittle, I think you have a proposal for Mr. Blakely. Why don't we start from there? And please speak softly. You don't want to attract any more attention than you already have."

Whittle opened his briefcase and produced a two page letter. He gave copies to Ambassador Walsh and Ian. The letters referred to the earlier documents he had presented to Ian. The message was simple. Ian's renunciation of his American citizenship was based on tax fraud. But the US government was willing to settle with Ian and dismiss the case provided he paid $100 million US dollars to the special fund to be operated by the Office of Dollar Defense.

"This is a joke, right?" Ian said after reading the document. "I've gone over this over and over with my lawyers and accountants. I have paid all the US taxes I owe. And I've talked with some senior officials here in Singapore. They will not cooperate with your attempt at my forced rendition. If you try it the government here will make this a huge embarrassment for the US. You will have stepped in a giant bucket of shit."

"Let me put this to you in another way, Mr. Blakely. I read how you have portrayed yourself in Myanmar. You're Mr. Integrity, Mr. Clean. Well if you don't pay the one hundred million, the US Government is going to go super public that you are a financial, tax evading renegade. Then what happens to your Sovereign Wealth Fund? The Myanmese – or whatever they call themselves – are going to kick your ass out of their country. And we'll be waiting."

"You're blackmailing me."

The Ambassador tried to calm things down with some small talk. "Clarence, you were with the IRS before your current assignment?"

Clarence didn't mind being called Clarence when the attractive female ambassador was the one doing the calling. "No way," Whittle replied, "I was with the FBI. And I still am. Dollar Defense is not an IRS operation. Although they cooperate with us." Whittle glared back at Ian. "I didn't come here for bullshit or small talk. Ambassador Walsh tells me that your participation in Project Zafar is furthering the interests of the United States." He turned to the Ambassador. "Well I'm here to tell you that the Office for Dollar Defense has interests which are more important to the United States than some gas pipeline in Myanmar."

"It's not a pipeline project," Ian corrected. "And just what are those interests that justify your blackmailing expats?"

"Call it whatever you like, Blakely. You pay the $100 million or you become an international renegade."

"This is bullshit," Ian said. "I'm lucky to make $100 million on Project Zafar. Forget it. Make me an international renegade. I don't give a rat's ass. My clients in the Blakely Funds will probably step up their investments. None of them are American. The US has been creating an evil empire financial image of late. You're providing me with good publicity." Ian sat back and smiled.

Kim's hand jabbed his knee under the table. *The conversation was not going the way she wanted it to.* "Perhaps," Kim said, "There is a number that could be mutually agreed upon by both sides? One hundred million seems a bit much, Mr. Whittle."

Whittle said nothing. For a few moments nobody said anything. Then he spoke to Ian. "I don't believe you want to be an international renegade." He said this slowly. "We may not get you in Singapore but we'll get you someplace. You'll always be looking over your shoulder."

"I'll take my chances," Ian said.

"You were lucky in Myanmar. Your bodyguards were at the right place, at the right time. We only have to get lucky once."

Ian couldn't believe it. *His bodyguards? So Whittle didn't know who Adrian Cairncross was and he didn't seem to know about Su Myat.* Ian looked at Ambassador Walsh. "He doesn't know?"

"No," said the Ambassador. "He hasn't asked to be briefed."

"Do you know about the Royingha?" Ian asked Whittle.

"Who are they?" Whittle said.

The Ambassador had a puzzled look on her face.

It was Ian's turn to poke Kim's knee. A liberty he had been dying to take. Ian lowered his voice and looked around to make sure nobody was listening. Then he bent over and whispered. "They are Moslems who live in Northern Myanmar. They are opposed to Project Zafar."

"So what," Whittle said.

Ian took out a piece of paper and wrote in big letters "AL-QAEDA" on it. He showed the paper quickly to Ambassador Walsh and then handed the paper over to Whittle. "Those bodyguards as you call them were their" – he pointed to the paper – "agents who wanted to kill me. Ambassador, you really haven't briefed Mr. Whittle on this?"

The Ambassador cleared her throat and then spoke. "No, we have not." She leaned over to Whittle and spoke in a whisper. "Mr. Whittle, this is a top secret matter. Project Zafar is not just about India or Myanmar. It's really about Al-Qaeda. We have been working at top secret level with Homeland Security on this. You might not be aware of this Mr. Whittle, but you saved Mr. Blakely's life in that hotel lobby in Yangon. You stopped a major Al Qaeda operation. They are determined to stop Project Zafar."

Ian was instantly impressed. Kim had picked up on his little ruse like they had rehearsed.

"You're kidding me," Whittle replied.

"I'm sure you are aware that the defeat of Al-Qaeda and its affiliates is *the* number one American priority," Kim said. "Even over chasing expats and tax evaders."

"I certainly agree with that. But where are we going with this, Kim?"

"Where are you from, Clarence?" Ambassador Walsh asked.

"Detroit. Why in hell should that matter? "

Kim reached over and put her hand on Whittle's arm. The female charm offensive was in full swing. "Clarence, I'm not trying to be condescending or patronizing. But you are in a different world out here. And believe it or not, you're like the guy who jumped out of the airplane without a parachute and lived because he landed in fifty feet of cow manure."

Ian restrained a laugh. He thought *he* was that guy.

"What do you mean?" Whittle said.

"Clarence, by threatening to expose Ian as a disreputable tax evader and trying to kidnap him, you have seriously jeopardized a top secret US security op against Al-Qaeda. But amazingly, you showed up just at the right time to save Ian's life and keep Project Zafar going. Whether you meant to be or not, you are a hero – unless you insist to the contrary -- in the war against these terrorists."

Whittle smiled. "I get it. So I'm a hero. Do I get some positive recognition for this Ambassador? Like with my Director?"

"I will personally write a special letter of commendation to be read by Director Sullivan. He's actually a friend of mine. I can assure you it will help your career."

"You'll only write it provided I ease up on money boy," Whittle said, his glare back and directed at Ian. "That's what you mean, right?"

"Precisely, Clarence. No publicity, no $100 million."

"I think this is a bullshit story, Ambassador. I think you made this up. You think I'm this dummy from Detroit."

"Clarence, I am not making this up. And for you, it's a career enhancer."

Clarence still wasn't buying. He was a man on a moral crusade. "This bastard walks out on his country, avoids paying taxes and lives la dolce vita in Singapore."

"I've done nothing illegal and I've paid a fortune in taxes as an exit tax already. I'm not apologizing for anything," Ian said.

The Ambassador put her hand on back on Whittle's arm. "Clarence, you may never get a free career boost like this again. Play the cards the way they're dealt. You've already helped your country."

Whittle shook his head no. "Kim, where I grew up to survive you needed to develop street smarts. I can't figure out how, but I think in some way you're bullshitting me. I don't believe your Al-Qaida story. It's too simple. You State Department people are clever with words."

"Clarence, I'll write this up. It will help your career. Make Ian a serious offer. Don't think too much."

Whittle wasn't happy. "He has to pay something. He can submit one of those bullshit lawyer disclaimers that he admits no guilt."

"Clarence, don't jeopardize your chance."

At that moment, the waitress in the green headscarf brought out their club sandwiches. It gave Whittle a little time to think.

"Okay, Ambassador. He pays fifty million. No publicity, no rendition, everything in confidence and in writing. And you write your letter."

"Fifty million! For what," Ian practically screamed. "This is pure protection money. The US government is in the protection racket. This is blackmail!"

The Ambassador looked at Ian. "Pay it."

"It's the principle," Ian replied. "I could invest that $50 million in something that does more for humanity than the US government."

"Fuck the principle, Ian. Pay it. Cost of business. You have no choice. Pay it and move on."

Ian hesitated for a moment, then shrugged. "This is bullshit... Okay."

"You're one smart operator, Ambassador," Whittle said. "Make sure you don't forget that recommendation." He laughed. "So now I'm a hero in the fight against Al-Qaida?"

"Don't worry. You will be a hero. The letter will be in by the time you get back to Washington."

"I want to see that letter before I go. It's not that I don't trust you but..."

"You don't trust me. Stop by the Embassy in the afternoon."

Whittle got up and left a $50 dollar Singapore note on the table. He had taken just a few bites of his sandwich. "That's for my meal," he said. "I've got another lunch." He headed out of the hotel. Tall, muscular, handsome, he attracted glances as he walked out. While the three had been talking, another middle aged Chinese couple had come and taken the table next to them. As Whittle walked by, the woman said something very loudly to her husband in Chinese while staring at Whittle.

The Ambassador began to laugh.

"What's so funny," Ian asked.

In a low voice, the Ambassador said "They're tourists from the Mainland. The Mainlanders never cease to amaze me. The woman said no Chinese alive was as big and strong as that American man. The husband then said it was because Americans grew up eating meat while the Chinese ate rice. Chinese must eat more meat in the future."

"Chinese always say that when they run into somebody bigger than they are," Ian said. "It's a national lament."

"No doubt some Chinese lady has said that while she was admiring your muscles."

Coco had said exactly that. But Ian was not going to admit it. "It certainly would make me happy if I became the object of such admiration," he said. "But I don't think I win any medals in the muscles department."

"And what is your department"? Kim asked with a flirtatious smile.

Ian normally would have had a flirtatious follow up for a flirtatious question. But this time Ian suddenly got serious. "The Blakely Funds own the stock of Monsanto. The Chinese want to eat more meat, the cows need to eat more corn and the cows don't give a shit if it's genetically modified and grown from Monsanto's seeds. I think it's a great idea. I'm doing good. I'm helping make the Chinese bigger and stronger."

Kim shook her head. "You're always thinking about stocks and money, aren't you?"

"Money can change the world for the better as much as any politician. That fifty million is exactly what I was going to put into a genomic research institute in the Philippines."

"I'm sure you can find another fifty million somewhere. Ian, whatever made you think of Al-Qaeda? That was brilliant."

Ian smiled. "What did I have to lose? You picked right up on it. We never got to rehearse. You were brilliant."

"Whittle didn't believe our story. But he got away with fifty million and he got his recommendation."

"Kim, considering how he screwed up in Yangon, he made out like a bandit. Anyway, I appreciate your doing this. I know you solved a big problem for me."

"You could say I saved you fifty million."

Ian rolled his eyes. "Thanks a lot."

"Ian, I didn't do it for you. I did it for the United States. We need to balance things here in Asia. The Chinese are the supermen. We've got to balance them. The Indians aren't in the same league as the Chinese but in Southeast Asia they're the only country resembling a superpower. Zafar is in the interest of the United States. I did my job."

"The Indians are coming up," Ian said.

"Yes, but India is a collection of countries and cultures that the British put together. China is a homogeneous organic whole that's been growing and expanding for five thousand years."

"Kim, you should write a book on this."

"I would like to but I could never do that in my current position. By the way, I do feel bad about one thing."

"Besides my fifty million? What's that?"

"Those poor Royingha," Kim said. "We sort of used them. They are one of the mistreated peoples of the world. The US is putting heat on the Myanmar government to protect the Royingha, but they tell us it's not our business. There's no serious Al-Qaeda presence there, as far as we know."

"But probably your report will circulate through the secret bowels of Washington and some poor Royingha will wind up being incorrectly classified as Al-Qaeda. Collateral damage."

Ambassador Walsh wasn't laughing. "On another subject Ian, your Dragon Lady really put on quite a show. Those pictures of her with her cigarette lighter held high in the air and then sitting there holding that goddamn cigar were too much. And then the grieving widow pictures. She's become a legend overnight. She's inherited her late husband's stature. I still don't believe how she pulled that off. She was one step away from going up in flames."

"Her cigars give me a headache," Ian replied.

"Maybe you've had to put up with them in more intimate circumstances?" The Ambassador was smiling. "Don't complain. It's like the fifty million. Sometimes you have to put up with things to get what you want." She briefly put her hand on Ian's as she said this.

"Kim, as a politician you are a natural. So what do I have to put up with you?" Ian asked.

She withdrew her hand but not her smile. "You're forbidden fruit for me. It's a cross we both will have to bear. And I don't smoke cigars even in the most intimate of moments."

"Sometimes forbidden fruits taste the best," Ian replied.

"Forbidden fruits *are* the best. But I shall refrain. Besides, let's face it. Ian, you and I think differently. And we are going in different directions."

"I'm sorry. I really am. I think under other circumstances, well, you and I could make a good team. I can even put up with your misguided view of the world."

"Am I better than some lithe and lithesome Asian lady in a longyi?"

"Lithe and lithesome. I hadn't heard that expression."

"But apt." The Ambassador smiled. "Ian, in a few months I'll be gone. Maybe to a bigger post, Russia, Nigeria, who knows. While you will be stuck in Asia making unconscionable amounts of money. Actually there is something else."

"What's that?"

"Can I trust you to hold something in complete confidence?"

"Of course."

"I have been approached by some influential people to run for the Senate in my home state of South Dakota. It's a big risk. I would have to give up my State Department career."

"Is it something you really want to do?"

"Yes. It's in politics where I think I can do the most good. My grandfather was Senator from South Dakota. Of course, he was a Republican. But I have name recognition. Our Senator Stonehill is ninety years old. He will be retiring next year. It's now or never."

"I should have googled you. I didn't know you were from a political family. But to answer your question. Go for it! Screw the risk. You are intelligent, attractive, well-educated and you have the resume. And you have the name recognition, as you say."

"This little Zafar gambit, by the way, if it goes well, will give me a nice little push. I'm being honest."

"It will go well," Ian said.

"I am going to need a lot of money if I'm going to run. Unfortunately, foreign nationals are prohibited from contributing to US political campaigns. So you are off the hook."

Ian had vowed that, unlike so many businessmen, he would never donate money to a politician with whom he disagreed. But he knew he couldn't say no to Kim if she asked. "You've already given away fifty million of my money. Of course I will contribute if it's legal."

"I suppose it's the thought that counts." She smiled.

It was Ian's turn. He reached over and for a moment held her hand.

"I will miss you," Ian said. "And I have one regret."

"What's that Ian?'

"I'm never going get to make love to you on a bathroom sink."

"Who knows?" she said smiling. "Certainly not in the Fullerton." She started to get up. "I'm late for my next meeting." But then she sat down again. "There's one more thing, which I should mention to you."

"What's that?"

"We've gotten word from our sources that there's a group of Hindu fanatics opposed to Project Zafar. Remember the Emperor Zafar was a Muslim.

This group has a history of violence. They may try to disrupt the opening ceremony. Supposedly they want to assassinate the Indian President."

Ian shook his head. "Never a dull moment in the Mysterious East. Are you sure about this?"

"Very sure. Just be careful." The Ambassador got up, shook hands with Ian and left.

Chapter Twenty-Six

Devangar Saravanan was on the phone. Ian had been waiting for his call. He wanted to talk to him about Hindu terrorists. But Devan was all excited. "Ian, the President will sign the final approval and the PSC for Project Zafar tomorrow. And not only that. Three weeks from now the President of India and the President of Myanmar will hold a ceremony at Bahador Shah Zafar's tomb in Yangon to inaugurate the project. This will be a great day for India and Myanmar."

"Devan, the American Ambassador just told me that some Hindu extremists are going to cause trouble. Zafar was a Muslim. They want to assassinate the Indian President."

"No, no. Don't worry. In India whatever you do there's always somebody opposed. It's part of our national character. The Indian government will take care of them. We know who they are. They're just a bunch of assholes from Bihar. Bihar is India's poorest state. It's the center of Hindu nationalism or the "Cow Belt" as we call it. Don't worry about this crap. We're going to make a fortune. Think about that."

"I hope you are right."

"Bahador Shah Zafar is respected by the majority of Indians and considered a nationalist in our independence struggle. He is considered a martyr against British Imperialism. His mother was Hindu Rajput. He was a very tolerant man, especially towards Hindus. He was a poet. And he is considered a Sufi saint. The Sufis were kind of mystics. Don't be such a buzzkill."

"Buzzkill? Is this another one of those Anglo-Indian words?"

"Ian, the Indian government wants this to happen. The Congress and the BJP are in favor. Those are the two national Indian parties. The President of India is a figurehead, but so what? No idiots are going to be allowed to screw this up."

"I hope you're right."

"Have you been to Bahador Shah Zafar's tomb in Yangon?"

"No."

"Well it's not exactly an architectural monument. It's really what looks like a modest size house. But you are part historian. It has great historical interest. Downstairs there are what look like several big beds with multicolored quilts. These are the tombs of the Emperor, his wife and I think another relative. I guess the body is in one of them. The house is considered a dargah. A dargah is the tomb of a Sufi saint."

"Wasn't the body accidently discovered about twenty years ago?"

"Yes, the British tried to hide it. But finally it was dug up right on the grounds of the current house. The British exiled the last Indian emperor in Burma and the last Burmese emperor in India. Your ancestors could be very nasty. Some people have suggested the two should be brought back to their home countries for reburial but apparently that's not going to happen."

"Sounds like a nice symmetrical arrangement to me. Sort of a fair trade."

"Symmetrical? Be careful. The Burmese haven't forgotten how your armies conquered their country. Neither have the Indians."

"Don't forget, Devan, the British armies were staffed by sepoys, Your ancestors."

"I told you. I'm Chettiar. We don't shoot people. We're just evil money lenders."

"I guess one crime is enough." Ian said smiled into the phone.

"This is going to be a big India/Myanmar love in. And we get rich. Oh, and by the way, Coco will personally accompany the two Presidents."

"She's certainly moved up in the world," Ian said.

"She's become a hero, almost a saint. The politicians want to be seen with her. She complains to me that she hates being called a saint. But for now that's great. I told her to play the cards the way they are dealt. She's very hot politically."

She's actually pretty hot, period, Ian thought, checking an impulse to say this aloud. Ian laughed. His mother was Catholic. He had gone to a Catholic grammar school. In the Catholic world, saints traditionally didn't go around sucking dicks and chomping on men's necks. Or making fortunes on LNG projects. But times change. *May the saints come marching in.*

Coco stared out the window at the pond. She had already decided. Man-made ponds don't last forever. She would have it filled in one day.

This hero shit was getting on her nerves. She didn't want to become President of Myanmar or become a local saint. One An San Su Kyi was enough. She just wanted to make lots of money. And travel globally. So much in the last few weeks. Project Zafar, the testimony, her husband's death and funeral, dealing with Major Nyan Myint's disappearance. She was tired.

She went back to her office and turned on the BBC news on the new TV she had just bought. The announcer, an attractive woman of obvious Indian descent and, to Coco's Americanized ears, with a really overbearing British accent, was talking about how archeologists had just dug up the bones of Richard III. He had been the last Plantagenet king and was killed in the Battle of Bosworth in 1585. "Fuck," Coco screamed aloud. She had a Richard III problem. She was really pissed.

Her iPhone beeped. She was about to become even more pissed. It was a friend of her husband's, an army guy. Another rich ex general who had made a fortune while on active duty. This General was now speculating in real estate in Yangon and reportedly making an even bigger fortune.

"Madame," he began politely in Burmese.

"Coco," she interrupted him. She was liking her chosen name more and more. The original Coco was no saint and neither was she.

"Yes, Coco, I hope things are settling down for you. We are all very proud of you. And of course we miss your husband very much."

"Things are settling down. No one will ever replace him. General Maung Myo was a towering figure. Everyone admired him."

"Yes, that is true." There was a short silence. "Perhaps this is not the best time. But I want to plant a thought with you and perhaps take some pressure off you with all your responsibilities."

"I have much to do now. That's true," Coco said. *Get to the point, asshole.*

"May I tell you something in the strictest confidence?"

"Of course."

"You should be aware that the area you live in will be redesignated for commercial use."

"I was not aware of that. I didn't know there was even a designation system."

"It's a new system. It hasn't been announced yet. But it is definite. I have this on the best authority."

"I see," Coco said. *If this son of bitch is telling me this, everybody else of any importance must already know.* All the elite were insiders in Myanmar.

"I tell you this out of respect for you and your husband. The value of your property is leaping upward. The city is expanding in your direction."

"Really."

"Yes. Well, it may be indelicate of me to mention this at this time. But I represent an investor group who wants to pay forty million in US dollars for your property. We would leave part of the house standing as a memorial to you and your husband and build a hotel. We already have a world renowned architect lined up."

"It's too soon for me to think about such things," Coco began slowly. "But I can tell you I will never sell this property. It is where my husband and I spent our married life. It has a great deal of meaning for me." *Plus I've got this Major buried under my pond.* She began to cry. She had gotten good at crying when it was required. "I don't need the money. Honor counts for more than money. But thanks anyway."

"I'm sorry to upset you. But if you ever change your mind, give me a call."

Coco slammed the iPhone down on the desk. Fortunately it didn't break. Its gorilla glass face glass was not that delicate. But she was really pissed. Her husband was barely dead and the wolves were already calling about his house. But it wasn't this indelicacy that bothered her. This guy was offering her no less than forty fucking million US dollars for her house and the grounds! He wanted to turn it into hotel and tourist attraction. She was dying to take the offer. But the only answer she could ever give was NFW -- *no fucking way*. Not now, not ever. Goddamned Major Nyan Myint was buried under the pond. What would happen if somebody accidentally dug him up? She remembered watching an episode of *The Sopranos,* when she was in the US. The Mafia thugs had to dig up some murdered stiff because the property on which said stiff was buried got sold to build condos. The incriminating evidence had to be removed. But who could she trust to do that job? She couldn't call Tony Soprano. *Fucking Richard III. My kingdom for U.S. forty million?*

She was really angry. The Major was getting his revenge. *Was this some kind of fucking karma?* She would have happily taken US forty million. Actually she probably could have held her husband's friend up for more. Yangon real estate prices were going through the roof. The property the house was on was at least five hectares. And she wasn't a U. S. citizen – no capital gains tax. She could easily buy a property in London with the forty plus million U.S. Or maybe something in the south of France. The bastard—her husband's friend -- probably stole all his money anyway. No, the house had to remain in her hands until she passed on. *That sucked.*

Then Coco's Chinese business mind clicked in. Her mood brightened immediately. Things weren't so bad. She could keep the old house, convert it to a hotel herself. And build a new annex on the grounds. Great idea. She'd make sure nobody disturbed the lovely little pond in the back. Or she'd just fill it in first.

There was no rush on this. But one day she would do this.

Of course, one day maybe a few hundred years later her hotel would have to be torn down. That's the way of most modern hotels. They don't last forever. But she'd be gone. Then they could dig up the ground and build condos, or a shopping center or a new hotel or whatever. And discover the remains of Major Nyan Myint. And the Glock. And the remains of her Chanel bag. And the sanitary pads. Let them figure that out. Some forensic expert could speculate as to how the Major met his mysterious end. How he wound up with three bullets in him while dressed like a monk. The newspapers had already dug up that she was a dead shot at Brown. They could trace the Glock ownership in the United States. Of course they would think she did it. That gave her a certain satisfaction.

She lit up another cigarillo. She was going to have to give these things up. Next Chinese New Year. She turned on her computer. She started to read the Myanmar Times. Always good for laughs. The last place to look for inside information. Except her eyes alighted on something that wasn't that funny. It was a small article, easily missed:

The Ministry of Defense announced today that General Sein Soe would be resigning his position and would be taking the position of military attaché to Argentina and Uruguay. General Sein Soe said that while being so far from Myanmar would be painful, he looked forward to his new post. His wife would be accompanying him on this mission. The General and his wife, Su Myat, would be departing for Buenos Aires by the end of the week.

"Fuck," Coco said aloud, "they buried this news. But the military are letting the bastards get away with exile. The fucking military protects its own." The fake monks from the hearing had according to Coco's sources confessed to everything and provided a clear link to Su Myat and her husband. The fake monks and Adrian Cairncross were going to be tried. The fake monks including Adrian Cairncross would probably be executed for blasphemy. Or at least get life. But the Big Fish were being allowed to go into exile.

To return another day? Coco drew deep on her cigarillo. Well, what of it? Maybe Su Myat and her husband would both get Hoof and Mouth disease or *aftosa* or whatever the hell it was the cattle get down in Argentina. Project Zafar would be approved by the end of the week and everything was all set for the ceremony with the Presidents of India and Myanmar at the tomb of Bahadur Shah Zafar. She would make a fortune on Zafar. Her husband's Singapore apartment – now hers—had already doubled in value. Three commercial properties he owned in downtown Yangon were up by some greater multiple. She had convinced her husband to leave all his property to her as his daughter was unquestionably richer than he was. And she had saved his life, after all. Coco was getting everything. For a guy who always said he didn't care about money, her husband had done quite well.

Coco laughed and spoke again out loud, this time in Mandarin. "Five thousand years of Chinese history counts for something. Five thousand years of Chinese treachery. This fucking Burmese princess picked on the wrong Madama Butterfly. Next time Su Myat should find a Japanese Butterfly. Japanese women are into torture. They like to be tied up. They make better victims."

All Coco had to do was protect that pond.

Chapter Twenty-Seven

The big ceremonial day had come. The formal signing of the agreement between India and Myanmar inaugurating Project Zafar by the Presidents of India and Myanmar. The Presidents of India and Myanamar were going to visit Bahadur Shah Zafar's tomb and hold the signing ceremony there. Coco and Advaita would accompany the Presidents.

Ian, Coco, Advaita and Devan had assembled in Ian's suite at the Strand. A limo was to pick them up and take them to the old Secretariat where they would be included in the Presidents' motorcade which would take them to the tomb. They had discussed leaving Devan in the hotel, but Coco insisted he come. "Enough with this Chetty crap," she had argued.

"How do I look?" Coco said to the three men. Coco was outfitted as a demure Burmese maiden with a green flower colored longyi and sandals. But with a few accessories. Starting with a beautiful green jade stone hung from a gold chain. And matching gold jade bracelets, earrings and a gold ring with another giant jade stone. "It's Myanmar jade, dark green as you can see. I just got it. I found a new Yangon designer who did the whole thing. I'm going to make her a star."

"You look great. But didn't you already have a jade necklace from Myanmar?" Ian asked.

"Now I have two," Coco said.

"Coco," Devan said, "Isn't this look a little too luxurious for Myanmar? After all, you're now considered a saint in some quarters."

"Fuck this saint bullshit. That's not the image I want."

"And what, pray tell, Madame, is the image you want?" Advaita asked smiling.

"Coco Chanel of course. And Eva Peron or Sheryl Sandberg. I want the women of this country to look up to me, to want to aspire to something more. I'm no Mother Theresa. She can stay in India and help the poor. We want to get rid of the poor here in Myanmar."

"You're not the next Mother Theresa nor were you meant to be. That's for sure," Advaita said.

Coco looked at him with her curved grin. " You got that line from someplace. You Indians are always so clever with words."

"I'm Indian. I haven't the foggiest notion what you are talking about," Devan said.

Ian rolled his eyes. "T.S. Eliot."

Coco looked at Advaita. "At Brown I had to read *The Selected Works of American Feminists*. I don't remember anybody named T.S. Eliot. Was she a woman? " She looked at Ian. "Or was he a dead white guy?"

Ian shrugged. "It doesn't matter," he said. He shook his head. *To think Coco graduated Phi Beta Kappa*. Then he spoke. "Can we focus on the subject at hand and put off the literary discussion for another time? Coco and Advaita are going to be accompanying the Presidents of Myanmar and India. That's what we should be thinking about."

Coco took out an outlandish set of sunglasses and put them on. "It's going to be sunny today. What do you think?"

"Are you really going to wear those?" Ian asked.

"Of course. They are the latest D&G. Am I supposed to squint?"

Ian smiled. "Coco, okay, you can be Eva Peron or Coco Chanel. But those glasses? I don't know. They project a Dragon Lady image. A teenage Dragon Lady. Maybe something a little more mature and less outlandish?"

"Evita wore sunglasses. I've seen pictures of her with them on."

Ian replied. "Couldn't you wear transparent ones where we could at least see your eyes? Already we have to deal with that New York magazine article." A female former classmate of Coco's at Brown had just done a nasty article on her for the New York Magazine entitled, "Myanmar's New Dragon Lady." Ambassador Walsh had called Ian to express her unhappiness with the article.

"Ian, I told you that bitch hates me. I stole her boyfriend in college. She's never forgotten. All this stuff about Dragon Ladies is racist. A figment of horny Western prejudices. I'm going to wear these glasses. I will not be the demure Madama Butterfly of your fantasies."

"Madame Butterfly was Japanese," Devan said.

"Chinese, Japanese, Vietnamese, Burmese. We all look alike to you. You, Devan, have an 'ese' problem."

"You do look alike," Devan said, in a serious tone.

"But you are all so beautiful. The women I mean," Ian added, smiling. "That's why God made so many of you. He was so pleased."

"*She* was so pleased." Now Coco was smiling. "You are all male racist pigs. At Brown my Woman's Empowerment Group would castrate you both for those remarks."

"They would castrate us anyway. They don't need a reason," Ian said. "Getting back to the sunglasses. This is politics. I read somewhere that Jack Kennedy never liked Jackie to wear sunglasses in public."

Ian had gotten lucky. Coco was a big admirer of Jackie Kennedy. Another one of her female heroes. She loved Jackie's style. "Really?" she said. She reached into her bag and took out another pair of semi-transparent, a little less outré, sunglasses. She took off her D&Gs and put on the new ones. "This better?"

Ian laughed. "You fill up your bag with a backup pair of sunglasses? Yes, they are better."

"It's not a bag. It's a clutch. A Marc Jacobs. I bought it in Singapore. A bargain." She smiled. "I knew you would hate the other glasses."

Advaita interjected. "I think Madame looks perfect. Shall we go downstairs. Our car is ready."

Ian was nervous. He was sitting in a car that was part of a short motorcade procession that had originated at the old Secretariat and ended at the tomb. Devan was in the car too. He consoled himself that in modern Myanmar they don't shoot Chettys anymore.

Ian hadn't gotten the idea of Hindu terrorists out of his head. The Ambassador had called him again to warn him. "Something is going to happen," Kim insisted. Be careful." Of course she was there too. In a car directly behind the Presidents. She made sure the press took *her* picture. *Would they like this in South Dakota?*

Ian's eyes darted out the car window looking for snipers. The sound of the sirens of the accompanying police escorts didn't help his nerves. But all he saw were crowds of people in longyis, and dirty looking children gawking at the passing cars. And the occasional monk. *Real ones, he hoped.*

Up ahead in an open lead car, accompanied by Coco and Advaita, were the Presidents of India and Myanmar. The open car seemed like insanity to Ian, but politicians everywhere like to reach out to their people. Coco and Advaita didn't need to reach out to anyone.

The procession was winding its way to a special ceremony at the tomb. The tomb wasn't that far from the Secretariat but the procession was strictly for show. Only the Presidents, Coco, Advaita and selected media representatives would be allowed into the building. Its small size limited occupancy. Chairs had been set up outside the building for honored guests, and loudspeakers were positioned so that the guests could hear the Presidents' speeches.

Ian sat still, his eyes searching the nearby trees for snipers. It turned out there were some people in the surrounding trees. But no snipers, just children.

So far. The hot sun boring down on the honored guests. Crows cawed overhead. Then the speeches began.

It was as if the two Presidents' speeches were written by the same person. The speeches – both partly in English – went on and on about the evils of British Imperialism, and how British armies had despoiled ancient traditions and ancient monarchies. And how the hereditary monarchs of both countries had died torn from their native lands. "So much blood was shed by the rapacious British," said the President of Myanmar. "But now, the peoples of Myanmar in the future will be linked by Project Zafar. And they will go forward as equals and brothers and not be manipulated by a colonial power," said the President of India. One good anti-colonialist tirade deserved another.

This was too much for Ian who whispered to Devan, "I thought this project was a blow to the Chinese, not the British. As far as I know, the Brits aren't coming back."

"It's all very nineteen fifties," Devan said. "All this anti- colonial stuff. It's like an old song from when we were young. We love hearing it again and again. Anyway, British, Chinese—they all look alike. We can't tell them apart."

Ian resumed scanning the trees.

But the ceremony went off as planned. No incidents, no terrorists. The highlight of the ceremony was not actually the speeches by the two Presidents but rather the marching display put on by a contingent of Indian soldiers. The soldiers were borrowed for the occasion from the famous marching Indian Border Force at the Wagah border crossing with Pakistan. The Indians kicked their legs high in the air, engaged in what could qualify as Olympic gymnastics, and exuded a self confidence that inspired the crowd. A crack contingent of soldiers from Myanmar performed too, but they were definitely outmarched by the Indians. *At last India wins at something,* Ian thought.

Project Zafar had the blessing of the two governments.

It was only a few hours later, celebrating at a small party in his hotel room, that Ian learned that Hindu fanatics had shot and killed two custodians at the tomb of Bahador Shah Zafar in India. The tomb Bahador Shah Zafar never got to occupy.

Chapter Twenty-Eight

Pleasure is none, if not diversified.

— John Donne

Ian was at a lunch in Singapore, listening to a boring speech on ASEAN economic integration. The speech was about to end. He glanced at his iPhone. An SMS from Kim Walsh. Could he come to her office at 2:30? He could just make it. He wondered what she wanted. She had announced that she was leaving the State Department to run for Senate the following year in South Dakota. He had attended a formal party in her honor two nights before. It was a nice function but he had no opportunity to talk to her alone.

Twenty minutes later his car pulled up to the American Embassy. The Embassy is set back from the road with a high fence around it and built fortress style like all the new American embassies. Terrorist bombs, typhoons, earthquakes—all had their work cut out for them here.

He entered the front gate and his identification was checked out by the Marine guard. He went through a metal detector and two additional identification checks after he actually entered the building. Finally he was just outside Kim's office. Her secretary, a white middle aged American woman, then signaled for him to go in.

Kim was standing behind her desk. Her office was quite large – much larger than Ian's – and had the usual paintings of Obama and the Secretary of State on the walls. The carpet was lush and the couch and furniture did not have the usual government-issue look. She herself was fashionably but casually dressed in a black skirt that covered her knees and an off white blouse. Ian immediately noticed that, uncharacteristically, she wasn't wearing a bra.

Kim came around her desk. "Thanks for coming," she said. She took his hand. "I'm still getting compliments from Foggy Bottom regarding Project Zafar and how well things turned out."

"That's great," Ian said. "Your help was crucial." He was wondering why he was there and why she was holding his hand. And not wearing a bra.

"I have a little present for you," she said. "A going away present."

"But you're the one going away. You're the one supposed to be getting the present.'

"If you live up to your reputation, you'll be delivering your own present."

She took Ian's hand and escorted him into an adjoining room. Ambassadors it seems have their own bathroom. At least Kim Walsh did. She pulled Ian into the bathroom, turned the latch to lock the door and then leaned back on the sink. She unbuttoned the two top buttons on her blouse. "As head of the embassy here, I've reviewed your request to fuck me in a bathroom. Your application has been approved," she said in her always authoritative voice.

"I just died and went to heaven," Ian replied, as his hands immediately got to work. He finished the unbuttoning. Off came the blouse. Ian couldn't help but notice the Ann Taylor label. He pulled up her skirt. She wasn't wearing underpants. No bra, no underpants, Kim had come undressed for the occasion. He pulled the skirt straight up over her head. She pulled off Ian's clothes with such eagerness that she ripped off one of the buttons on his shirt. He grabbed her by her butt, held her up and she wrapped around him.

Twenty minutes later they were done. They were dressing. Ian was exhausted. "Holding you up by the butt for twenty minutes is a job for a younger man," he said.

She laughed. "You performed as required. They don't have beds in bathrooms. It was your choice of venue."

"Indeed."

"I'm going to miss you, Ian. But I'm pursuing my life's dream," she said. Her blue eyes were suddenly sad. They showed she was really hurting. That she was attracted to Ian. But that's the way life was.

"I'll miss you too, Kim. But I can't move to South Dakota. Or Washington. And you couldn't get elected dogcatcher in South Dakota with me by your side." Ian was hurting too, although maybe not quite as much. He had already resigned himself to her leaving.

"Ian, tell me one thing. That Indian fellow, Devan, told me that Coco had strongly pressed for you to be involved with the Zafar project. How did she come to select you?"

Ah the painting. It still has to be a secret. "I don't know. She could have picked so many other money managers."

They walked out of the bathroom and sat down on the Ambassador's big couch. Ian didn't want to leave just yet. Kim didn't want him to leave just yet.

"I am going to set up a foundation," Kim said. "It would contribute to Native American higher education. In South Dakota and nearby states. Foreigners can contribute to that. It's legal. It will look good politically. Anyway it's something I would like to do."

Ian laughed, while fingering the ripped spot on his shirt where the button was. "That was an expensive trip to the bathroom. But I'll put in a million. That should help you get started."

"Thank you so much." She leaned over and gave him a peck on the cheek.

"On another subject, have you ever heard of a Chinese painter named Wang Qiang?" Kim asked.

Where was she going with this, Ian wondered. "Yes, the one who was murdered."

"It seems he was an art professor at the Rhode Island School of Design. He was kicked out for recruiting young students as models and then having affairs with them. Some of his paintings were pretty sexy and pretty realistic. Nudes and all."

"Why a you telling me this?" Ian asked, holding his breath.

"Of course we did a background check on Coco. Brown is right next to the Rhode Island School of Design. It seems she was one of his models. Did he do any paintings of her that she or her late husband might be embarrassed by now?"

"She hasn't mentioned any," he lied. "She doesn't embarrass easily." He was hoping that there was nothing more than female jealousy that was driving these comments. Any way to make Coco look bad. "Does this make any difference now? Who's going to care?"

"Probably nobody," the Ambassador said.

She leaned over and gave Ian a long and tender kiss.

They both knew. Ian would be bad for her career.

Chapter Twenty-Nine

A Year Later...

Coco wasn't looking forward to the day's event. But she felt like it was something she had to do. She stood looking out at the pond in the back of the house. The two lotus plants she had placed in the pond were doing really well. One pink, one white, their flowers commanded attention and no doubt brought down blessings on those visiting the pond. The lotus of course is revered by Buddhists and Hindus alike. A floral testimony to the Major who lay secretly below? Coco had placed the lotus plants in pots so their rhizomes – their root system – could not spread out over the pool lining and damage it. But sooner or later the pool would have to go. No need to rebuild it, no unnecessary digging. The lotus plants and the goldfish, that had made the pond their home, would unfortunately close out their days with the pond.

The Army, after a year of investigating, had decided to declare Major Nyan Myint legally dead. The suspicion remained that General Sein Soe and his wife had somehow done in the Major. But the Army didn't want a scandal. And the late General Maung Myo, his reputation enhanced in death, and his wife, Coco, her courage displayed the year before with the raised cigarette lighter, were heroes.

Coco was holding a memorial ceremony for the Major in her house in Yangon. Assembled in her main living room were Major Nyan Myint's wife, his two girls, ages eight and ten, several Army officers, a senior Buddhist monk and several reporters. Ian, who happened to be in Yangon attending a Zafar Board meeting, had accepted Coco's invitation to attend. A giant picture of the Major was placed on a table in the front of the room with flowers and rice and fruit placed before the picture. All attendees were hand a little scroll with a Buddhist prayer written on it. This ceremony wasn't supposed to be a funeral – a full scale Burmese funeral can take a week – but in some ways it resembled one.

The ceremony began with the monk offering prayers. As the monk prayed, Coco again looked out the window towards the pond. She wondered if the Major could hear what was going on. Lately it had started to get worse. There were nights when she couldn't sleep. Nights when she thought the Major, like a zombie would come crawling through her window. Like a zombie he would arise in the darkness, bullet hole in his head. She would have laughed at this at Brown but her Asian heritage was stronger than she thought. She was no different from her husband and all the other Asians. She was afraid of ghosts. One particular ghost.

It was Coco's turn to speak. She had at her side a Chanel bag like the one she had hidden the Glock in that night. But no Glock. Bullets have no power against ghosts. Or at least they don't in the movies. And she wore a new pair of the same cheap high heeled shoes. They looked a little incongruous with her longyi. Of course only she knew the significance of this.

She stood up and, speaking in Burmese, looked mostly at the Major's wife and children.

"Major Nyan Myint was a great man," Coco began, "loyal to his family, loyal to my husband. I can think of so many times when my husband relied on him – his intelligence, his honesty, his courage. I'm sure whatever has happened to him has been in the service of his country."

She looked directly at the children. "You can be very proud of your father. Nobody knows this, but the Major once saved my husband's life from assassins who had come to kill him. Enemies of the Burmese people. The Major said it was just his duty. It had to remain secret for security reasons so I will say no more." Actually nobody knew about this because Coco had just made this up. She turned again to the children. "Your father was a very brave man. You can be very proud. In your father's honor, and on behalf of my husband, I am setting up a special trust valued at four hundred thousand US dollars for your education, here or abroad. Mr. Ian Blakely will manage the trust. By the time you are ready for college, God willing it should have appreciated substantially. As young women coming into a world different from that of your father, you will have the opportunity to do something great to make your father proud."

The two little girls looked up at Coco, smiles on their faces. Coco was happy the Major's children were girls. Not because of any feminist inspired prejudices. Rather Coco felt that as females they would be less likely to want to revenge their father. She forgot that ladies could be good with a Glock.

The Major's wife began crying and came up to thank Coco. She knelt down before her. Coco held her hands. For the first time in her life she felt genuine shame. The hypocrisy of it all was too much. Coco looked out the window. She fully expected the Major to come through. Then she felt anger and impatience at herself. *Why am I letting this bother me? It was me or him. Four hundred thousand for his fucking kids. That should be enough.*

After the event was over, Ian approached Coco.

"I know you don't want me to ask. But what really happened to the Major?" Ian asked. "I know he was spying on you in Singapore. I'm not stupid. And that time he rescued me from Adrian Cairncross in the temple? That was too cute. He was an enemy, was he not?"

Coco's eyes were cold. "It was me or him. I shot him before he could shoot me."

Ian didn't need to know the details. "It was either you or him. Better not you."

Her face changed. Tears suddenly welled up behind her sunglasses. "He's buried out under the pond."

"So he's not coming back," Ian said.

"He comes back in my dreams. He's a fucking evil *Nat*."

"What's a *Nat*?" Ian asked.

"It's a Burmese thing," Coco replied. "I can't explain. Burmese believe in a spirit world filled with *Nats*."

"That's something I didn't know."

"I hate this house," Coco said. "He comes in through the windows. I have nightmares."

"I thought you said you didn't believe in all this Asian fear of dead people."

Coco caste her head down. "I'm not as tough as I thought."

The next day the newspapers carried stories praising the outstanding generosity of Madame Maung Myo.

And pictures of the widow of Major Nyan Myant, on her knees, thanking Coco. .

Chapter Thirty

A Year and a Half Later...

A slim Anita sporting a tight new miniskirt walked into Ian's office. Anita was now a young mother of a young baby boy. It had taken her awhile to regain her old shape.

"Wow. You look really hot again," Ian said. The Blakely organization was not a politically correct U S bank. Ian could say whatever he pleased. And Anita could wear whatever she pleased.

Anita beamed. "Thank you."

Ian had just finished a meeting with a company CEO. Anita was smiling and handed Ian a sheet of paper. "This just came off of Bloomberg. I think you're going to like this."

Ian began reading.

Supreme Court Declares Executive Order 99,876 Unconstitutional

In a unanimous decision just announced, the Supreme Court declared significant portions of Executive Order 99,876 to be unconstitutional. It declared that the President and the Office for Dollar Defense had no authority to levy a special wealth tax on foreign holdings of US citizens or to review the tax returns of former US citizens who had properly renounced their citizenship and complied with all the requirements of the Internal Revenue Service. All taxes and penalties levied in this regard must be returned to the individuals involved and all penalties, renditions or other punitive acts must cease. The Court, however, did not invalidate the prohibitions on the holding of gold or bitcoins.

"Anita, this means I get my fifty million dollars back."

"The United States is a country of laws," Anita said. "After all. It's still number one in the world as far as I'm concerned."

"This is a big deal. The Court did its job. That doesn't happen in most countries. I have to say that any obituary for the United States is a little premature."

"But you left."

"I'm a special case. I needed a bodyguard in America. And I love Singapore."

"Singapore wouldn't exist without its umbrella of American support."

"Anita, come on. That's an exaggeration. At any rate this Supreme Court ruling isn't perfect. The gold and bitcoin prohibition stands. Franklin Roosevelt by executive order banned the holding of gold in 1933. He got away with it. I guess the Court was bound by that precedent."

"So what are you going to do with all that loot?" Anita asked. "You could give it to some charity. It's sort of a windfall. You never expected to get it back."

"Charity? If you mean handouts to poor people, never. No. I'm going to give it to that genomics institute in the Philippines. I can't imagine a better use for this money which would help humanity more. Or Asia. Biotech is at the cusp of major breakthroughs. Extending life, improving health, raising agricultural productivity, raising intelligence. Nothing against the Mother Theresas of this world, but this genomics institute will be a better use of this money."

Anita laughed. "So Mother Theresas need not apply."

"Well, actually now that you mention, I will give another million to Senator Walsh's foundation."

"She did help you, didn't she?"

"Yes. But I follow my own ideals. I don't care what anybody thinks. And this institute will provide venture capital ideas for our new biotech fund."

Anita laughed again. "Help yourself by helping others."

"Why not?"

"So, who's going to run Blakely biotech fund?"

"Sorry. I forgot to mention. They just accepted last night. That young Indian professor who visited here last week and his Chinese wife. He has Ph.D. in biology from Yale. She has an M.S. in computer science and an MBA, both from Carnegie Mellon."

"Congratulations. They are brilliant," Anita said.

Ian couldn't resist teasing Anita. "You told me you thought he was handsome. For an Indian, that is. You said that's why he was able to get a Chinese wife. Even if he was a little dark."

Anita laughed. "From her picture she's a little mousy looking. But in person she looks better."

"My, my. You women can be so sexist when you want to be."

Anita just smiled.

"I don't care if she's got only one eye and a wooden leg," Ian said. "She's brilliant and so is he. If I were starting over and their age, I would get degrees in biology and computer science. Screw financial history. Technology is accelerating at an accelerating rate. Science is exploding. And Asia has joined the party. All of Asia."

"Viva capitalismo!" Anita said.

Ian ignored her. "Each group brings its own pluses and minuses. The top Indians have a special advantage. They are always arguing, always thinking. Chinese have to labor under the Confucian yoke of obedience. The Confucian ethic fits in well with the Communist one party state's desire to control. Admittedly, China with its Confucian discipline has done a great job at building roads and airports and apartments and catching up with the West. Certainly better than India. But going forward, China may be at a disadvantage in a global knowledge society, where information needs to be free. Luckily, China is filled with bright, hard-working people."

Anita rolled her eyes. "You can't stop being a professor and giving lectures."

"Back to more important things," Ian said. "You've just about regained your old weight."

"It's good to be slim again. But my husband wants another baby."

"And you?"

"I don't know."

"But it's your civic duty," Ian said with mock solemnity. "Singapore needs more babies."

Anita rolled her eyes. "Good God. You should run for Prime Minister. Why don't *you* have a couple of babies? You can afford it."

Ian smiled. "I'll have to think about that."

"Getting back to the US," Anita said. "The world needs a US that is strong and follows the rule of law. And treats all its citizens including the poorest with justice. That is after all what Obama stands for, even if in this case he overstepped his authority. This Supreme Court decision shows the United States' strength and wisdom, not weakness."

"Can't argue with that," Ian replied. "I just wish Uncle Sam would treat the richest with justice as well."

"Nothing like a sense of moral outrage. You can lead your fellow one percenters to the barricades."

Ian laughed. "Plutocrats of the world. Unite!"

Chapter Thirty-One

Coco and Ian had slowly grown closer even as they worked together on Project Zafar and other business ventures which included a new on-line bank in Myanmar. Coco usually stayed in Ian's apartment when she came up to Singapore. But tonight she said she had an extra treat for Ian and she wanted him to come to her flat. As he ascended in the elevator, memories of her opening the door just in her tiny shorts, with a dagger soon to be pointing at his crotch, filtered through his mind. He was not to be disappointed.

It was déjà vu all over again. The door to Coco's apartment was slightly ajar. Ian pushed it open. There was Coco, attired only in her half opened shorts and high heeled cage shoes. Ian raised his hands in mock fright. "No dagger, please," he said.

Coco took Ian by the hand. "Come," she said. She led Ian into the bedroom. There, leaning against the wall, in its full splendor, was *Bad Girl*, the painting of the near-naked Coco that had caused so many problems. The painting had stayed fully wrapped and hidden in the vault of Standard Commercial for two years until Ian had personally carried it over.

"I finally had to unwrap it," Coco said.

"The painting is like the girl. It yearns to be naked," Ian said.

"Here's the treat. As promised, you can look at the painting and fuck me."

Ian was standing behind her, his hands on her bare shoulders. "I dare not ask if I'm the first," he said.

"Which do you like better?" she asked. "The young slut in the painting, or the old one you have your own old lecherous hands on?"

"You look even better today than you did then."

"You're a fucking liar."

They both knew he was lying. There's something about an twenty year old girl – the tautness of her skin especially – that a now thirty three year old, no matter how beautiful, no matter luxurious the oils in which she bathes her body, cannot compete. Wang Qiang, perverted genius that he was, had caught it all, the never-to-be-duplicated, twenty year old Coco. That Coco was just too much competition.

But Ian was going to give it a try. He put his hands on Coco's face and gently let them cover her eyes. "Your eyes are as beautiful as ever," he began. "And so is your face."

She leaned back on his shoulder. "Ian, stop talking and fuck me. And bite my neck."

He complied. With the painting actually on the floor leaning against the wall, he didn't have to strain his back as he gazed at the painting. Good thing. His back had been bothering him lately. Too much sitting in front of a computer screen.

"So what are we going to do with this painting," Ian asked after he had caught his breath after their lovemaking.

"The Macau court has convicted the two triad guys of murdering Wang Qiang and his assistant," Coco said. "He owed them a great deal of money."

"Yes, I know," Ian said. "So nobody is going to connect Wang with Myanmar."

"That's good. Wang Qiang always told me my painting would be the new Mona Lisa. That I was the representative of a new age, just like she was in her day."

"You believed him, of course."

"For about a week. But I really don't want this painting to stay hidden forever. I'm really proud of it. I'm safe. They can't connect it to Myanmar."

Ian looked at her. "Maybe. You are such a bad girl."

"I am."

"But somebody may recognize you. And that would connect the painting to Myanmar. Remember what Senator Walsh told me before she left. She guessed you had posed for Wang Qiang." Ian's iPhone beeped. It was Henry Ashton. "Of all people," Ian said.

Henry sounded really excited. "Ian! I know this is bragging but it's good news for you too."

"Tell me."

"Remember my Wang Qiang painting, *Woman in Mercedes?*"

"Of course, Henry. How can I forget it. You got there just seconds before me and snatched it away."

"I snatched it fair and square. Anyway, the casino guys have chipped in and are building a new museum in Macau. The Central Government in Beijing wants them to diversify away from gambling. They want to build a permanent collection of Wang's works. He's a local hero now. They've got loads of money. They've offered me five million US for my painting"

"Wow."

"Ian, your painting is probably worth even more. People pay for flesh. No matter what artistic bullshit they hand you about the nude being art. And besides, your painting is so representative of a new age. It's like a new Mona Lisa."

Ian could hardly keep from laughing. He hit mute on the phone and said to Coco, "Henry Ashton thinks *Bad Girl* is another *Mona Lisa*. That new museum in Macau is buying up Wang's paintings. They've offered Henry five million US for his painting."

"I want ten million," Coco said immediately. The *I told you so* look on her face took over the whole room.

"You're hopeless," Ian said." He released the mute button. "Henry, perhaps you could do me a little favor."

"Of course," Henry said.

Of course indeed. The Blakely Funds had moved substantial business to Henry's bank.

"I would prefer that my ownership of the painting remain anonymous. Could you negotiate the sale? We – I – want ten million US. Not a penny less."

"You can rely on me," Henry said. "Not a word from my mouth. I'll get back to you." Henry clicked off.

"People will be speculating who the model was for the painting," Ian said to Coco. "I don't want them to figure out it's you. If nobody knows I own it, that's safer."

"I don't want to deny I'm the model forever," Coco said looking up at him with her best cat-ate-the-canary smile. "Remember, that's my painting, not yours."

"What are you going to do with the money," Ian said. "You must be worth a hundred million anyway with Zafar and your real estate."

"We need to save for the baby," Coco said.

"The what?"

"The baby. Remember that little trip we took two weeks ago to Sri Lanka? Don't worry. We don't have to get married."

Ian took a breath. He actually liked the idea. "So I'm a father again. And you Coco…"

"Mother, slut, entrepreneur, Burmese hero…"

"And Mona Lisa," Ian added.

Chapter Thirty-Two

"That fucking bitch!" Coco said. "Those are my tits. I'm the Bad Girl." Coco was reading the *South China Morning Post* on-line. It was Sunday morning and she and Ian were relaxing after eating a breakfast of *huevos rancheros* that Ian had prepared himself.

"What's the problem?" Ian asked.

"That lying bitch Lolita Chin says she was Wang Qiang's model for *Bad Girl*. She says she's Wang Qiang's Mona Lisa. She says she was Wang's girlfriend." Lolita Chin was a B movie Cantonese actress from Hong Kong.

"Really. She does look a little like you." Ian was laughing. "Of course she isn't six months pregnant."

"Life is so unfair."

"Look, there's 1.4 billion Chinese. Not counting the overseas ones. Half are women. The Chinese are a relatively homogeneous group. There's got to be somebody out there who looks a little like you."

"Stop the bullshit," Coco said. "She sucks Wang Qiang's dick a couple of times and she gets to be Mona Lisa." Coco was pouting. It was hard to tell how serious she was. But then she smiled.

"You are already Coco. Now you have to be the Mona Lisa too?"

"Why not?" Coco replied.

Ian put his arms around her, taking care not to disturb the nicotine patch which he had finally persuaded her to wear. Coco without a cigarillo was a difficult achievement. And hugging her wasn't so easy either. Her skinny model's body made her baby bump look like a really big bump. "Darling, let it go. Now the Major's *Nat* or whatever you call it can go after Lolita Chin."

Coco's face turned serious. "I hadn't thought of that."

"Let it go. We are good for one another. We have a new world to build in Myanmar." He rubbed her giant baby bump and thought he felt a little kick. "And a child to raise."

END

Author's Bio

Peter T Treadway has had a varied career as economist, educator, money manager and novelist. Peter graduated in 1964 from Fordham College with a degree in English. He then went on to get an MBA from NYU (1967) and then a PhD in economics at the University of North Carolina at Chapel Hill (1971). He is a rare breed – an economist who can write!

Over the years since leaving Wall Street in 2001, Peter has developed a special interest in Asia and technology. He has served as an Adjunct Professor of Finance at the City University of Hong Kong and visiting professor at the Shanghai University of Finance and Economics. Peter has also presented a number of financial workshops in Southeast Asia. He is currently principal of Historical Analytics LLC, a firm dedicated to money management with a particular interest in the technology area and Asia. A regular blog entitled The Dismal Optimist is produced for clients and interested readers. In 2013 he co-authored a book, Investing in the Age of Sovereign Defaults, How to Preserve Your Wealth in the Coming Crisis. He has written two novels, the latest Coco's Gambit.

From 1965-2000 Peter had a distinguished career on Wall Street and with major American financial institutions. For example, from 1978-81 he served as Chief Economist at Fannie Mae. From 1985-1998 he served as institutional equity analyst and Managing Director at Smith Barney. He was ranked as "all star" analyst eleven times by Institutional Investor Magazine.

A resident of West Palm Beach, Florida, covid virus permitting, he normally spends about half his time in Asia.

Printed by Libri Plureos GmbH in Hamburg, Germany